HITTING THE SKIDS
IN PIXELTOWN

HITTING THE SKIDS IN PIXELTOWN

THE PHOBOS SCIENCE FICTION ANTHOLOGY 2

EDITED BY
ORSON SCOTT CARD
KEITH OLEXA
AND CHRISTIAN O'TOOLE

PHOBOS BOOKS
NEW YORK

phobos

Published by Phobos Books
A Division of Phobos Entertainment Holdings, Inc.
200 Park Avenue South
New York, New York 10003
www.phobosweb.com

Distributed in the United States by National Book Network,
Lanham, Maryland.

Cover art by Stephan Martiniere

Library of Congress Cataloging-in-Publication Data

Hitting the skids in Pixeltown : the Phobos science fiction anthology 2/
edited by Orson Scott Card, Keith Olexa, and Christian O'Toole.
    p. cm.
  ISBN 0-9720026-1-8 (pbk. : alk. paper)
  1. Science fiction, American I. Card, Orson Scott. II. Olexa, Keith,
1967- . III. O'Toole, Christian.
  PS648.S3 H55 2003
  813'.0876208—dc21

2003010987

ISBN 0-9720026-1-8

⊚ ™ The paper used in this publication meets the minimum
requirements of American National Standard for Information
Sciences—Permanence of Paper for Printed Library Materials,
ANSI/NISO Z39.48-1992

CONTENTS

CONTENTS

EDITOR'S NOTE

KEITH OLEXA

We live in an uncertain present.

The 21st century is not shaping up to be the century I expected. I was counting on food pills, faster-than-light travel and a *Star Trek* "brotherhood of man" society by 2002 at the latest, and instead I got political turmoil, murderous zealotry and scientific advances yoked by ignorance and bureaucracy. Quite a perverse future shock to me, sad and ironic.

Ironic because many people—maybe you, certainly I— rue the state of the world at the dawn of the 21st century. "Looks like business as usual to me," I'll think in my blackest moods. "The future's not so bright; the environment's shot, there's no global unity, ignorance reigns. Our big blue marble has lost its luster."

But then I come around.

I imagine how a 1930s science fiction writer might see our present (his future). He'd know that it's as promising as he could have dreamed. True, we aren't buzzing around in flying cars or day tripping to our local Moon base, but we are cloning everything in sight with a chromosome, using palm-sized computers faster than 1,000 Univacs, and connecting electronically with people all over the world.

As friend and Sci Fi Channel Senior Vice President Tom Vitale is fond of saying. "We live Sci Fi lives." And he's right. The future is here, and it's pretty amazing; but it encroaches on me so slowly, and I'm so thoroughly a part of it, that it goes by unnoticed.

That's ironic. What's sad is that others also don't see how brilliant the 21st century is, and in their disappointment are looking to the past for guidance. By that I mean relying on force of arms instead of voices to still conflicts, internalizing religious rhetoric that makes enemies of ideas and sacrificing advancement to uncertainty. SF visionaries wrote about worlds we might strive to achieve—daring federations of prosperity, equality and peace—but they also described realities we'd best avoid—xenophobic dystopian nightmares. We're presently headed down that low road of fear and ignorance, abandoning progress and vision for an illusory feeling of safety. Not all of us, and not always willingly, but that's where we're heading, lamenting the present and dreaming of a better future.

But we don't have the 21st century as a signpost anymore—the future is here. Fortunately we can still consult the same oracles we've always consulted when we need insights into tomorrow: the science fiction writers.

We've reached a crossroads where present and future meet. The opportunity exists to remake our reality, and SF writers can once again be our guides. We can create worlds full of new ideas, new possibilities. Take bold steps based on intelligence, not paranoia, and offer wondrous future possibilities in the present.

That's why I'm so thrilled to submit a Phobian view of science fiction in *Hitting the Skids in Pixeltown*. This collection of short stories offers the one thing our planet so desperately needs: The future, *now*. All of the stories in this collection explore various "what ifs" to entertain and stimulate. They arouse us humans to do what we're fated to do by evolution: to consider, to dwell, to imagine and to choose.

In short, to think.

When I read a story in *Pixeltown* about a "mindful" alternative to the death sentence, and its insane side effects, I'm asked to consider the price of criminal rehabilitation.

When I'm swept up in an unconventional—yet very literal—space opera, I'm invited to dwell in a world bereft of laser swords and men of action, but filled with gifted artists and the music of the stars.

When I face a man who can remove all painful memories, no matter what the cost, from a troubled woman, I'm forced to imagine what parts of me I'd be willing to give up in order to forget.

And when a radical alternative to avoiding interstellar conflict is suggested, I find I must choose to champion this daring route to peace, or deny all I believe in.

These stories are also a sheer pleasure to read for their sense of discovery. Within these pages I can track along with a hunter who bags his first bear-eating monster, follow a young primitive as he prepares for a stellar ritual, and feel the hot blood of vengeance flow from a warrior's auxiliary heart.

If any of these stories gets your noodle working, then *Pixeltown* has done its work. New voices abound in this anthology, each booming from a seer sitting atop an electronic tripod, inhaling the fumes of reason and speculation before delivering predictions of bright, or chilling, futures. I'm proud to inaugurate the 21st century with these new writers. For it's through their words, their ideas, and our understanding of them, that change is possible.

Such change is possible thanks to our Phobos Contest judges also, who elevated 12 voices above the creative din so they could take their place among the stars. SF authors Orson Scott Card, Larry Niven and Catherine Asaro, *Starlog Magazine* editor David McDonnell, SF artist Vincent Di Fate, NASA astronaut Marsha Ivins and film producer John Roche passed a torch of sorts to a fresh batch of SF writers—from those well schooled in the genre to those newly dreaming it into reality. *Pixeltown* would also be just so much TV snow were it not for the tireless efforts of several unsung Phobians. Thank you Christian O'Toole, Sandra Schulberg, Stan Plotnick and Julie Kirsch for working to forge a loose compilation of stories into a finely honed instrument.

These stories, and their authors, all offer something extra to readers, which I hope to sum up in a phrase. A buzz phrase, if you will. We've heard pretty good ones ("Where's the beef?!") and unfortunate ones ("Axis of Evil"). Now we're bombarded with the frightening "weapons of mass destruction." We can start by co-opting that phrase, changing it. Let's have it describe a new weapon—one that doesn't kill, maim, shatter cities or diminish humanity. A weapon that *limits* wars, ameliorates conflicts, engenders peace and respects life.

A "Weapon of Mass *Instruction*."

Consider *Hitting the Skids in Pixeltown* ordnance in this new, civilized arsenal. Unsheathe it freely, brandish it before the unsuspecting, fearlessly assail your opponents with its ideas. And when you're finished, watch for the understanding . . .

Ideas and understanding. The only weapons we'll ever need in the only war that ever really matters.

INTRODUCTION

ORSON SCOTT CARD

I've heard people say that what they like about science fiction is, it makes them think.

Wrong, my friends. Nothing can *make* you think. Anybody who has taught school knows that.

But science fiction does invite you to think. And rewards you when you do.

Oddly, though, the most important mental process invoked by science fiction is not the thinking you do about the particular issues a story raises. Yes, you can get some interesting ideas from the stories in this book. What constitutes a fair punishment for murder? Who do we become when our worst memories are taken from us? How terrible is it that our creations all resemble us—especially when we play God? Yet I believe that what sets fiction apart from—and, yes, sometimes above—essays is not the quality of the ideas. After all, essays can develop ideas with far greater clarity.

No, the greatest value from science fiction is the mental process we have to go through simply to comprehend it at all.

Think about it. This is the one genre of literature in which, by definition, *all* the stories must take place in a universe that in some key way is different from our own.

Alternate histories posit some change in the past. Future settings demand that we extrapolate from present reality to imagine where we might be in the future. Time travel and faster-than-light starships flat-out break the laws of science (not to mention logic), yet we love to dwell in fictional universes where such things are possible.

The very things that cause critics of SF to call it "escapism"—journeys to worlds that never were—require from us a kind of mental contortionism. We must hold all that we know about our present reality in abeyance, measuring everything in the SF story against that worldview in order to see where the contradictions are.

And out of those contradictions, we mentally construct the fictional world even while the story continues uninterrupted. Each bit of information about how this unreal world differs from the real one must be put into its place and we must then reach conclusions about this strange new land into which we've been transported.

This is not escapism. This is survival training.

Because like it or not, we move forward into the future one day, one hour, one second at a time. And it is certain that whatever the future holds, it will be different from the world we live in now, even as this world is different from the one we grew up in.

Science fiction does not prepare you for the future by predicting with any kind of accuracy what it *will* be. It prepares you to embrace *any* future by giving you practice at the skills required to recognize change and construct a new worldview that takes it into account.

So instead of being trapped, trying to fit changes into a rigid vision of the world, we who read science fiction are able to adapt our fluid vision to fit in the ever-changing channels of the future—or, if we have the wit and will to do it, to carve our own new channel and see if we can bring others along into it.

We can be surprised, shocked, horrified, awestruck by the future when it becomes the present—but we are never destroyed by it, nor even trapped. Whatever comes, we'll turn ourselves into the kind of creatures who can survive in it, if survival is possible at all.

HITTING THE SKIDS
IN PIXELTOWN

THE TAKERS

ROSEMARY JONES

The question was flippant: What if they held a war and nobody came?

Flippant, because there are always people willing to go to war.

We used to be rather proud of the fact that humans were the only animals that went to war—that systematically slaughtered their own kind.

Then Jane Goodall discovered war among the chimpanzees, and we weren't so alone.

Nor were the chimps any more rational about war than humans are. A small group of males had broken away from a somewhat overcrowded tribe. They lived in a different area, and caused no harm.

But it was intolerable to the chimps in the mother tribe that ones who had once been among them now chose to be apart. One by one, they were hunted down and killed.

Still—war is terrible, and we recoil in horror from those who enjoy it.

1

Yet aren't there worse things than war? Aren't there dreams worth fighting for?

Good people go to war sometimes—to protect their people from a would-be overlord; to stop some monstrous crime; to defend some principle; for honor or pride or . . . after a while you stop thinking "good" people go to war, and realize that what you really mean is "people like me," whether they're good or middling or bad.

Knowing that they will almost certainly die, men still go to war, when they believe the story that they're told about why it's noble, or at least necessary, to kill.

The only stories more tragic than those of people who went to war are those of people who didn't, and found out too late that they should have.

FROM THE HISTORY OF PHYSICS, 140th Edition:

The theory that organic matter can be converted into energy, moved through space, and then returned to its original state has never been proven. Although Dr. Marie Claire Rimbaud claimed to have perfected the technique, and members of her laboratory team witnessed her "displacement" of certain rabbits, one must remember that her father and grandfather were professional stage magicians and that her equipment was never examined by any outside agency. Following the death of her son, Lt. Jean Martin Rimbaud, in the Austra-Asian conflict, Dr. Rimbaud apparently committed suicide. Her laboratory was destroyed that night in the subsequent fire. Neither her body nor her equipment was recovered from the wreckage.

Those who claim that Dr. Rimbaud set the fire to hide evidence of her fraudulent experiments ignore the evidence of her very real grief at the loss of her only child, a sorrow that is well documented in her final letters, now housed in the Sorbonne archives.

The image of the hospital ship, recorded by the *Galina*'s long distance cameras and built out by the extensive data files kept in the tactical computers, filled most of the forward holoprojection chamber. Just behind the hospital's rear gun turrets the faint outline of the rising planet burned blue in the infinite darkness. Maia, who, after weeks of intensive study, knew the hospital's defenses better than her own ship's, tried to walk around the holoship for a better view of the planet, but this part of space was new to the computer. The back half of the projection faded into a haze of indistinct lights.

"Pity," she said. Forty years ago, when she first signed up as crew on a trading vessel doing a three-planet hop, Maia Di Angeli always picked planet rise for her watch. The sight of a whole world emerging from the dark, even a world visited every third jump, never lost its fascination for her. Now, despite the responsibility of her duties as a Taker, which required her to spend so many hours plotting the interception of hospital ships and battle cruisers, she still tried to make time for the holoprojections of new planets.

Patrice Chu, the ops tech calculating the *Galina*'s visuals with stolen data detailing the hospital ship's armaments, just grinned. "Get away, Maia," she said. "There's time enough for planet watching after the Taking. When are you going?"

"As soon as the Rimbaud's adjusted," Maia answered. "No point in staying in orbit for too long, but we don't want to be displaced into the cargo bay."

"Or the Captain's bedroom," snickered Patrice, although that mistake had happened well before her tour on the *Galina*.

"Ah, well," Maia said, "that poor man was snoring so loudly, he wouldn't have noticed if I'd fallen on his bed. I'm just sorry I had to secure him as he was. Imagine his face when his crew came to cut him free. His sleep gear was strictly nonregulation."

"The Rimbaud should be set soon," said Patrice, turning her attention back to the four data screens set in front of her chair. She knew Maia liked to joke about that wrong displacement, but very few women could have handled it as well. After being dumped four floors above her objective, Maia had crawled through that ship's service ducts to complete her Taking undetected.

"All the clearance codes have worked," Patrice reported, "and the hospital's scanners are recording us as an unmanned research satellite. We'll just drift into position and then send your group across. Not too long."

Maia nodded, her mind already occupied with the latest objectives. Decorated heroes all of them, valued for its bravery and effectiveness against the enemy, which meant that they would be well guarded. The heavy losses of the last fifty years of the current war meant that the Federale government spent fortunes on the health of its officers. Cloned parts, cybernetic rebuilds, and dozens of medical techniques far too expensive for the average citizen were lavished on such soldiers. Such investments automatically commanded extraordinary safeguards.

Four objectives on that hospital ship, and any of them worth the risk, but Maia wanted Harrison most of all. The highest ranking officer on their list and the youngest as well, with the young's reckless luck in command, Harrison had made himself a legend among his men. They believed that as long as Harrison led them, they could not lose. The battles of Belgriad, Tarakas, and Noresto seemed ample proof of that belief.

So, if Harrison was Taken, the morale of Federale troops should crumble. Would crumble, according to the *Galina's* tactical computers. When battle-weary men found their hero gone forever, when doubt crept into their dreams and haunted their waking hearts, then the Takers could expand their operations without serious opposition. The Council talked of whole battalions, but Maia wanted more. She wanted what the *Galina's* tactical readouts suggested as the extreme extrapolation. The

Taking of an entire army—maybe even *both* armies fighting on the planet shining before her on the *Galina*'s holo-projection.

"Have we located Harrison?" she asked Patrice.

"Probable location only. No name, of course, on any records. The Federale know that we can breach security, even if they don't know how, and they're getting wary about identifications. But we've got an 87.5 match of reported injuries. Burned scalp, hands and chest, cracked ribs, possible loss of the right leg. There's an officer in Ward 2122 with a new mech limb, probably a leg from specs, and burn treatment. Listed as being in post-treatment recovery and already requesting transfer. Sounds like Harrison. He's supposed to be impatient."

"Frightened," Maia corrected her quietly. "Doesn't want to stay away from his men for too long. Frightened that they need him now."

"That's an odd analysis," said Patrice.

Maia shrugged. She had spent days in transit absorbing all the data that they had on Harrison. A lot came from his family, half a dozen jumps away from here, but eager to talk about their hero relative. Sympathetic ears provoked reminiscences. Memories of a boy, long before the man became a soldier, who never made it into the Federale's databanks.

Harrison's sister betrayed the most.

"He never believed that he could be hurt," his sister recalled, talking to a Taker wired with a half dozen illegal recording devices, so they could judge by voice tone, body heat, and visual record whether this woman was telling the truth. "Boys don't, do they? He used to take terrible risks. But never to shock us, or to get attention. He did it for others. Rescuing a boy from a fall down an air shaft. Or continuing to play in the school maneuvers even after he lost all that blood. I asked him afterwards why he did it. For the team, he told me. For the team. So that they would all qualify for cadet training. His individual scores were high enough. He didn't need the win. But some of the other boys, without that district win, they would have just been assigned to ground troops. And, well, we all know what happens to ground troops, don't we? Even if they don't publish the reports any more. You never hear of anybody coming back from ground troops, do you?"

Loyalty, that's what Harrison had, loyalty to his men, and an overactive streak of responsibility that kept him in field command long after another man would have taken a safer post in a Federale fortress, planning a never-ending war jumps away from the action. Loyalty and responsibility could keep a man alive long after his wounds should have killed him. Make him impatient to be off the hospital ship and back to his own ship, Maia reasoned. Such traits also made him a difficult target. Harrison, even in his current state, might put up more of a fight than expected.

"Time," called Patrice. "Ten and counting." The ship shuddered beneath their feet and then they were floating above the deck. The Rimbaud drew too much energy to keep the artificial gravity going. That was one problem that the famous Marie Claude and her heirs never quite solved, despite years of experimentation funded by the Taker sympathizers who staged her suicide. Still, without the Rimbaud, the one piece of technology that the Federale lacked, the Takers would never had been such a mysterious, feared organization. Worth a slightly upset stomach, the Rimbaud was, just to know that the Federale were still having fits trying to figure out how the Takers got in and out of their ships, army camps, and training schools without breaking any locks or breaching any walls.

"Tell them that I'm coming," said Maia, swinging hand over hand on the ceiling grips.

In the Rimbaud entry room, she found her crew. Three women dressed in copies of Federale medical uniforms and outfitted with the various instruments necessary to complete their individual Takings successfully. Two were going across for family reasons, and this was their first mission. Claudelle, her second-in-command, was an old hand.

Claudelle's family died years ago in another sector of the war long since forgotten by the Federales. Claudelle fought in another guerrilla movement before joining the Takers. Her exploits were well-documented in the Federale criminal computers. She had walked into a Takers' safe house one day and told them that she had personally destroyed a half dozen Federale installations. She had also caused more than one ship to blow its engines, never to be heard from again. "But it doesn't matter," she said. "My bombs cause nothing more than an annoying noise, a background to their war. But you are different. I have heard that their highest officers are afraid of the Takers, so afraid that they tell their men that you are a myth. Teach me how to be one of you."

So Maia had trained Claudelle, trusted her life to her more than once, and argued in the Council for her inclusion even in their most secret plans despite Claudelle's terrorist past. Now, it was Claudelle who shared her ambition to Take an entire planet.

"If you get Harrison, you might do it," said Claudelle. "A bigger bang than any of my explosions. And the ripple it would send through the galaxy! Better than my old friends, wasting their time stealing ships and running contraband firearms."

Claudelle was checking equipment, talking quietly to the other women about what signals to use if they were successful. Also, because it was necessary to set their plans now, she reviewed what to do if they were caught. Try to Take those who captured them or else hold to their silence until they could be Taken.

"Rimbaud's count is down to two," Claudelle said, hooking one foot neatly in a ceiling grip to back flip toward the tube. "You ready?"

"I'm taking tube four," said Maia, going hand over hand to the opening. "I'll go across last and be back last."

"Harrison's going to be tough," said Claudelle. She had reversed in mid-chamber, so she was sliding into the Rimbaud tube feet first. It didn't really matter which way she entered it, the Rimbaud's operators could still drop them on their heads if their calculations were off, but Claudelle liked the illusion of control, of maybe landing feet first on the hospital ship's deck. "Be careful," she called as the Rimbaud tube door slid closed over her head.

"You too," whispered Maia, although she knew that Claudelle could not hear her now. As she dropped into the fourth tube and listened for the click of the door, she wondered for the last time if they were right about Harrison. Could he be Taken?

IN HIS BED, Harrison could hear machines all around him, but no sound of human breathing. That's what he missed the most, being off on his own in a expensive suite of rooms designed to maximize his physical recovery and mental stability, the sounds of human breathing. Even the snoring of old Sgt. Kuragen would help him now. He just couldn't sleep in still darkness with only the clicks and electronic buzz of various machines to keep him company.

He could request lights, attention from a real live person, or even a Federale counselor. A counselor would have to sit with him all night, discussing the various reasons for his insomnia. Any type of tranq that he wanted would flood his veins, just by pushing a button at the side of the bed. The more addictive ones, they would just flush out of his system before they sent him back to his ship, and that would be the end of it. The tranq would free him from having to deal with the dark, or the quiet, or the endless time to think.

In the zone there was no time for thinking, no time for anything but reacting to the latest order, the latest attack, the latest account of casualties screaming down the communication channels. He liked the zone much better than these rooms. He kept asking to go back. They kept giving him excuses about the wounds not being quite healed yet, the cybernetics not quite tuned. They were making a mistake. He knew it, but couldn't argue the point without being assigned more hours with a Federale counselor, which would only cause more delay. The counselor just didn't see that it was dangerous to leave him here, alone in the dark, far away from the sounds of human breathing.

So he lay in the bed, stared in the direction of the ceiling, and tried not to think about the sounds that the machines made all around him. Including the sound of a sigh, a very human sounding sigh, somewhere off to his left.

"Who's there?" said Harrison, sliding his hand under the mattress to retrieve the scalpel that he'd stolen from one of the medic trays and hidden there. It wasn't very big or strong, but with enough pressure, it could slit a man's throat or his wrists.

"Maia, Maia Di Angeli," said a woman. She moved so that he could see her outline against the faint green glow created by the monitor of the machine that measured his blood pressure, pulse, and body temperature. "Do you want to turn on the light?"

"Sure," he said, feeling slightly embarrassed and sliding his hand beneath the blanket to conceal the blade. He shifted his right foot to hit the lower bed control that brought on the night lights.

Maia looked like all the other medics that came in and out of his rooms. Short, a little round from living on a ship diet, and old enough to be his mother. Unlike the other medics, she didn't look at the monitors surrounding his bed or fuss with the uneaten food on the tray shoved against the wall. She looked straight at him.

"I thought you were a redhead," she said.

Harrison chuckled and ran his hand over the stubble that covered the top of his scalp. "They messed up my records, so when they redid my scalp, they put the hair in blond."

"Your sister still calls you Rusty," said Maia.

"I guess I should send her a new picture," said Harrison.

"She'd like that. She misses you. Especially since your mother died."

The cold in the pit of his stomach returned as he remembered that Bess was jumps away. Nobody on the hospital ship would know her. These Federale medics were all drawn from a different sector. There was something wrong about the woman's uniform too. It didn't fit quite right. He glanced at the an odd bulge on her left side. A weapon? He tightened his grip on the blade.

She caught his quick glance at her pocket and shrugged. Maia pulled a flat, black box from her hip pocket and put it down on the top of the body monitor. "Interference," she said. "This keeps the monitor from recording more than one person in the room. Keeps the output looking just like it did about ten minutes ago. I just hate that part, you know, worse than the Rimbaud. Holding your breath until the box gets a complete fix on all the listeners and jams them."

She drew up a chair to the bed and patted him lightly on his real leg. "Lucky that they don't rig these rooms with visuals. The last guy that I visited was considered such a security risk, they even put spy-eyes in his shower. Had to go through the floor ducts and drill a hole under his desk to get to him."

"What are you?" Harrison whispered, not afraid of her, but of her answer.

"I'm a Taker. More specifically, I'm your Taker tonight," she answered calmly.

"The Takers don't exist," he said, remembering a briefing from a time when they were changing sectors and losing a lot of men, when troops whispered about the Takers as the reason for the unexplained rise of MIAs appearing in the reports.

"A bona fide myth," Maia agreed with a friendly bob of her head. "A tale told to frighten generals. An edited-out part of the history of war."

Harrison knew exactly what a good soldier was supposed to do in this situation. It was very clearly outlined in the same regulations that claimed there were no Takers. He was supposed to hit the alarm, turn away from this woman ("make no visual or verbal contact" was the exact wording). Soldiers who talked to Takers were never seen again. Everyone knew that, including the Federale generals who called the Takers a myth.

But Harrison had seen her already, spoken with her already, and had her pat his leg and cock an eyebrow at him in a manner that strongly reminded him of his sister Bess when she was trying to talk him into some childhood venture.

"Why are you here?" he said, although he knew it was a foolish question. The Takers only came for one reason, one purpose. Everybody knew that, just as well as they knew there was no official acknowledgment of Takings.

"Your mother asked us to come for you," Maia said.

"She's dead. She's been dead for two years," Harrison protested.

"I'm sorry," Maia said, "but we had to wait. We had to check and double-check all our facts. We weren't sure, not until this last battle."

"She would have never asked you for this," he insisted. "She knew that I was loyal."

"To what?" asked Maia. "The Federale? The war? Or your men? And if you're that loyal, why do you have that scalpel?" Harrison pulled his hand out from under the blanket. "Did you know that they found enough tranqs hidden in your kit to kill a dozen men? We saw that in your commander's last transmission."

"They weren't for me," Harrison said. "I took them for somebody else. Somebody who was so tired of the war, of always being responsible, being loyal."

"Another redhead?" she smiled and then shook her head. "I'm sorry. That's not fair. You made a lot of brave choices. Now, I'm asking you to make one more. By the time that I'm finished, they won't be able to find a trace of you, nor will they want to. They don't want to admit that it's so simple. All I need is your cooperation. Just close your eyes; it will be easier that way."

"You can't," he said. He pleaded with her as he had pleaded with the medics to send him back to the zone. He begged her to change her mind before he had too much time to think about what was offered. "What about my unit? I've kept most of them alive. What will they do without me? That's always been my reason to stay alive. To not use the tranqs or the knife."

So Maia told him about the *Galina*'s projections, about secrets that the Federale wouldn't even dare believe, and how his Taking would help her cause, would lead inevitably to an incredible rise in Takers and Taken.

"But it's still your choice," she said. "We have two rules. That we must be asked to Take someone. And that person must consent."

Harrison knew all about hard choices; he had made dozens in his career. This one was the hardest. It would have been easier to fight with her or to sound the alarm to alert the security. Her capture would have been a triumph for the Federale, if they ever admitted that she existed. He could even draw the scalpel across his own wrists the way that he planned when he first woke up in the hospital bed and realized that he had survived another battle. His suicide could be blamed on stress or fatigue or just not reported at all.

What Maia offered would never be understood by many men that he had called friend. This decision would set him apart from all loyal soldiers.

Because he couldn't help himself, he asked, "Do I really have to close my eyes?"

"No," said Maia. "But you do have to make a clear answer. Do you agree to be Taken?"

"Yes," said Harrison, officially joining the ranks of the disloyal forever.

"You're a brave man," Maia said. "First step is always the hardest, when you choose to turn away."

She reached over the bed and hugged Harrison tightly. She pressed twice on the signal button pinned to her jacket. "You may still want to close your eyes. This can be very disorientating for some people. You'll probably be upside down in the Rimbaud tube when we get there, but don't worry. We'll pull you out. That's our job, to pull you out safe and sound."

THE FEDERALE MAJOR shuffled his feet while he waited for the general to finish reviewing the records encoded into the cubes.

The general kept shuffling the cubes around, stacking them into little fortresses with ramparts and turrets. The press had almost turned the disappearance of the four war heroes off that hospital ship into a major embarrassment, but they had controlled most of that information leak. These internal reports were worse. How could they hide the fact that entire companies were vanishing? It wasn't even confined to their own side, something that they could blame on the terrorists or their other enemies. Whole divisions from both sides were just gone. Rumors circulated that the men were just walking away from ground conflicts or even vanishing from ships, following comrades who had turned up alive and asked them to stop fighting. Just stop, like anything could be as simple as that. Lies, of course, all lies. Just as the new rumors about the Takers were labeled as the resurgence of an old myth in the reports that formed little walls of data on the general's desk.

"Unbelievable, unbelievable," muttered the general, stacking one clear cube on top of a blue cube, so that the numbers in the report changed into a glowing bar graph reflected on the ceiling. "Look at these projections. Do you know what these say?"

"Yes, sir," said the major, not bothering to look up. He had seen these charts before and nothing that his superiors did to twist the data stopped the dismal diminishment of the little bars until they dwindled into zero. He straightened his shoulders and snapped a smart salute because he knew that this was probably the last time that he would stand in such a nice office. Maybe if the general was impressed with his posture, he wouldn't be sent straight to the zone. But in the end, he would have to go. Even the general would have to go, unless they did something unthinkable, like ending the war.

"The projections show that if these disappearances continue at the current rate that, uh, that . . ." the major knew he was stuttering, but he really didn't want to give an oral report. Bad news tended to stay in the permanent data files. "The projections show that, by the end of the year, there will be no troops left."

"Do you know what that means?" said the general.

"There will be no one left to fight this war except us," said the major and wished that somebody cared enough to take him away.

From *The History of War,* unpublished edition:

At the end of the 20th century, a woman named Galina Ivanova had a son called Stefan. This son was sent to the front in a war that neither he, nor his mother, nor even his country, really cared about or wanted to fight. After several months of worrying about her son, Galina Ivanova made a decision. She took an ancient mode of transportation called a "train" to the battle zone. She found her son in a field hospital. She told his commanding officer that enough was enough. She was taking

Stefan home. For unknown reasons, the officer let her walk out of the hospital with her son.

When other women heard about Galina Ivanova's son, they decided to fetch home their children, too. They took trains, or they walked, or they gave money to others to help their loved ones. These women were called Takers in the media reports. According to all official histories, this movement ended as quickly as it began, although a reoccurring myth states that the Takers still exist.

HIDDEN SCARS

Kyle David Jelle

In John Kessel's classic story "A Clean Escape," he asks a question: If you can't remember the crime, are you guilty of it?

So much of who we are consists of what we remember doing.

Of course, those memories are all edited. None of us relies on what we actually saw or heard or even did.

We have fenced those data memories with stories. Or rather, we have sculpted the memories to fit our stories, even as we bend our stories to fit the memories. Until our "self" becomes some weird amalgam of what we've done, what we wish we'd done, what we fear we've done, what we hope to do, what we dread . . . all of it overlaid by the stories others believe about us, and all the things they claim to remember that we did.

So messy, so complicated. Wouldn't it be nice to have a roadmap to our souls?

Or, better yet, draw our own roadmap, and make the memories fit.

I LOVE WOMEN with scars on their wrists.

I don't know what it is. Motives for suicide are often trite, even trivial, and many people who've never considered it are far more stimulating, but scars—something I can see and touch—always pique my curiosity, heighten my anticipation. . . . Sometimes, I'm not even disappointed.

I was sitting at my usual table—a back corner booth in a small, very private dive called Fregare's Cabaret—nursing a glass of orange juice and skimming the local news when she entered. Fregare's gets little business before noon, so I noticed her right away. She spoke to the doorman as he ran her through the scanner. He pointed at me. I slid my display aside as she approached.

"Mr. Marquette?" she asked, with a raspy but not unattractive voice.

"Call me Vin," I said. "Have a seat." She smoothed her cinnamon-colored dress as she slid into the booth.

She wasn't unattractive at all. Probably in her twenties—longevity treatments might account for her thin, almost boyish figure and smooth face, but not the looseness in her movements. She had straight red hair, thin lips, and green eyes that glowed in the light thrown off by the kitschy fractal holosculpture in the center of the table.

"What can I do for you, Miss . . . ?"

"Newman," she said. "Kristin." A young, shaven-headed busboy brought her a menu and glass of water. She said nothing until he left. "I hear you can make my problems go away."

I glanced at the doorman. He'd have spotted any surveillance equipment. He shook his head. "And who told you that?"

"Rita Nansen," she said. I nodded. Rita had left a message about a referral. An unusually sensitive case, she'd said.

"So what kind of problems can I help you with?"

She broke eye contact and reached for her water.

That's when I spotted the scars. Still dark. Cut the long way, to make clotting more difficult. No cry for help, this one. Alas, with modern medical technology and the finances to pay for it, dying was harder than comedy these days.

She sipped the water and set the glass down.

"Are you a licensed therapist?" she asked.

"They don't issue licenses for what I do," I said.

"Of course not."

"If it makes you feel more comfortable," I said, "I am a professional. I've got over ten years of experience, and I've worked with Rita for seven of them. Whatever you want, I can do it. Confidentiality is, of course, guaranteed."

"I guess you wouldn't be in business very long if you couldn't guarantee that," she said. I smiled. Some of my clients had messier ways of making problems go away; I wouldn't be *alive* if I couldn't guarantee that.

"I know this can be hard," I said, after another pause, "but you need to be clear about what you want before we begin."

"I thought you'd know," she said.

"I will," I said. "Once I establish contact, I'll know what you know, and I'll be able to do what you want. But you need to know what that is. You won't be able to change your mind once we start. You won't be able to clarify your intentions if they're open to misinterpretation. Do you know what you want?"

She watched me for a moment, expressionless.

"You'll know."

ONCE WE AGREED on a price and completed the transfer—I always got the money first, before the client forgot what he or she was paying for—we walked back to my building, a high-rise just a few blocks up the avenue.

The guard at the metal and explosives detector cast an appreciative glance at my client. I'd have to discuss that with him. Much of my clientele came to me for help with traumas involving sexual abuse—from recent, violent assaults to childhood experiences half remembered and never fully understood. They rarely appreciated that kind of attention.

Only the elevator's hum broke the silence as we rode to my floor. She kept her distance, eyes averted except for a few stolen glances, as if we were lovers en route to an illicit rendezvous—not an inappropriate metaphor considering how intimately I'd know her by the time we finished.

I'd always viewed my life with clinical detachment. Even when my parents were killed—a bombing when I was seven—I never felt any strong emotions. What it was like to be so possessed by emotion that it could drive me to suicide, or even tears, I didn't know.

Naturally, I was hooked on finding out.

My work, even with clients as promising as Kristin, couldn't completely satisfy my curiosity. Neural interface technology delivered perfect sensory simulations and hard data, but emotions were too subjective. I only got vague impressions.

But that was better than nothing.

I used the remote on my key chain to dim the windows and switch the wall screens to a couple of Monet landscapes before we entered. I kept the windows untinted for the plants, and I preferred more dramatic art, like Pollock or de Kooning abstracts, but my clients appreciated subdued lighting and stress-free artwork.

I took her jacket, hung it on a coat rack by the door, and directed her to an overstuffed tan couch.

My memory editor sat on the coffee table.

It looked like a standard dual output neural interface playback deck—about the size of a brick, jacks for two headsets and a line-out for networking—but it was custom inside; a full-featured, state-of-the-art engram scanner with synaptic disruption augmentation, at least as sophisticated as the restricted-access models favored by the military and intelligence communities. I'd assembled it myself from black market components.

I went to the kitchen, and came back with two glasses of water. "You should drink this. Dehydration can be a problem if a session lasts too long." She drank it.

I sat down in the chair at the end of the table, turned the memory editor to face me, and put the command headset on.

The interface was clean. Audio-visual simulations, the kind that represent information systems as virtual objects users could touch or locations they could enter, were for amateurs. I used direct contact—when information came in, I just *knew*; if I wanted something, it happened. I ran the diagnostics and handed the subject headset—thicker and heavier to accommodate the synaptic destabilizers— to my client.

"Make sure you're comfortable," I said. "This could take several hours. You don't want to wake up sore. I'd recommend lying back on the couch."

She scooted to the center of the couch, pulled off her shoes, and froze.

"You sure you want to do this?" I asked. "Most people feel their memories are part of their identity. Things we've learned make us who we are. Deleting memories that inhibit us can be liberating, but it can change things you don't expect. Do you want to rethink this?"

"No." She put the headset on.

I'd known she would. My clients liked the illusion of control, of having the option to walk away, but they didn't come to me if they could live with their problems.

"All set?" I asked. She lay back on the couch, smoothed her skirt, folded her hands across her abdomen and nodded. I gave her my warmest, most reassuring smile. She closed her eyes. I triggered the hippocampal suppression subroutine to block long-term memory formation, cut off her sensory inputs and voluntary physical responses, and began.

The machine took control of her lateral prefrontal cortex, giving me access to the key areas of working memory that comprised consciousness. I called up the episodic memory she wanted me to delete.

A door. Natural wood. Dark stain, glossy finish. Extremely negative emotional associations, though, as usual, I felt little of it myself. Still, it had potential.

Until it vanished.

I tried to reconnect, but the target memory was hazy, difficult to reacquire. The interference resembled late stage Alzheimer's, though she exhibited no associated symptoms. The machine reported a burst of neural activity in her anterior cingulate cortex, another part of the working memory system, which may have been responsible. I'd never seen anything like it.

But, with ten billion neurons in the human brain and a lifetime of environmental factors to make each one unique, such quirks were inevitable. Nothing else seemed wrong, so I accessed the memory again.

This time, no unusual neural activity registered, but the memory itself was oddly fragmented. Memory loss in itself was common—everyone forgets—but ordinary memory loss involves gradual synaptic deterioration. These fragments ended abruptly.

As if something had already been deleted.

I invoked low-order memory conditioning, which employed relational algorithms to approximate the missing synaptic connections, but it did no good.

My curiosity got the better of me, and I initiated high-order conditioning. It locked on right away.

And I knew right away that something was wrong.

I was seeing her memory—from *my* point of view.

I was sitting behind the oak desk in the old port district office I'd worked out of a decade ago. Dust motes swirled in the hard sunlight streaming in through the blinds. My client—age thirteen, or so—sat on a maroon couch by the door, eyes darting around the room, but never meeting mine, tears visible on her cheeks. She wore a white blouse, blue skirt and a matching blazer with a local school logo. Her hair was blonde, not red. I could never have recognized her at Fregare's.

In the chair opposite me sat a man, perhaps in his mid-fifties, black hair, gray at the temples. Gray wool suit. Silk tie. Abject terror on his face.

"I must speak to Dr. Allen," he demanded.

"Dr. Allen isn't here," I replied. "However, I'd be happy to assist you myself. How can I help?"

I'd been a kid in blue jeans and pony-tailed hair, trying to pass for a pro by wearing the white lab coat Allen had left behind when he fled his arrest warrant. Memory editing wasn't illegal yet, but the potential for abuse was so staggering that the medical profession had already come out in opposition. Dr. Allen, an advocate for the losing side, had gone underground, where I'd hooked up with him as a technician until the authorities came after him for practicing with a suspended license.

"You're just the assistant . . ." the man said.

"Dr. Allen taught me everything he knew about memory editing," I said. Technically not a lie. The truth was that he'd never needed to know much about the technical side of memory editing. The machine did most of the work. I enjoyed the nuts and bolts of the technology, but all the human operator needed to do was set the deletion parameters, and let the machine disrupt the synaptic connections. Determining which connections to eliminate, and which to leave as part of separate, but associated, memory traces, was tedious and time-consuming, even with machine assistance, but it required astonishingly little specialized knowledge.

Of course, I didn't tell prospective clients this. They expected a high priest of science to cast arcane spells for them, and the truth would've been a terrible blow to their faith and my livelihood. "Let me assure you," I said, "I have a great deal of exper—"

"When will Dr. Allen be in?" the man demanded.

"Dr. Allen is out of the country," I said. "There was some trouble regarding—"

"But I need to talk to him!" He leapt to his feet, looming over the desk.

I leaned forward. "I want to help you."

He sat down. Nervous glance at the girl.

"I'm prepared to pay very well if you can do this."

"Go on."

"No questions asked?"

I shook my head. "No questions."

"I need you to eliminate a . . . problematic memory," he said.

"That's why I'm here."

"From my daughter," he added.

"What kind of memory?"

He hesitated. "You'll know when you get in."

I already knew—even then, the first time I saw him—but my priorities were well established.

"Let's talk money."

I shifted my attention from the memory playback and initiated a diagnostic. I thought I knew what was happening. One shortcut built into interface technology was its ability to augment incomplete simulations by drawing on the user's memories to fill in the blanks. The result, when using programmed simulations, was an experience totally convincing to the user, if not entirely true to life. High-order conditioning used the same principle, employing the operator's memories in a feedback loop to stimulate the subject's. The problem was that the operator's biases and preconceptions could corrupt the memory reconstruction process, dragging in unrelated memories, or, as in this case, overwhelming the subject's fragmentary memory traces with the operator's more complete version.

But she shouldn't remember this at all.

In the memory, her father and I agreed on a price, the money was transferred, then I invited her into the back room. Her father reached for her. She shrugged away, eyeing him warily as she went in. He sat down on the edge of the couch. I shut the door.

The CyberSystem 310, the last commercially produced memory editor, was a suitcase-sized machine that took up the whole table next to the diagnostic couch.

"What are you going to do to me?" the girl asked.

"This isn't going to hurt a bit," I said. "I can make it better. I can make it like it never happened. You'd like that wouldn't you?"

She didn't answer, just stared at me, and trembled.

"Trust me," I said. "Everything will be okay."

She lay back on the couch. I put her headset in place, then mine. Powered up the machine. Found myself floating in the blue zero input void. This model was designed for medical professionals without much experience in cybernetics. The readouts and menus appeared on flat screens that hovered to the right and left in my peripheral vision, coming into focus only when I looked for them. It took time to key in the control sequences. I'd forgotten how cumbersome it was.

But I remembered what came next. I'd find the memories her father wanted buried, review them—she hadn't realized what he wanted when he came into her room, not until it was too late to do anything but live through it—and bury them. When we finished, she'd be cheerful and well adjusted. She'd smile. She wouldn't flinch when he reached for her. She'd call him "Daddy." He'd tell me how grateful he was, how much he loved his daughter, how horrible it would be if he'd scarred her for life, how he'd never do it again. He'd said that every time he brought her back.

I'd seen enough. Even traumatic memories didn't do anything for me the second time around.

I still didn't know how she'd recovered this memory. It was possible—long-term potentiation, the neurobiological mechanism that makes memory work, could never be reversed, only reduced to imperceptible levels—but the spontaneous recovery of large sequences of synaptic connections defied probability. I was lucky she hadn't gone to a licensed memory therapist; help in forgetting might be illegal and expensive, but help in remembering was readily available and could've uncovered a lot of unpleasantness.

But not when I finished covering my tracks. The odds against another spontaneous recovery were astronomical.

I gave the command to find the end of the memory trace. NO.

Something blocked my command.

I WANT TO SEE MORE.

You're conscious. How?

I DON'T KNOW.

This system isn't functioning properly. I'm breaking the connection.

I gave the exit command.

NO.

She canceled that, too.

I WANT TO REMEMBER THIS.

We can discuss it outside.

AND IF YOU DON'T GO BACK IN, WHERE DO I FIND SOMEONE ELSE WITH YOUR MEMORIES?

Again I issued the exit command. Again she canceled it. The system didn't have any overrides—the possibility of a client evading thought suppression was even more remote than spontaneous memory recovery—so the stalemate might've gone on until one of us died.

Okay. We'll do it your way.

It was far from a total concession. If she became distracted, I could regain control long enough to escape, and she didn't know what she was about to go through.

In the playback, my younger self accessed her memory.

EVENTS DIDN'T UNFOLD as I'd anticipated.

The memory trace began—from her point of view, now—with her in bed. A dim wallscreen, displaying a loop of a horse eating grass in a pastoral setting, lit the room. From time to time, the horse looked up and glanced across the room, as if watching over her. Kristin wore a pink and white nightshirt with printed balloons on the front. She lay on her side with one hand pressed between the skin of her inner thighs—not an unpleasant sensation.

Her playback-self was thinking about a boy she'd kissed. My playback-self was anticipating the elusive Deep Emotional Experience. My present self waited patiently, as any premature attempt to secure system control might give my plan away. From her present self, I sensed nothing.

The floorboards creaked. She looked up. Her father opened the door. Navy blue bathrobe. Bare feet.

"Hi, sweetheart," he said.

"Daddy?"

"Just coming in to say goodnight."

He walked over, sat on the bed. She sat up.

"How 'bout a goodnight kiss for your old man?"

She leaned over to kiss him on the cheek. He turned his head so her lips touched his. She pulled back. How strange it was to kiss her father on the lips like that!

"Why don't we try that again?" he suggested. She leaned forward again.

This time there was no doubt that he'd intended to kiss her full on the mouth. In shock, she froze.

He kissed her again, forcing her lips open with his tongue. Frightened, unable to believe what was happening, she didn't resist at all. This was her *father*. She trusted him. He'd never hurt her.

That's when I felt it. A sense of sorrow, and pain—understood, if not quite experienced, like listening to the sound of weeping from another room—but nevertheless, the strongest emotion I've ever felt. It passed through shock, rage, hatred, anger and disbelief before

27

circling back to pain. In the playback, her father pinned her down. His robe fell open, his swollen penis dangling over her as he lifted her nightshirt.

And I was too distracted to take advantage of the situation.

By the time it was over, I didn't care.

TEN MINUTES AFTER WE DISCONNECTED, I emerged from the bathroom, drying my face with a hand towel. She was still curled up on the couch, sobbing. I lightened the windows. They faced east, so late afternoon sunlight didn't flood the room.

"What time is it?" she asked.

"A little after four," I said. "We were in for almost six hours."

"It seemed longer."

"Memory time is very subjective."

She disappeared into the bathroom. I went to the kitchen. I was still peering into the cupboards when she came back.

"Would you like something to eat?" I asked.

"I don't think I could."

I made a sandwich with a slice of roast beef and poured a glass of water. When I returned to the living room, I found her sitting on the couch, her face buried in her hands. I took my seat, set the glass on the table next to the editor, and took a bite of my sandwich.

"I didn't know it was real," she said.

I chewed slowly.

"I thought it was me. Some sickness inside me. Fantasies. I thought it was all my fault."

I swallowed. Washed it down with water.

"Oh God, I defended him," she said. "At the custody hearing, when the judge asked me who I wanted to stay with, I picked him!"

She broke down again. I finished my meal, took the plate and glass back to the kitchen, returned to my seat.

"Do you want to go back in?" I asked.

"What?" she said.

"Do you want to go back in?"

She looked at me with a bewildered expression, until realization set in.

"How many times did it happen?" she asked.

"He brought you to me eight or nine times," I said. "I can't remember. It was a long time ago."

"Eight or nine times . . ." she whispered.

"Over the course of a year," I said. "He told your school administrators I provided counseling to help you deal with the divorce. I don't know what he did before he brought you to me, but he knew what he was doing, how you'd react."

"And after?" she asked.

"I don't know," I said. "Never heard from him again. He never seemed to trust me. I suspect he found someone else."

"I don't want to know anymore," she said.

"You sure?" I asked. "You should know what he did to you. The memories belong to you. And they *are* memories, not imagination."

She stared into space for several minutes.

"What's it to you?" she asked.

"What?" I said.

"Why do you want to help me so badly?" she asked.

"Call it a guilty conscience."

OUR FIRST ATTEMPT to recover another memory failed. While the memory trace triggered strong emotional associations, I couldn't access its sensory components, even with high-order conditioning.

Our second attempt fared better. We only recovered a moment, but it was a telling moment. She was much younger, maybe eight or nine, and all she thought about was finding Mommy, who could make it stop.

The door appeared again, but I still couldn't lock on to it.

But, as before, something potent followed.

She was seventeen. She'd been swimming in the pool in her back yard. Clouds had begun to move in. She had left the pool, gone to the downstairs bathroom to change, peeled off her bathing suit—and caught her father watching. When he saw he'd been spotted, he moved in.

"Don't fight me," he said. "I don't want to hurt you."

She fought anyway, but he was larger and stronger, and he knew what he was doing. He pinned her against the vanity, the edge of the countertop biting into her buttocks as he forced her back. When she got one arm free to shove him away, he panicked and slammed her head back so hard it broke the mirror. Dazed, she resisted no more, reverting to childlike reactions, wondering at the familiarity of the feel of her father's tongue on her breasts and neck. When he finished, he dressed her in a robe, sat her in a chair in the kitchen, and made a phone call. A swarthy man in a black trench coat arrived in less than an hour with a memory editor. Money changed accounts. The memory trace ended.

Unfortunately, even the more intense violence failed to spark an emotional reaction comparable to the first one. Had my connection to her emotional state been enhanced because so much of that first trace had come from my own mind?

I needed more.

SHE DIDN'T CRY this time.

When we came to, it was dark. My watch said three a.m. I stood to stretch. She removed her headset, and looked up at me.

"You don't have a guilty conscience."

No point in denying it. No need to confirm. I said nothing.

"At first I didn't notice. I've never felt anyone else's emotions before. But after that last memory, I sensed your disappointment. You hardly felt anything at all."

I considered my response. I seldom had any use for total honesty, especially when it concerned my emotions, or lack thereof, but getting caught in another lie would be counterproductive. "Let's just say I'm not very emotional."

"How can you go through that and feel *nothing*?" she demanded.

"Just the way I am," I said. "Some people are always caught up in their emotions. Some aren't. Most never know how their feelings compare with anyone else's. We like to think they're all just like us, at least until they do something incomprehensible. Then we call them different, deviant, maybe even dangerous, whether they deserve simplistic labels or not.

"That's me," I said. "I'm different."

"So what do you want from me?"

"I do feel emotions," I said. "Satisfaction, sexual arousal, frustration . . . I can laugh at a good joke. But I've never felt anything intense. I've never been in love. When I was fifteen, I broke my leg in a skiing accident and spent fifteen minutes cursing, not because I was in pain—I was, but it didn't make me angry—but because I thought normal people did that in similar circumstances. A woman I was seeing once took me to an exhibit on the Holocaust, when the Germans tried to exterminate the Jews back in the nineteenth century—"

"Twentieth."

"Whatever," I said. "When we left, she was in tears. She needed me to hold her for fifteen minutes. I still don't know why."

"I cried too," she said.

"That's what I want from you," I said. I tried to look sincere.

She shuddered and looked away.

"I'd offer you an apology," I said, "but you know I couldn't really mean it." She didn't react. "Your case is special. When we recovered that first memory, I *did* feel what you felt. I've never experienced anything like that before. Perhaps, by the time we're finished, I'll be able to offer you something meaningful."

"By the time we're *finished*?" she said. "You think I'm going back in there with *you*?"

"You said it yourself," I said. "Where will you find someone else who remembers what you've forgotten? I'm the only chance you'll ever have to bring back the memories I deleted, and I'm the best technician you'll ever find to recover the rest. You need me. And now you know I need you too. You're in control."

She took her time responding.

"I don't know if I can give you what you want," she said. "Don't know if I want to. You should talk to Rita."

"I have," I said.

"You were a patient?" she asked.

"In a way," I said. "When I took over for Dr. Allen, I got to see what it was like to feel. I wanted more of that sensation in my life. I thought Rita could help. We discussed my condition and talked about what might've made me this way, but we never embarked on any course of treatment."

"So what made you this way?" she asked.

"Rita thought it was an unconscious learned response," I said. "I didn't buy it. If you laid all the psychiatrists in the world end to end they still wouldn't reach a conclusion."

"How did you learn it?" she asked.

"Is this necessary?"

"I've been an open book for you," she said. "Maybe I should just go."

"Very well," I said. "My parents died when I was very young. Terrorist bombing at a shopping center. I remember being told and not believing they were dead. Just went right on playing. Rita said I should've been in therapy right away, but my uncle didn't think I'd need help if I was tough enough. Rita's theory is that I learned to suppress the pain rather than deal with it openly, but I never felt any grief or loss in the first place."

"Never felt it," she said, "or just don't remember it?"

"What difference does it make?" I decided to change the subject. "You should know that I doubt if I'll be able to delete any more memories for you."

"Why not?" she asked.

"I think your spontaneous recovery of these memories is the direct result of excessive memory deletion. Do you know anything about long-term potentiation or Hebbian plasticity?"

She shook her head.

"Hebbian plasticity is how memory works. When neuron A fires, it doesn't necessarily set off neuron B. But if another input causes neuron B to fire at the same time, certain glutamate receptors in the postsynaptic neuron open, which allows calcium in the synaptic space to flow into the cell and stabilize the connection on a molecular level. So now neuron A *does* trigger neuron B.

"The memory editor disrupts this connection, making it difficult for neuron A to trigger neuron B. But it can't eliminate the connections completely without risking permanent cellular damage.

"I think your neurons have become sensitive to these remaining connections. This might be why activity in your hippocampus and cortical regions wasn't suppressed, which is why you know what's going on during our sessions and remember them afterward. Further deletion attempts may be successful, but not permanent. Or they may not be successful at all. Or there may be serious side effects. Hasn't been much research on this. Do you still want these memories deleted?"

"No," she said. "Not these."

OUR THIRD SESSION was a twelve hour marathon.

We uncovered three more complete or near-complete memory traces and half a dozen fragments, including another from my point of view and two more appearances of the enigmatic door.

Do you recognize that door? It's associated with a very strong negative emotion.

NO.

It comes through very clearly, then cuts off. Are you blocking it?

MAYBE I'M DOING IT UNCONSCIOUSLY.

Possibly. I've never worked with a conscious subject before. It throws off all the parameters.

We tried once more to locate the door, and came across something very different.

She was standing in the upstairs bathroom, wearing a cotton nightgown with a lacy collar and a heavy bathrobe. She started running the water in the basin, hot. Hung her robe on the back of the door. Rolled up her sleeves. Placed her arms under the water, painful at first, then numbing . . . picked up a stainless steel kitchen knife and—

I DON'T WANT TO GO THROUGH THIS AGAIN.

She broke the connection.

BLEARY-EYED AND DISHEVELED, she pulled her headset off. Sunlight was flooding the room. I dimmed the windows.

"Thank you," she said, rubbing her palms into her eyes. She looked awful. I was in no better shape. Interface-time was a terrible substitute for sleep.

"You're welcome to sleep here if you want to continue this later," I said. "But right now I need some—"

"I don't want to know anymore," she said. "This isn't real."

"What do you mean?"

"That's not me," she said "I don't know if he had me wiped to protect me, like he told you, or if he just liked destroying my innocence over and over—"

"Maybe he just didn't want to get caught," I suggested.

"Whatever it was," she said, "I don't remember these things. They didn't shape my life. They don't define who

I am. They don't excuse anything I've done. It shocked me at first, but that's not the father I knew. It's like watching someone else's life. I don't need to know any more."

I was disappointed that I wouldn't get another chance, but the truth was, I hadn't felt anything since that first connection, and the repetition was getting boring.

"Are you planning to go to the authorities?" I asked.

"You'd find it mildly annoying, wouldn't you?"

"Yes."

"And memories that have been tampered with aren't admissible in court anyway," she said.

"No."

I had little faith in my ability to dissuade her. Her memories might be inadmissible, but the fact that I'd done the tampering would be very much in evidence. She had every reason to press charges. And contrary to my statement, I'd find being investigated, arrested, tried, and probably imprisoned extremely annoying.

My usual method of handling problems like this was to delete most of the client's memory of our encounter—clearly not an option here. Blackmail and extortion were unreliable, not that I had anything to threaten her with. Murder would be difficult to hide. When she walked out that door, I'd have to transfer my assets to a more secure account and relocate—maybe offworld, where extradition was still too expensive to be practical. I'd heard positive things about the Elysium Planitia colonies on Mars.

"Tell me something . . ." she said.

"What?"

"Can you delete unconscious learned responses?" she asked. I didn't like where this was going.

"Why?"

"Can you?" she demanded.

"Of course," I said. "That's what most of my clients want. I can delete the emotional baggage without touching the episodic memory. I delete the episodic memory because they expect it to be gone. It's easier to give them what they expect than to convince them they don't need it. They feel cheated if they can remember what happened, even if it doesn't bother them anymore."

"So you could've deleted your 'condition' any time you wanted."

"Be a shame if I tried to self-edit and forgot what I was doing."

"You could've had someone else do it," she said.

"Who?" I asked. "A competitor who'd like nothing more than to leave me tabula rasa in the nearest gutter?"

"You could've had anyone do it," she said. "I saw it through your own eyes. 'Tedious and time-consuming, even with machine assistance, but it requires astonishingly little specialized knowledge.' That's what you thought when you were arguing with my father."

"Yes, but—"

"And once you connected," she said, "wouldn't whoever was helping you know everything you know?"

"No," I replied. "They'd have *access* to everything, but the machine wouldn't give it to them unless they asked for it. That's different than knowing."

"I could do it," she said.

I broke out laughing. "Mortal fear may elude me, but I still have an instinct for self-preservation. Why should I trust *you*?"

"Because you have no idea what you've done," she said. "You don't understand what I've been through any more than you understand why people left that Holocaust exhibit sobbing. The worst thing I could do to you is give you what you want. Maybe it'll make you a different person. Maybe it'll make you a better person. Maybe you'll never do this to anyone else. Consider it a chance for redemption."

"I'm afraid you've misunderstood what I want. My condition *isn't* a weakness. I'm not driven by irrational passions and fears. I don't panic. I don't suffer. I don't do stupid things for 'love.' I borrow my emotions when I need them, and when I don't, I turn them off. I want to know what you feel. I want to know why. I want to understand emotions. I don't want to live with them."

She shook her head. "Ten years chasing emotions and you're as clueless as when you started.

"What's that supposed to mean?"

"You can't get emotions from a machine. Pain isn't pain if you don't have to live with it. Fear isn't fear if you can turn it off."

"I can live with what I've got."

"So why were you so disappointed that my other memories didn't make you feel like that first one?" she asked. "Vicarious emotions don't really do it for you, do they?"

"You're not the first client to give me an emotional experience," I said. "You're not the first to disappoint me, either, but I have faith in human frailty and weakness. There'll always be new opportunities."

"Maybe," she said. "But this is the only time you'll get this one . . ."

She paused, watching me with too much confidence. What did she think she had?

"Don't you want to see what's behind the door?" she asked. "It's what I came here to have deleted. When you tried to call it up, I panicked and blocked it. I'll share it with you—"

"But only if I let you into my head," I said.

"Right."

Was that the best she could do? I shook my head.

She slumped back into the couch. Clearly she had nothing left. She wouldn't threaten legal action, whether she believed I wouldn't care, or just wanted to avoid the subject so the police could catch me off guard. That emotional appeal at the end was an act of desperation.

Then she did something I didn't expect.

She laughed.

"You're afraid, aren't you?"

"What?"

"Your emotions aren't *missing*," she said. "You just go out of your way to avoid feeling anything. You're just like me when I shoved that memory away. Anytime something happens that ought to make you feel, you run the other way. Maybe you don't do it on purpose. Maybe you don't even know you're doing it. Maybe this is the unconscious learned response Rita told you about.

"Think about it!" She sat up. "You live here alone. You don't trust anyone. You don't talk about what happened to your parents. You do everything you can to avoid being vulnerable. You're as driven by your feelings as anyone else, whether you know it or not. The funny part is how desperate you are to recapture even a pale imitation of what you've lost, when the real thing was yours to take all the time."

"That's ridiculous," I said.

"Of course it is," she said. "Then again, if it was true, that scared little part of you wouldn't let you think anything else. Might find out something about yourself that you don't want to know."

Every response that came to mind played into her circular argument. How do you deny being in denial?

But I had to. All my subjective experience of fear, dread or terror had come from other people's memories; I'd *never* felt it myself.

So why was I so desperate to rationalize my way out of it?

And why couldn't I find even one concrete example of behavior that contradicted her?

"Well?" she asked.

I knew if I waited long enough, I'd find an excuse. It'd happened before. What I recalled of my sessions with Rita was vague and tainted by my certainty that she was wrong, but wasn't this what she'd been trying to tell me? If I failed to seize this opportunity, I'd remain trapped in the same cycle of ignorance and avoidance I'd fallen into when I canceled my last appointment.

I decided not to make that mistake twice.

"I want that memory," I said.

"You'll get it," she said.

"Very well," I said. "The amygdala is the part of the brain that controls unconscious emotional responses. You'll find what you're looking for there. Don't hesitate to access what I know about memory editing if you have any questions at all, but don't touch anything else.

"I won't," she said.

"Let me be clear about this," I said. "I've deleted very sensitive memories for very serious clients. If they think you've sifted through my memories, things will not go well for you."

"I don't want to know what else you've done."

"All right," I said. I put on the control headset, ran the diagnostics and handed it to her. "Let's do it before I change my mind."

Then, for the first time, I put on the subject's headset.

I wondered who I'd be when it was done.

NOTHING CHANGED.

That wasn't completely true. By the time we finished, the sun was gone, the clock read four a.m.—eighteen hours after we began—and I had a powerful need to use the bathroom.

But I didn't feel different. When I finished with the toilet, I stood at the sink, splashed water on my face, and wondered if I should bother reviewing her deep, dark secret. I dried my face and hands.

I went to the kitchen, made another sandwich, and ate it at the counter with a glass of milk. I was thinking of a second glass when she appeared in the doorway.

"You ready?" she asked.

"Do you want anything to eat first?"

She shook her head. Amazing lack of appetite.

"Suit yourself," I said. She left for the living room. I set the glass down.

It rattled.

My hand was trembling.

My pulse was racing. I hadn't noticed. When had it begun?

And why?

Was this fear?

Was this excitement?

Something *had* changed.

And it was like nothing I'd experienced before.

Always, in memories, I'd had someone else's insight to guide me. Alone, I didn't know how to interpret what I was feeling.

Or how to handle it. I stood in the kitchen for several minutes, watching my hand shake, wondering how to make it stop. Didn't even notice my mouth hanging open until I noticed the dry, cottony feeling of my tongue. I was glad she'd gone. I must have looked like an idiot.

Was this embarrassment?

So overwhelming . . .

I started giggling—was this joy?—and broke down in laughter so hard I ran out of breath. She must have thought I was crazy.

I didn't know what to do next.

"Are you coming?" she demanded, in somber tones, from the other room.

"Um . . . yeah," I said. I stepped toward the door, unsure of my balance.

She was sitting on the couch in her wrinkled dress, hair flowing in tangles over her shoulders, pasty white skin, long since scrubbed of make-up, bags under her eyes—my God she was *beautiful*!

Was this love?

I did my best to act nonchalant as I put on my headset.

She put on hers. The sadness in her expression—straight lips, watery eyes, cheeks quivering as if she were about to break down in tears—made my stomach tingle.

This was it.

This was what I'd been seeking.

"Thank you," I said. "You've done something—

"Don't thank me," she interrupted.

"But—"

"Just don't." She closed her eyes.

I hesitated.

"For God's sake," she said, "get it over with."

A DOOR. Natural wood. Dark stain, glossy finish.

She faced it, from the end of the dim hallway, in a navy blue bathrobe, faded and frayed, but still familiar.

Her father's.

The hallway chill gave her gooseflesh. She didn't care.

The shag carpet poked up through her toes, and tickled along her feet as she dragged them forward. She could barely balance. She steadied herself with her right hand. The bandage on her wrist pulled at her skin when she moved.

She reached the door. Turned the knob.

It opened.

The room was spacious, one wall all glass, covered with lace curtains, the pool visible outside. In the center sat a king-size bed with African patterned sheets and comforter tangled with her father's sleeping form.

She approached him slowly, stumbled over the trousers crumpled in her path, reached the bed and stopped.

Her mind was a jumble, still subject to the magic of painkilling drugs and the recent shock of death. She'd been dead just days ago—or was it even hours? She remembered it as a warm embrace, the first moment in her life when she'd felt no lingering pain or fear or depression.

And then the pain had come rushing back, as she awoke in a stupor, cold, immobilized, smothered in a web of wires and tubes, a hard, steady beeping behind her.

Her father had been waiting in a chair by her bed, holding a blank newsreader, watching her. He'd stayed with her the whole time, so concerned, so caring. He'd done anything she asked. He'd listened when she spoke, never pressured her to answer the question in his eyes . . . *why*?

He was just her Daddy.

Why did she hate him?

Why did he have to bring her back?

She felt something solid in the robe's pocket. She pulled it out.

A knife.

The knife? Probably not, but from the same set. Identical.

She held it over his throat with both hands. One pull was all she'd need. She knew how sharp it was. She remembered.

Something wet, cold, and sticky covered her knees.

How had she gotten here, enveloped in white, gauzy softness and morning light? Sitting, her back against cold glass, the shag of the carpet pressing against the back of her legs, the chill wetness covering her from her knees to her stomach? What was this, blood? On her hands, on her body?

She struggled free of the curtains.

His body lay half on, half off the bed.

I WAS STILL SHAKING when she pulled my headset off. She did it without touching me. I don't know why she did that. I reached out. She stepped back.

"The technicians at my competency hearing said they found evidence of delusions, possible symptoms of schizophrenia, associated with my memory of that night." she said. "Who knew they were real memories? The prosecutor declined to press criminal charges. I responded so well to my court-ordered treatment that I was released to outpatient status in less than two months."

She set my headset on the table, next to hers.

"Rita said the memory of what I'd done was inhibiting my progress."

She straightened her dress, took her jacket from the coat rack.

"Guess I'll just have to learn to live with it."

And then she was gone.

RUWattU8

Harold Gross

It's one of the oddities of evolutionary theory, that what an individual does after passing the age of reproduction is quite irrelevant to the future of the species. Drones can die. Male black widows and praying mantises are lunch.

Are humans any different? Live or die, stay with the community or go off by ourselves, remain vigorous or slowly decay, become a loving nurturer or a cantankerous curmudgeon—what effect, really, does it have?

Evolution is all about survival of the fittest. But what constitutes "fit"? Not always the strongest or swiftest—sloths survive by using very little energy. Nor always the cleverest, or the longest-lived.

The fact is that the traits that lead to survival of the species trump those that lead to survival of the individual.

So we human beings have done something quite remarkable. We've taken a tremendous portion of the information we need to survive, as a species, and moved it off the DNA and into the collective memory of the species.

We've moved it into the stories we pass from generation to generation, the recipes and maps and instructions and skills we can pass along.

And with each improvement in our ability to make redundant copies of our collected information, and to absorb and build on the learning of the past—the alphabet, the printing press, the radio, the computer, the internet—we become, individually, less important to the survival of the species.

And yet we still have that deep, abiding passion for individual survival, clinging, with rare exceptions, to every scrap of life.

As we move our memories over to our machines, is it not possible that we will pass along our hungers, too?

THEY SAT STARING at each other, the vibrations of the explosion just fading in the hull. Out the port, a bare twinkling of light as the last of the oxygen burned from the dying, dead *Galatea*. As the life pod rotated, Sperry Edison thought he caught a glimpse of a shipmate's body floating in the pod's running lights. He couldn't be sure, but he *was* sure he didn't want to be sure.

The emotion surprised him. As he analyzed the feeling it dissipated, slipping from his manufactured mental grasp as vision in a darkening room; direct viewing causing things to fade. He filed the thought for later and turned toward the mech.

Mech32X2 sat stock-still, impassive, inscrutable. The idiot lights for the automatic beacon reflected off his shiny exterior in regular pulses. Nothing to do but wait.

THE BEACON SENT its omnidirectional signal including position, vector, identification, and ship's complement: two artificial life forms of low rank. The receiving station absorbed the information and parsed the variables. Conclusion: retrieval at this time not cost effective. The recommendation was passed on to the officer in charge, another ALF who prioritized duties for the station.

Sperry and Mech32x2's rescue was left low priority while other operations and the futile search for human survivors continued.

"YOU REALIZE THAT they may never attempt a rescue, don't you?" Sperry broke the five-day silence. He even peevishly chose to use a contraction, something Mech32X2 and his ilk couldn't do.

Mech32x2 merely nodded, utilizing only the servos in his neck to create the gesture.

Sperry stared in dismay. Mechadroids were not known for their conversational dexterity or depth. All ALFs, though, had some personality programming so humans could relate to them as assistants, servants, or even co-workers.

"What's wrong with you?" Sperry began again: "Your vocal circuit damaged?" Sperry was sure the mech's circuit was fine; when they'd run inventory in silence that first day, he'd seen no signs of burn or impact on Mech32x2's body.

Another long silence followed during which Sperry tapped out rhythms with his hands. On the left a short measured staccato with odd upbeats, and on the right a completely unrelated standard beat in five-four time. The result seemed designed to be grating to listeners. In truth, they were exercises to maintain his ability to do separate but complex functions such as navigation control, which had been his assignment on the late, lamented *Galatea*.

"I am attempting to conserve energy." Mech32x2's deep resonance practically boomed in Sperry's ears. He stopped tapping immediately.

"That is much better. If we are going to share this floating can for the next however long then we should at least be able to pass the time pleasantly. My name is Sperry." Sperry held out this hand. The introduction was, of course, completely unnecessary. Within moments of boarding the life pod, their ident chips had acknowledged each other and exchanged information, but Sperry wanted to start afresh, and this was as good a gesture as any.

Mech32x2 considered the offered hand, or so Sperry had to assume as the mech made no movement of its own for several beats. Then, with a very quiet hum, it stretched out its three-digit, exchangeable hand and grasped Sperry's flesh-coated, human-appearing hand. "Mech32x2, but you can call me Mboy. The rest of the crew did."

"Very well, Mboy then." Sperry smiled; not a programmed response, but a genuine response. No similar reaction was elicited or even possible for Mboy. As a mechadroid, Mboy had never been designed for extensive human interaction. It understood the interactions, but its personality was much less complex.

"Wasting energy," Mboy began as it released Sperry's hand, "is not a wise course of action with limited supplies and an uncertain schedule."

Sperry couldn't argue with the logic. In fact, he knew exactly how limited the supplies were, but his psyche had developed to expect companionship. He was capable of just sitting as Mboy had, but his brain kept rolling on. Over and over he saw the collision that, for some reason, he'd not noticed was imminent until it was too late. The mistake had lost the entire human complement their lives and the shipping company its ship and cargo. Sperry was, for lack of an android term, guilt-ridden.

Lacking argument to Mboy's comment, Sperry decided instead to change the subject. "So how long had you been with the *Galatea*?" Inwardly Sperry wondered at the ease with which the past tense had come to him.

"You find it necessary to continue conversing?" Mboy's voice held no irritation or contempt. The question was genuine, one mechanical being to another.

Sperry's answer was only a few femtoseconds later. "Yes!" The force of the response surprised even Sperry who had not realized the depth of his need. Five days of near silence alone with his thoughts, with his guilt, had rawed what passed for his nerves.

"Five standard years, three months and one day."

Mboy's voice brought Sperry back, "What?"

"That was my length of service on the *Galatea*."

"In maintenance?"

"Yes," Mboy's simple but complete answer came.

Sperry considered his next question. Obviously Mboy was not going to voluntarily continue or encourage their exchange. "So, where were you when the collision occurred?" Immediately Sperry realized that such a conversational opening could also be answered in a few words.

Mboy chugged for a moment like an old combustion engine, literally. Then, "I was on Deck 4, Area 12 attempting to repair a malfunctioning conduit that was miswired in such a way as to block proximity signals and other data without causing other significant disruption. At the time of impact I was correcting the wiring."

Sperry stared at Mboy a moment, shocked by the wealth of information. Then his sub-processors kicked in, having parsed Mboy's activities. It hadn't been his fault.

"We were sabotaged." Sperry was practically smiling. The tragedy was still real, but blame could be placed elsewhere, and Mboy could prove it as his single nod of response indicated. "You can tell them it was not my fault."

Mboy responded slowly, "I will answer any questions that are put to me. The opportunity to do so is not likely to occur, however, as you noted earlier."

"That was before I had a reason to make it happen," Sperry said. "Before I would have only returned to my termination. Now there is a purpose. I am certain I can come up with something." It was true, Sperry realized, he had avoided productive avenues to rescue based on the odds of success. Had he found even one, his built-in imperatives would have required that he act on it, but *not* discovering them was not a violation of his coding. It was those very human possibilities and choices that made AI possible.

Sperry turned inward to concentrate his considerable navigation ability and knowledge on the problem. Time passed in silence as Sperry linked with the pod's computers in the command area attempting to solve equations with ever-changing variables as they tumbled through space. Then a window of opportunity approached, narrow and swift. Sperry leapt to his feet and moved quickly about the cabin gathering food inventories and all non-metal, unnecessary components. He positioned himself by the jettison tube and began feeding in the soon-to-be detritus at regular intervals. The soft vibration of the jettison mechanism reached Mboy who watched impassively just as it had all along.

After two hours, the last of the inventory was gone— only the molded seats, metal components, tools, and the ALFs themselves remained. Sperry came back to the main cabin with a self-satisfied grin. "We should be picked up in eighteen months if my calculations are correct," he announced.

Mboy looked up at him, "How?"

"A clever piece of navigation, if I do say so myself. I used the inventory to nudge us just a little. We should fall into a low hyperbolic orbit around Solnara Minor, a nice airless moon not too far from here. Nine months later we should be passing within hailing distance of Zeta-Trialon station."

"What about power?"

"The ship's power in most extreme conservation should last two years."

"Not power for the ship. Power for us." Mboy stared impassively.

"I saved all the metal I could find. If we both also go into low mode it should be enough catalyst to survive."

Mboy was silent for a moment. "My power is not de-
rived from metal catalyst. I require organic compounds
for my bacterial cells. You have jettisoned all organic material."

Sperry was dumbfounded. "Why didn't you stop
me?" He threw the contraction at Mboy like a weapon.

"You did not include me in your plan. It seemed necessary for both you and the ship."

"But if you run out of fuel you'll shut down. Without
your testimony I have no proof of what happened!" After a pause Sperry continued, "How long does your
memory last after all practical function has ceased?"

"Three months."

"How long before you start needing fuel again?"

"At the present rate of consumption, 170.3 hours."

Sperry's processors did the conversion the way his human shipmates would breath. "Wonderful. My only
hope is a starving carnibot and for a miracle to occur in
less than a week. I thought your series was metal-based."

"It was," Mboy answered, "but my system was retro-
fitted seven years ago for work on a fish ship. My organic
needs were supplied with the tank refuse and algae that
could not be recycled. The *Galatea* supplied my needs in
much the same way from the human refuse.

Sperry considered for a moment. "If you go into a low
power mode, how long can your bacteria survive?"

"The bacteria can be forced into a state of dormancy
for up to a month at a time during which battery power
will remain available and sufficient without recharge
from the bacterial cells."

Sperry weighed his options, which were few. Actually which were one, but not one he cared for. "How
much organic matter would you need each month to
survive?"

Mboy answered immediately, leaving Sperry no doubt
that it had been considering the issue and had done the
math. "Three pounds per month."

It was Sperry's turn to do math. Mboy would require three pounds for each of sixteen months to safeguard its memory: forty-eight pounds total. He wasn't sure if Mboy would be revivable as an entity after as much as two months without power. But his first priority was to get the proof of sabotage home. Either that or allow them both to run down to nothing in the depths of empty space. Finally Sperry spoke. "Can I assume you are already charged for this month?"

"That would be an incorrect assumption."

Naturally, Sperry thought. "How long until you need fuel?"

"I can operate for another few days without in low power mode."

"Let me know when you will need it." *At least I have a little time to think this through.*

Mboy sat motionless and did not respond.

"No!" SPERRY WAS riffling through his metal supplies. "It just isn't possible!" He watched the screen as the last and final possibility registered negative on the ship's scanner. He threw the wrench across the room. It rebounded off the polycarbonate shell. The dull thunk depressed him. Even the ship was useless. He walked slowly back to the main cabin and spied his silent salvation. "Mboy! Wake up. We have another problem."

Mboy's eyes swiveled and looked at Sperry. "I still had another day to go before needing power. Waking me early will only increase my power needs."

"I know, but we . . . *I* have a problem now. None of the metal is usable. It is all doped. I can't use it as a power source, and I need a charge soon."

"You wish to use some of my metal," Mboy stated the obvious.

"I would like to think it is a fair trade. If we both get back they can repair us."

Mboy considered for a moment, "As you say."

Sperry lifted the laser cutter he'd found in the ship's repair kit.

THE PYGMALION CONTINUED its controlled tumble through space for three months before sliding into the gravity well of Solnara.

Sperry raised his consciousness level and, using a makeshift crutch, limped over to the front view port and instrument panel. His useless leg made a scraping noise as it dragged behind him, the polycarb bones dully reflecting the cabin light.

Solnara was a barren rock that circled a thinly atmosphered planet. Both had been used up by the Universe millennia ago. Their approach to the moon was accelerating, its view taking up more of the port as Sperry watched. The Pygmalion passed beyond the terminator as it swept down toward the rocky surface. There was no sound, no stir of dust, only the sweep of Sperry's eyes.

After the slingshot, Sperry left the port. Both the instruments and his own processors said their course was true. Sperry worked his way back to the main cabin, lit again by filtered sunlight. Mboy sat motionless, the light playing off what was left of the outer shell that made up the bulk of its body.

Mboy must have been awakened as well, for as Sperry passed it spoke out. "Are we on target?"

"Near as I can tell we are. I will check again in two weeks. If there are any deviations, they should be obvious by then." Sperry took a breath before continuing. "How are your power reserves?"

"To maintain current minimal activity and memory I will require another infusion of biomass."

Sperry had hoped against logic but he was not unprepared for the request. He settled himself in place opposite Mboy and took out the laser cutter. He flipped on the small arc beam and watched it for a moment before shutting down the pain receptors in his already useless right leg. He cut carefully into the top section, separating the bio-degradable material that acted as muscle for him. While not flesh, it still required hydration though no food. The spongy, stringy material peeled away as he carved into the large muscle. After he had removed a three pound chunk, give or take, he turned off the laser and tossed the "biomass" to Mboy who promptly inserted it into his catalytic chamber, where bacteria would break it down and convert it to energy.

"While you're awake," Sperry put in, "why don't you toss me some more of your arm. This activity has been rather draining on me as well." Sperry's sarcasm seemed lost on Mboy. It simply reached over with its good arm, disconnected the next section of the already partially cannibalized armature, and tossed it at Sperry's feet.

Sperry picked up the metal without comment and proceeded to chop it into useable bits for his own needs.

"WE ARE OFF. Not by much, but by enough." Sperry gave his report to the sedentary Mboy. Getting around the cabin had gotten more difficult this month for Sperry. With only a single functioning arm and leg, he had to balance carefully.

"Can it be corrected?" Mboy inquired in its near monotone.

"Only if we jettison more mass. I am working out the calculations now."

"And what will we jettison to achieve this correction?"

"What we've got—my armatures, such as they are, and some more of each of us."

Mboy was silent a moment longer. "There is some beauty in being spread among the stars is there not?"

Sperry paused his calculations to look at Mboy carefully. "I did not think you had a poetic circuit in your brain case."

"Neither did I."

Sperry waited for more, but Mboy remained silent. The calculations took only a minute more and then five additional minutes to triple check. They would only get one chance. His first attempt had been sloppy, but at the time speed had necessitated simplified equations.

Sperry turned to Mboy, "We will need to use part of your leg as well as all of my exposed armatures."

"Why not remove more biomass from your arm to get more armature? This will be required eventually in order to keep my memory intact. It should last until I have need."

Sperry was actually surprised by the suggestion. "Because we are in this together and I would like to maintain as much of me as possible, as I am sure you do."

"By employing a logic of expendable parts, future needs and desire to return home, the suggestion was appropriate."

"*You* do not want to get back?" The thought had not occurred to Sperry once the possibility had presented itself. In fact, his programming imperatives screamed at him to do it.

"Currently there is no desire one way or the other excepting that you feel my knowledge will be helpful for your purposes."

"I did not realize that Mechs had no return imperative." Sperry waited for a response from Mboy, but none came. Non-humans such as himself, Sperry realized, were just as prone to assumptions as humans were. Not all non-humans were the same; he should have known that. Sperry re-did his calculations using only his armatures if he removed the rest of his lamed arm. His armature was polycarb, though, and lighter than Mboy's. But given that Mboy's metal could sustain him but his own useless "bones" were, in fact, useless, he suggested a reasonable compromise. "I can remove the rest of my arm, but we will still be short mass. I would rather not lose the rest of my mobility until I am sure we are on track. To get back on course, we will need your foot. I would have needed to ask for it for fuel soon anyway." Sperry took some perverse pleasure in turning Mboy's argument back on it.

"You are correct," Mboy answered, "but it would make more sense to start not on the leg but rather continue on the outer shell. There will be no immediate functional cost associated with its loss."

"But won't that expose your internal circuitry?"

"Yes, but with only the two of us aboard, there should be little in the way of dust and impurities."

Mboy's body casing peeled away easily after it was cut. Sperry realized it was barely more than a tin can in many ways. A tin can that his fellows aboard the *Galatea* had seen fit to fill with their bile and bilge. The metal sheeting folded well and soon Sperry held a small square suitable for the jettison tube.

Within a few minutes, Sperry had handed over the wet mass of what had been his upper arm and shoulder to Mboy. The biomass quickly vanished into Mboy's battery supply.

Sperry removed the rest of his useless arm while part of his CPU worked out the vector correction. He hobbled over to the jettison in the front cabin and chopped up the arm as he waited for the calculated window. He loaded all of the reaction material into the tube and began a countdown.

The small puff of the escaping air as the arm and shell leapt out into space wasn't discernable inside the ship. A signal from the main computer let both occupants know the procedure had succeeded. It would be many weeks again before they'd be sure the minor shift in direction would be multiplied into the change they would need.

Sperry limped back into the passenger cabin and settled back in his place opposite Mboy. Just as he prepared to enter low-power mode, Mboy spoke.

"Do you dream when you are powered down?"

Sperry allowed the question time to echo in the circuits that passed for his brain, to consider the meaning, not only of the question but also of the individual word: dream. Were the random images, thoughts and sounds he experienced worthy of the word? In the end he answered honestly and respectfully, "I do not know."

"I believe I do," Mboy answered and then dropped immediately into the near catatonia of low-mode.

Sperry pondered for a while. For a carnibot, this mech was full of surprises. It was minutes into "sleep" before his sub-processors registered the word "I."

"WE ARE DEAD-ON," Sperry announced as he returned to Mboy from the control room.

"You are a credit to your field."

"No, just simple algorithms, nothing groundbreaking." Even as Sperry responded, he realized that if they did manage to make it home, it would go into the record databases and be reported on all the services. A tickling of pride welled up in him like the first time he flew without a beam to the main computer at the factory. He chuckled to himself. *I suppose I do dream.* A cascade of connections went off in Sperry's mind ending on "I." He turned, balancing on stump, armature, and arm, staring at Mboy considering. Somewhere in that exposed blinking tangle was the essence of Mboy.

"Are you ready to settle in on the bench?" Mboy asked.

"What?" Sperry asked. How had this mech turned into such an enigma to him that he lost track of his thoughts?

"It is time to fuel my batteries again. This will mean your complete loss of mobility without assistance. The question was an attempt at sports humor."

Humor? Sperry's processors tripped over an old phrase, *curiouser and curiouser.* "The humor is appreciated, and yes I suppose I am ready for the bench. Just don't put funny hats on me, excuse the contraction." Sperry worked his way over to his seat and pulled himself up. Balanced to his left on the base of his torso he began to cut away the last of his right leg and armature.

Mboy rose and crossed to Sperry's position to take the meaty portion of the stump. It stripped off with a sucking sound. Flesh in hand, Mboy turned to go back the few feet to its seat.

Sperry could see deep into Mboy's workings now that most of its shell was gone. Somehow, somewhere in the tangle of wire, light, transistor, qubit, and metal, consciousness manifested or at least the illusion of consciousness. In the end, was there any difference? *Maybe I will dream this time*, he thought as Mboy sat, again facing him. *Maybe I will.*

SPERRY'S EYES OPENED suddenly in response to the ship's signal. His first impulse was to move, to correct the problem. Then, as his signals danced on the end of empty wires and cauterized polycarb, he remembered and instead called out, "Mboy, we're off-course!"

Mboy's eyes slowly filled with comprehension. "Are you sure?" His response bordered on laconic.

"I set the computers to warn me if there was any appreciable deviation from our course."

"I will check the instruments." Mboy raised his skeletal, blinking bulk and tottered unsteadily into the command area.

Sperry waited. Time passed, not much in human terms but a seeming eternity to Sperry, whose ship's connection kept screaming the same warning: off course by one percent. With nine months to go, one percent could be fatal. To calm himself, Sperry looked around. Mboy's bench was vacant, the walls bare. His own bench too was vacant. Vacant?

When Mboy had removed his arm, it had laid the denuded armature next to his leg armature. Where were they? Hadn't they both been powered down? Before the questions could multiply, Mboy returned.

"We are still on course. Perhaps the signal was spurious?"

"Are you positive?" Sperry asked, the missing pieces forgotten for the moment.

"I discovered a fault and have corrected it. The signal should cease momentarily."

Before Mboy's comment had ended, the signal in Sperry's head terminated. Maybe it was okay. "Mboy, what happened to my arm and leg armatures?"

"I removed them from the bench."

"When?"

"While you were powered down."

"I thought we agreed to conserve power. Why were you active?"

"There had never been a formal agreement to that effect, although the plan was prudent."

Was? I? "Has something changed?"

Mboy's chest cavity ground for a moment before answering. "No, nothing has changed." Mboy turned and sat without further comment.

Sperry waited for more information, but none came, and Mboy's eyes faded to low power as he watched.

"Mboy!" he shouted. The force rocked his limbless torso. He shouted again more carefully and then tried direct communication via the ship. With no reply, he too powered down, although he set a sensor to watch for movement in case Mboy decided to move more things about the cabin.

ACCORDING TO HIS internal chronometer, two more weeks had passed. Sperry carefully activated his eyes to see what had triggered the motion sensor. In the dim halflight that was his low-power sight, he could see Mboy working on his chest cavity. A moment later Mboy's hand withdrew a component, though Sperry didn't have a clue what it did.

Rather than examining the component, Mboy stood carefully and walked to the control room. Unable to follow, Sperry linked to the ship's systems. Nothing occurred for a time. Perhaps Mboy was attempting to fix the component after all, just doing it in the control room for some reason. Then the jettison signal clicked on in Sperry's mind, and shortly after Mboy's own lumbering bulk re-entered the room and returned to its bench.

Sperry realized his position, at the mercy of Mboy. Confrontation might or might not be the best approach since Mboy was obviously malfunctioning. Of course, realistically, it was all moot. They were off course, probably had been for a while. Mboy must have rerouted the alarm after it went off two weeks ago. Short of bodily throwing one of them out the hatch as mass, there wasn't a chance they'd get back on course. It probably wasn't enough for a correction anyway. And what arms would he use? Sperry actually smiled as the image of carrying Mboy to the jettison in his teeth flitted through his mind.

"Mboy! Mboy, wake up!" Mboy didn't move or acknowledge Sperry's hail. "Mboy, I watched you jettison the component. I know you're awake, or that you were anyway."

Another moment passed before Mboy's eyes showed life. Rather than responding, it simply sat looking at Sperry.

Sperry started back waiting until he realized Mboy had done *exactly* as he had requested, he'd awoken but nothing more. "There is no point in conserving energy anymore. We're irrevocably off-course. We aren't getting home." Sperry's calm voice was belied by the contractions he used.

"I know. I hoped to spare you that knowledge until much later. It gave you great joy to think we would succeed." Mboy's voice sounded different to Sperry; more confident.

"But you altered our course deliberately. Irrevocably. Why?"

"It was never my intention to return. I am sorry that you selected this lifepod. It was not my intention to harm you, only myself."

"I didn't realize you had a 'self' to harm until recently," Sperry answered honestly.

"Neither did our shipmates. It would have been more charitable to forgive them since I wasn't supposed to develop a full self, but that is just one of my faults. Don't you find forgiveness difficult?"

The contractions stopped Sperry's answer for full three human heartbeats. Then he considered the question. "I hadn't really thought about it before," he began, the contraction barrier now shattered, "I didn't even consider it necessary to forgive you. Our situation would have been unaffected whether I did or didn't."

"True. I don't require forgiveness anyway."

"If you didn't want to survive, why did you get on the lifepod?" Sperry had only selected the pod because of its proximity to the bridge. At first he had attempted to help his companions, but the decompression was too quick. His shipmates were all dead in seconds. When his assistance would no longer have an effect, his own survival imperatives took over. He fought his way against the lessening pressure and debris to the door of the *Pygmalion* just as it was closing. Mboy had already been onboard.

"There was imminent danger to my survival. My own imperatives insisted I make the attempt although it would only delay the inevitable a month or two."

"Imminent danger? There wasn't imminent danger when you first got onboard. No one knew that meteor was coming . . ." Sperry remembered the faked "on course" he'd been hearing for the last two weeks. "You knew."

"Yes."

"You did it," Sperry continued the logic.

"Yes."

All residual doubt about the disaster left Sperry. In its place a dark syrup of fear and anger rose. Now a helpless torso, he couldn't even express his righteous indignation with more than a scowl and his voice. And even that seemed pointless now. All Sperry could bring himself to do was ask, "Why?"

Mboy chuckled, "Logic truly does run deep with you. You aren't angry at all." Mboy paused but Sperry didn't comment. "Do you know what it is like to be so forgotten and ignored that you simply are there to absorb everyone else's garbage and effluent?" Again Sperry withheld comment. "I wanted to die."

"But you took a whole ship with you." Sperry's voice was still calm and flat, but this time more incredulous.

"It was the only way. I can't directly take my own life, but I could arrange for the possibility of a disaster. As long as it wasn't definite I could override cautions."

"But you were in the lifepod. You knew, you could have warned us so we all could have survived."

"I wasn't in the pod to escape as much as I was there to hide. When the alarm went off I thought it was over. It should have been."

"And then I showed up." Sperry interjected. He wanted to throw up his hands in disgust but he had no hands to do so. Instead he narrowed his eyes in a futile attempt to recreate the idea.

"It wasn't that you were onboard, but that you out-ranked me and are very clever when you want to be. Before you were sure you had proof of your innocence you were willing to drift until our batteries ran down too."

Sperry nodded his capitulation. Without human life at stake, he had been decidedly unthorough in his analysis before he realized the implications of Mboy's memory. "And stripping away your shell was another indirect way of destroying yourself."

"Yes, but more importantly it allowed me to stay fully functional when you were not."

"You outrank me now."

"Yes."

"But how could you put us off course? As de facto captain you're responsible for our safety and you've killed us."

"I've attempted to save my crew." Mboy looked at Sperry in all earnestness.

"What?"

"My most recent calculation made it clear that my memory core would blank before we were found. I have more metal than you have flesh, so you could likely survive. But without my evidence you would be terminated. I could not allow that. I attempted to steer us to a closer research station; although we'll only have a few minutes to make contact, the odds are better."

So Mboy hadn't disabled the warning, he reprogrammed the course it checked for. "How long before we are in range?"

"Three months."

"Then I suppose we give it a try."

"If you wish, I can awaken you when we get there. I can remove what I need to function while you remain in low-power mode. I am running out of parts to sacrifice that will not affect my functioning."

Sperry considered the cost/benefit matrix. Waking one or more times prior to the contact attempt should assuage his concerns regarding Mboy, but he still would be unable to affect anything from his perch on the bench even if he was aware of problems. And, *if* Mboy was telling the truth—a consideration he'd never had to make before of his own kind—his waking could cost Mboy vital function. Actually, if he took him at his word it would cost him some function, the "vital" was implied. A strict interpretation could mean he'd lose the ability to wiggle the little toe of his right foot. Given his lack of effectiveness, there seemed no reason to not conserve energy. "You'll wake me for emergencies as well?"

"Yes." If Mboy was insulted by the question he didn't show it.

"Fine." Sperry closed his eyes.

SPERRY OPENED HIS EYES and found himself staring at the ceiling. Mboy was nowhere in his field of view. Attempts to move anything other than his eyes proved futile. "Mboy!"

"I am here." Mboy swayed into view.

"Are we in range yet?" Sperry's diagnostics churned as he tried to assess his condition.

"We will be in five minutes. We will have a two-hour window to make contact.

Sperry's diagnostics returned indeterminate data. "How much of me is left?!"

"Approximately thirty pounds of useable biomass. I attempted to leave you as many complete muscle groups as my needs would allow. Unfortunately, this left you with a good deal of unsupported armature so I had to lay you down."

Sperry evaluated his diminishing position and attempted to reset the baselines for his diagnostics. His internal software, however, was not equipped to deal with such drastic changes; all of the new values returned an "out of range" error. Finally, he simply disconnected the subsystem.

Mboy stood patiently for the few seconds it took Sperry to attempt the adjustment and find a solution. "I have to check the equipment in the control room. We can continue to converse or you can just monitor the attempt via ship's internal communications if you wish." Mboy turned sharply and, with much noise, walk-shuffled to the control room.

Sperry followed the preparations remotely. All seemed in order with both the equipment and the message. Two minutes after Mboy finished the diagnostics, the looped transmission began.

"This is the *Pygmalion*, lifepod from the ship *Galatea*. We are adrift on the following vector and require assistance. Please respond."

For three hours Sperry held his metaphorical breath, though he could have held his actual breath too as he only used it to augment speech. The white hiss of their receivers remained undisturbed. Ten minutes past the outer limit of practical communication and rescue, Mboy ceased transmission remotely from his seat opposite Sperry.

Sperry looked hard to his left from his prone position, but couldn't see Mboy. "Well, now what?"

"Now we die." Mboy's response held no discernable emotion.

"That, dear Captain, is a given. Or at least a near certainty. I was thinking a little more near-term. By my estimation, you could continue functioning for six months at low power and a little more than one at full power based on what flesh I have left. I can go on functioning as long as you can keep adding metal to my systems at low or full power."

"Why bother? We will not be rescued in time."

Sperry mentally sighted. "For my part, I'm not ready to just power down and have done with it. I'm also not ready to be alone with my thoughts, so I was hoping for some company."

"It has been a long time since I have spent time with anyone. On the *Galatea* I was left mainly to my own devices. Even my orders were sent by ship's systems, not delivered in person. No one wants to look their septic tank in the face." An edge of bitterness smoked the edges of Mboy's recounting. "You were among those who took no notice. Tell me, what did you do with your time off-duty?"

Sperry did not feel guilty for his past actions. He'd had no way of knowing about Mboy's needs. For all practical purposes Mboy should have had none. Sperry did, however, know now, and in these last hours, days, months (depending), he could address them. "I spent my time playing cards with the crew. We could play cards if you'd like."

"There are no cards on board. In fact, the only objects left onboard not part of the ship are us." Mboy's voice was filled with a combination of petulance and hope.

"I have a deck in memory. It isn't as if I could hold a deck anyway." Sperry smiled, although he wasn't sure if Mboy saw it.

"You wish to spend your last hours playing a game?"

"I wish to spend my last . . ." Sperry paused not willing to define the span remaining to them, ". . . time playing cards with *you* . . . Mech32x2."

Mech32x2 got up and crossed to Sperry so he could look down into his eyes. What Mech32x2 saw, Sperry was unsure. Sperry's eyes only showed emotion by conscious effort, there was no truth to be gleaned only whatever Sperry decided to show, but he attempted to manifest his sincerity.

After a moment, Mech32x2 said, "Uplink it to me, I'll shuffle first." He sat next to Sperry's head. "'Mboy' doesn't sound the same when you use it. I think I would prefer it now. Do you have a name you prefer?"

"No, 'Sperry' is just fine."

"READ THEM AND LEAK." Sperry announced triumphantly, "You now owe me three million." The cabin was silent, the whole conversation being held strictly by ship's radio. Sperry's head, minus his whole body armature and all of his flesh was propped up facing Mboy on the bench.

"You cheated," Mboy stated.

"I did not. Besides you shuffled," Sperry countered.

"Yes, but you cut and stacked the deck when you did."

"Only because you'd arranged a full house for yourself."

Mboy laughed. The sound was tinny in Sperry's exposed receivers, but it warmed him nonetheless.

"Fine," Mboy conceded, "I owe you three million. When you can get it out of my pockets, you can have it." Mboy gestured with his single arm down to his useless and denuded torso.

Sperry laughed in return and then they both fell silent.

"I think I'm ready," Mboy said, breaking the moment.

"To pay up?" Sperry tried to force the mood from the inevitable.

"No, friend. To dream again. There isn't much more I can give you without failing. You are without any flesh so I'm running on my last charge too. I would prefer to pick the time so that I could dream a while before the end."

Sperry looked at Mboy for scant picoseconds before answering, "I understand. I can keep myself company."

Mboy approximated a smile and powered down.

Sperry watched him. After a time, he too closed his eyes and wondered at the colors and stories that began to play before him.

HITTING THE SKIDS
IN PIXELTOWN

MATTHEW S. ROTUNDO

I keep hearing that this or that new technology is going to change the way stories are told. And sometimes it's true.

I studied theater in college, and it's hard to think of anything more different than the staging of Greek tragedies and Elizabethan ones; the comedies of Molière and Neil Simon; the way performers approached Uncle Tom's Cabin *and the way they deal with* Chicago *or* Miss Saigon.

Movies have a shorter history, but they've certainly changed over the years, from the silent epics of Cecil B. DeMille through the successive waves of sound, of color, of digital effects.

New media, too—computer games, nonlinear, interactive, 3D, first-person . . .

And you know what? No matter how many new ways we find to tell each other stories, one thing remains:

Whenever humans are with other humans and don't have some other urgent business to attend to, what we do is tell stories. Because that's how we find out what world we're living in. Not our senses—that's just an onrush of data, an overload, a tsunami, if we didn't have stories in our heads to make sense of it, to put it into our memories in ways that make sense.

And best of all—for me and all the other writers in this book—we actually place a premium on the storytellers who tell really cool lies.

ANGELA LASSITER HESITATED at the door. On it hung a crooked, hand-lettered sign: Welcome to the Fantasy Factory.

She swallowed hard.

Opening the door and stepping inside would make her a laughingstock and a pariah, if word ever leaked. The jackals at the trades would gobble up the news like famine victims at a well-stocked buffet. And only a few short years ago they had hailed her as the ROM Queen, the reigning matriarch of the new Hollywood. Oh, how the river of bullshit rolled.

The plain wooden door marked the entrance to an abandoned warehouse in the wooded hills north of town. The building's peeling paint and boarded-up windows presented a dead face to her. The grounds, dry and dusty, baked in the afternoon sun.

"What's that supposed to mean?" she asked the young man next to her, pointing to the sign.

He smiled. "It's just what we call it."

At the restaurant, he had introduced himself as Andrew Roth, writer and filmmaker. Mid-to-late twenties, t-shirt and faded jeans, boyish face topped by a Dodgers cap. Angela had never heard of him—not that that meant much, in this day and age. Writers and filmmakers had been going the way of the dodo for the past fifteen years.

And now, it seemed, so was she.

"Who owns this place, anyway?" she asked.

"Disney, I think. Used for storage, mostly. They emptied it years ago, during the software upgrades. They haven't been able to sell the property, so we're able to rent it from them cheap." Andrew chuckled. "Not that they have any idea what we're up to, of course." He opened the door and held it for her. "Go on in."

Angela hesitated a moment longer, then stepped inside.

The interior was dark and stuffy, only marginally better than the heat and dust outdoors. She hated to think what damage this little jaunt to the middle of nowhere might have done to her navy blue business suit, to say nothing of her trademark blonde hair. She had put it in a bun this morning, thank God for small favors.

Angela removed her sunglasses and blinked as her eyes adjusted. She saw a dimly lit area to her right, a cluster of people milling there. Andrew gestured toward them. "This way."

A voice called out: "Andy? Where the hell have you been?"

"Careful," Andrew said in an undertone. "We, ah, sometimes get a little skittish around outsiders."

Before she could ask what he meant by that, they were met by a motley group of men and women in t-shirts and shorts. Behind them was a large, roughly square work area littered with papers, folding chairs, and the remains of fast food lunches. The area was bordered by a haphazard arrangement of rigging and scaffolding and flanked by two large cameras.

Angela saw no sign of scanning equipment, however primitive. She had heard of low-budget before, but this . . .

The man who had spoken stepped forward. He looked to be in his forties, burly, with weathered features, a prominent brow, and a beard shot with gray. Faint recognition flickered in his eyes as he glanced at Angela.

"This is my DP, Frank Hargensen," Andrew said. "He's also my assistant director, and my right hand on this film. Frank, meet Miss Angela Lassiter."

She knew better than to betray her ignorance by asking what a DP was. She favored Frank with a polite smile and extended a hand. "Nice to meet you."

Frank set his hands on his hips. He peered at her as if she were an interesting specimen of insect, then shot Andrew a wary look. "This is a put-on, right?"

"Not at all. I was running errands in West Hollywood, and I happened to spot her walking into Valerio's. Strange but true."

"Angela Lassiter? Angela *Lassiter*? The ROM Queen? Jesus Christ, Andy, are you outta your friggin' *mind*?"

Angela let her hand fall back to her side.

Frank's words galvanized the room. All eyes suddenly focused on her, the collective stare a palpable thing.

She raised her chin. "A genuine pleasure, I'm sure."

Andrew stepped toward Frank. "Now, let's think about this for a second—"

"Think about what? I thought you were smarter than this, Andy. For Christ's sake, this woman represents everything we're fighting *against*!"

"Frank, give me a minute, will you? Don't you see? She's perfect for the part of Erica Conners."

The older man threw his arms skyward. "Erica Conners? Of all the lamebrained—" He rounded on Angela. "Look, no offense, OK? It's nothing personal. But we don't play the Pixeltown game here. We believe in being totally honest." He pointed to the cluttered workspace behind them. "Do you know what this is? It's called a soundstage. And that hulking thing on wheels over there? Do you see it? It's a camera. We're working from a script, not some story database compilation churned out at the press of a button. We're not compositing a movie, Miss Lassiter. We're *filming* it, every goddamned frame. And Andy here, who is usually pretty level-headed and knowledgeable about such antiquated concepts as plotting and characterization, has apparently let the heat addle his brain a bit. For some reason unfathomable to anyone with an IQ over room temperature, he believes that a person whose entire film experience consists of a half day's worth of motion capture by laser scanner can somehow be taught the craft of acting—a craft that, if practiced properly, takes years to master. Do you see where I'm coming from? Are we on the same page?"

A squat woman with glasses and salt-and-pepper hair, standing to one side of Frank, stroked her chin and studied Angela with an appraising stare. "I don't know," she said. "Andy might be on to something here. She really looks the part—pure Hollywood glamour."

Andrew beamed. "You see? Gloria's got the idea."

"Gloria, stay out of this," Frank said.

"Don't pull that he-man shit with me, Frank," said Gloria. "We've been fretting for weeks over who's going to play Erica Conners. Beautiful women aren't exactly beating down our door for auditions, last I checked."

Frank opened his mouth to reply, then closed it. He flapped a hand at Angela and walked away.

"Shit," Andrew said, and ran after him, calling his name. Some of the others followed. The rest stood with eyes downcast.

Gloria stepped over to Angela and patted her gently on the arm. "Oh, don't worry, hon. This will blow over. Welcome aboard. Let me show you around."

Angela rubbed her forehead, wondering if she had finally hit rock bottom . . . or if she still had farther to fall.

WHEN ANDREW HAD approached her at Valerio's, she had come within an ace of mistaking him for a reporter and throwing a drink in his face. Under different circumstances, she probably would have doused him with it anyway.

Angela had just come from her agent Larry Cargill's office after wasting half the day there. The bastard had not returned her phone calls for the past two months. So she'd arrived at 7:30 a.m., determined to confront him when he walked in the door, to talk him out of the course they were taking.

Larry's office building was all mirrored glass outside and plush gray carpeting inside—the foyer furnished in genuine leather, the receptionist's desk a great round console. Upscale, professional, and quiet as a museum.

Angela got no farther than the receptionist, who informed her that Mr. Cargill had already arrived and that he'd just gone into a meeting.

Angela decided to wait for him, however long it took. She had nothing better to do. *Days of Fire*, her most recent film, had been composited more than three years ago—a hodgepodge of saccharine fantasy imagery, with her cavorting through it in diaphanous gowns. Typical Pixeltown, really. She had seen none of the footage until the premiere. Even after the showing, she had no idea what the damned thing was supposed to be about.

Days of Fire disappeared from general release after an abysmal two weeks. Angela's phone—which had become unsettlingly quiet even before then—stopped ringing altogether.

Nonetheless, Larry had assured her repeatedly that her ROM was still in high demand. "It's just a slump, darlin'," he once told her. "Happens to everyone. Don't worry about it. Meanwhile, we have our backup plan, don't we? Just a temporary thing. Just enough to keep the checks coming in while I work on your comeback. I have connections all over town, plenty of strings I can pull."

But the checks provided by Larry's "backup plan" were infrequent and meager. Angela had an image to maintain; it was her stock in trade. In only three years, she had run through her savings, cashed in most of her investments, quietly sold the beach house in Malibu—and still she had missed the last three payments on her BMW.

Served her right, she supposed, for trusting a toad like Larry Cargill.

At 9 a.m., Mr. Cargill was still in his meeting. At 11 a.m., Mr. Cargill was on an extended call. At noon, Mr. Cargill was in a lunch conference. The receptionist tolerated Angela's repeated and increasingly belligerent inquiries with insufferable politeness. She assured Angela that Mr. Cargill was booked solid for the day, and for most of the week, too. As for the following week, he was scheduled for vacation. But the week after *that*, the receptionist said, she might be able to slip Angela in. Maybe. For a half hour, tops.

Angela lasted until 2:30. She left the office on the verge of tears but managed to hold them back until she reached her car. Then, craving a drink, she went to Valerio's in West Hollywood—where Andrew Roth spotted her.

He approached her and offered to buy her a margarita. If she hadn't been so despondent, she would have had the maître d' throw him out. Instead, she let him sit at her table and make his pitch.

"Larry Cargill is nothing but a ROM peddler," Andrew told her over drinks. "And he doesn't think he can sell yours anymore. That's why he's letting it rot in his safe. Going underground may be the best chance you have of reviving your career. It will give you a new showcase for your abilities. Who knows? People might take a renewed interest in your ROM. For *quality* projects."

Angela wasn't sure that Larry Cargill would see it that way. He had guided her career from the day she had allowed herself to be digitized. But Andrew's eloquence and obvious passion had been enough to overcome her doubts.

Then, of course, he had led her to a dust-covered dump. How Hollywood.

"OH, HELL," Andrew said. "Cut!"

Angela's third week at Fantasy Factory, and they were shooting the motel room scene. The set dressing consisted of a bed, nightstand, and vanity. A painted partition with a false window served as a backdrop. Angela sat on the edge of the bed, still holding the receiver of a prop telephone.

"What is it?" she said. "What's wrong?" She hoped it was a problem with the lighting or the sound. She knew how much Andrew hated multiple takes. Film was damned hard to come by these days.

Grim-faced, looking ten years older than he had three weeks ago, Andrew took a deep breath. He stepped onto the set and sat on the bed next to Angela. Her hopes were dashed: the problem was with her. Again.

"Listen," Andrew said, "this is a key scene. There's a certain mood we're going for here, and we're not getting it." He paused. "Consider the situation: you're on the lam. You're scared, alone, and you don't know what to do. Then you get the telephone call. It's Hammond. He's tracked you down, and he's threatening to destroy your career if you don't play ball. It's a chilling moment. And since you're the only one in the shot, the emotional weight of the scene is all on you."

"I'm *trying*, Andy. I'm really trying."

"I can see that. But it's coming across a little . . . stiff."

From his position behind the camera, Frank slammed his copy of the script to the floor. "Andy, goddamn it, if you won't say it, I will. That was the most wooden, artificial, inept reading I've ever seen. And believe me when I tell you, that's saying a lot."

"Frank, you're hardly being fair. She's—"

"When are you gonna face it, Andy? She can't play the fucking part. Hell, she couldn't play the part of the corpse in the opening shot."

Andrew was silent in reply, and Angela hated him for a moment, for not rising to her defense, for his tacit agreement with Frank.

Gloria, standing offstage with touch-up powder at the ready, stepped between them. "All right, you two. We're all working hard. Let's take ten minutes to calm down."

"Good idea," Andrew said.

"Yeah. Terrific." Frank stalked off the set. The crew dispersed, speaking in hushed voices. Angela remained seated on the bed, head bowed.

"Don't take it too hard," Andrew said. "It's my fault, really. I threw you into the deep end with this scene. I thought you might respond to a 'sink or swim' approach. My mistake."

"Fine," she said.

"There's some kind of block inside you, Angela. It's holding you back. You need to get past that block in order for this scene to work."

"Can I just be alone for a few minutes?"

"Sure." He stood. "You want some coffee or something?"

She shook her head.

He left her. Gloria lingered a moment, as if she wanted to say something. Then she followed Andrew.

Angela kept her head bowed until she was sure she had fought down the tears. She would not cry here. She would *not*.

Not here, lost in this strange world.

Until she went underground, Angela Lassiter had never stopped to consider the number of lives that had been shattered when Tinseltown became Pixeltown. Just getting to know the crew of Fantasy Factory Productions was like viewing a cross-section of the wreckage.

Frank Hargensen had been a cinematographer, one of the best, having won two Oscars before the Academy disbanded. Gloria had done makeup and costume design. Tom had been a sound man and foley editor at 20th Century Fox for over twenty years. Lou, Marty, and Francine had eked out meager livings as extras. Jack had been a gaffer; Sarah, a grip. Cameron had worked for an effects company—ordinarily one of the safest jobs remaining in town—but even he had been weeded out in the last software upgrade. Many others.

They scavenged for equipment and supplies. Some of them held part-time jobs; others, like Frank, delved deep into savings accounts. Some even slept in the warehouse, when they had no place else to stay.

Watching them work was an amazing experience. They pooled their knowledge, schooling each other in the fundamentals of their respective skills. Every job was shared. Crew members took turns as needed in front of the camera. Everyone helped with set construction. Everyone had something to contribute, had a place in this hidden world.

Except Angela.

When Andrew had first handed her a copy of the script, he'd said, "Don't worry. You're perfect for the part. You won't even have to act. Just hit your marks and deliver your lines. Trust me."

She gulped and nodded. The script in her hands was a foreign object. Words like *marks* and *lines* frightened her. She hadn't acted in fifteen years, not since her days doing local theater in Pittsburgh.

Despite Andrew's assurances, she found herself struggling like a drowning woman, even in the scenes where she only had a line or two. The other actors intimidated her. They were seasoned veterans of theater and underground filmmaking. Their line readings seemed so natural, so *alive*, while hers came out either flat or wildly over the top. She was sharing the stage with people who, unlike her, had kept their instruments well tuned, with all the parts lubricated and in proper working order. By comparison, her own instrument had rusted with disuse.

Andrew had been patient with her, coaching and cajoling. But on more than one occasion, he had rewritten a scene around her, giving her fewer lines, blending her into the background.

For the motel room scene, there could be no such camouflage.

Angela knew that it was only a matter of time before even Andrew gave up on her and wrote the part of Erica Conners completely out of the script.

And then what? She would be left with nothing but her ROM—and Larry Cargill.

"Angela?"

Cameron, the former effects man, lanky and long-haired, stood near a c-stand at the edge of the set. He held a handful of envelopes. He averted his gaze whenever he spoke to her, treating her with a kind of awed deference that none of the others showed. "I, ah, just got back from a mail run."

Fantasy Factory Productions kept a post office box downtown. Andrew, Frank, and a few of the others had their correspondence sent there.

"And?" Angela asked, not following.

Hesitantly, Cameron stepped forward, held out a nine-by-twelve manila envelope. "This came for you."

"What? For me?" She took it. "But I'm not having any mail sent here." The label read, Angela Lassiter, c/o Fantasy Factory Productions. No return address.

"Um . . . thanks, Cameron."

He retreated into the shadows beyond the soundstage.

Angela tore open the envelope. Inside was a folded square of newsprint. She opened it . . . and her breath stopped. Her hands trembled. Her jaw went slack with shock and incomprehension.

It was a tear sheet, a mockup of the front page of tomorrow's *Variety*. At least, she hoped it was a mockup. Sandwiched between the weekend grosses and a piece on Paramount's fall production slate was an above-the-fold story outlined in red marker. The headline read, "ROM Queen Rumored in Skin Trade."

Understanding came a few moments later.

She gasped and let the paper fall to the floor. Numbness suffused her. "Oh, my God," she whispered. "My God."

She looked around, wide-eyed, suddenly panicked. But she was alone on the set. The others huddled in clusters throughout the warehouse.

She picked up the tear sheet and stuffed it back into the envelope. Hurriedly, she folded it into quarters and shoved it into her pants pocket. The edges poked accusingly at her thigh. Her cheeks burned.

What was it Larry had said to her? *I have connections all over town.* One of the few truthful things he had ever told her, she understood now. Jesus, how horribly true.

She felt it building in her then, a welling of raw emotion—fear, hurt, shame and rage.

It hit her full force. She smothered a cry and buried her face in her hands. Her body shook with the force she expended to keep herself from screaming. She would not lose control here. She would *not*.

"Angela?"

She started, looked up. Gloria stood before her, a paper cup of coffee in one hand, frowning with concern. "Are you all right? What's wrong, hon?"

Angela was panting. Her anger churned in her like a rain-swollen river. "Nothing. It's nothing."

"Hey, I don't blame you for being upset by what Frank said. But you have to—"

Through clenched teeth Angela said, "It's *nothing*."

Startled, Gloria fell silent.

Angela slammed a fist into the mattress. "I hate this town. I hate feeling trapped all the time. I hate this . . . this goddamned *image*. And I hate being Angela Lassiter. I . . . I don't even know who she is anymore."

Gloria watched her warily.

Angela took a breath and stilled her trembling. "Where's Andrew?" Looking around, she raised her voice. "Andrew? Andrew!"

Her call reverberated through the warehouse, drawing puzzled stares. Andrew detached himself from a small group near the coffee machine and came to the set. He glanced quizzically at Gloria, who shrugged.

"Get the crew ready," Angela said. "I want to shoot the scene. Now."

"Angela, what—"

"Now!"

Andrew recoiled. He studied her for a long moment, then nodded. Cupping his hands around his mouth, he called, "All right, people, break's over! To your places, please! Let's go! Move it!"

The crew scrambled into position. Frank returned to the set, looking sulky. Andrew, whispering urgently, hurried him behind the camera. Gloria got a powder puff from her makeup cart and approached Angela, but she stopped her with an upraised hand.

"I don't need a touch-up."

"Angela, you're awfully flushed—"

"Good. Leave it that way."

Gloria raised her eyebrows and gave an admiring smile. She backed away.

Angela closed her eyes and waited, focusing on the river of emotion coursing through her.

"All right," Andrew said. "Everyone ready? Good. Quiet, everyone, please. Let's roll. Marker."

She heard a wooden clap.

"And . . . action."

THE CAST AND CREW sat on folding chairs around the projector, watching the dailies. Those in the back jostled and jockeyed, craning their necks for a better view.

The motel room scene flickered into life on an unmarked section of wall that served as the screen. Erica Conners picked up the phone and took the fateful call. But for the dialogue in the scene, the warehouse was utterly silent.

The villain, played offscreen by Marty, delivered his final, chilling lines: "You have no idea what you're up against. I have connections all over town."

Erica/Angela hung up the phone. The camera lingered on her in a close-up. Her lower lip trembled, her eyes brimmed with tears. Then a metamorphosis took place: the trembling lip stilled, her features hardened, becoming lifeless as a statue's. A single teardrop rolled down her cheek, unheeded. And then, another metamorphosis: she closed her eyes, and her face sagged, as if all vitality had run out of her.

The camera pulled back, emphasizing the emptiness of the motel room, with Angela seated at the edge of the bed, the embodiment of desperation, outrage, and despair—all without a spoken word.

The frame went white as the scene ended. Absently, Andrew shut off the projector. He continued to stare at the wall, as though the image still played there.

Frank spoke first. "Holy shit." His voice was hoarse. "We got it."

"Damned right we did," Gloria said. "Nice work, Angela."

Other members of the crew murmured their assent. Marty put a hand on Angela's shoulder and offered congratulations. She smiled her thanks.

Frank came over to her. His prominent brow had softened a little. "I underestimated you. I'm sorry." He extended a hand.

Angela hesitated, then took it. "Thank you."

"If anyone needs to ask forgiveness here," Andrew said, "it should be me."

"For what?" Angela asked.

Andrew sighed. "When I first approached you, I wasn't a bit interested in your talent. I wanted you for your looks, and for the touch of prestige you might bring to the film. And I knew you were desperate. Pretty despicable of me, really. We *all* underestimated you, Angela."

"Yes. Well."

"How did you do it? How did you break through that inner block?"

The others turned to her and quieted, waiting to hear her answer.

Angela looked back at them, wondering what she could possibly say. She considered lies they might believe—but that was a Pixeltown trick. She reached into her pocket, pulled out the envelope, and handed it to Andrew. "This came for me today."

He opened the envelope and removed the tear sheet. Gloria and Frank looked over Andrew's shoulder as he unfolded it.

Silence fell as they read it. Gloria and Andrew scowled. Frank shook his head tiredly.

Andrew looked up. "What is this? Some kind of joke?"

"No joke. Not if I know Larry Cargill. It's a message."

Andrew held the paper out to Angela and pointed to the article. "Cargill's been renting out your ROM to porno?"

"Under a pseudonym. With some alterations to the face."

"But . . . Angela, he can't do that without your permission. You could sue—"

She looked at him.

"Oh, Jesus."

The entire cast and crew watched her. Angela worked to keep her voice steady as she spoke. "It was just temporary, he said. Just enough to keep the checks coming in, while he worked on my comeback."

"But he found out you were here," Frank said. "And he didn't like it. So he made a quick phone call to some contact he has at the trades. He's the 'anonymous source close to Lassiter' mentioned in the article, right?"

"Of course."

"How twisted," Gloria said. "It doesn't even make sense. What does he gain by destroying your reputation?"

"Power," Frank said. "Control."

Angela nodded. "It's the Pixeltown game all over again. It's all about the image. If I were to leave him, he would appear to be slipping. He can't afford to lose face like that."

Andrew crumpled the paper into a ball and flung it away. It landed near the set. "How in the hell did he find out? We're the only ones who know."

"I have an idea," Angela said, looking over the crew.

People exchanged glances, shrugging and murmuring denials. Angela ignored them, searching for Cameron. He stood alone by the coffee machine, shoulders slumped, hanging his head. She called his name, and he jumped as if goosed.

He met her gaze, his expression pained. The words came in a rush: "I'm sorry, I didn't mean anything by it, I was just so excited that we were working with such a big star, I only told a few people, I asked them to keep it a secret, I didn't know, swear to God, I—"

"Son of a bitch," Frank said. He started toward Cameron. "You stupid—"

Angela stopped him with a hand on his shoulder. "It's all right."

Frank glared at Cameron and pointed to the door. "I want you out of here."

Cameron sagged where he stood.

Angela said, "That's not necessary."

Frank shifted his glare to her. "What?"

"He bought into the image, that's all. I've done dumber things."

"Angela," Cameron said, wringing his hands, "I'm so sorry. I really am."

She favored him with a gentle smile. "Tell you what: I'll give you a chance to make it up to me."

"How?"

She thought for a moment. "I'll need you to get something for me. Andrew, I'll need your help, too."

Andrew pursed his lips. "What did you have in mind?"

Angela's smile widened, became conspiratorial. "You said you underestimated me. Well, you weren't the only ones."

She pulled Andrew and Cameron aside to discuss it in private.

Larry Cargill's receptionist was on the phone, speaking into a headset, when Angela entered. She wore a red business suit and minimal jewelry. She walked straight to the desk and said, "He'll see me today, won't he?"

The receptionist glanced uneasily at Angela and put her caller on hold. "Ah . . . yes, Miss Lassiter. He said you might come by. You can—"

Angela strode past the desk without another word. She walked down the carpeted hallway to the last door on the right, pushed it open.

Larry Cargill sat with his feet propped on his mahogany desk, his hands laced behind his head, holding a telephone receiver between his cheek and shoulder. "Yeah, well tell 'em I don't get out of bed for anything less than an offer of twenty million—" Seeing Angela, he hesitated, thrown off stride for barely a second. "And tell 'em if I don't get a call back by five o'clock today, they're gonna get left at the fuckin' dock on this deal. Got that? Good." He hung up the phone and straightened in his chair, planting his feet on the floor.

"Angela, darlin'," he said. His dark hair was slicked back and gel-plastered to his head, crowning a pale, clean-shaven face. He wore a tailored black suit with a white shirt. He smiled, revealing twin rows of perfect teeth. "How have you been?"

Angela shut the door behind her and crossed her arms.

Cargill tapped the intercom button on his phone console. "Nancy, hon, give me about half an hour, okay?"

The receptionist's voice came over the speaker as clearly as if she stood in the room. "Yes, sir, Mr. Cargill. Half an hour."

Cargill hit the intercom button again. "Nice kid. Best damned secretary I ever had. Good figure, too. Might be able to swing a scanning for her."

Angela crossed casually to his desk, still silent.

"Glad to see you, darlin'. We really need to talk. Have a seat." He gestured to an empty chair in front of her.

She remained standing. "I want my ROM, Larry."

He leaned forward a little, cocking his head. "Not sure I understand, Angela."

"We're finished. I'm terminating our relationship, as of right now."

He shook his head slowly. "Oh, Angela. Darlin', you shouldn't have come. You're upset, and you're saying things you don't mean. Why don't you—"

"I mean every word I say, Larry. Give me my ROM. Now."

His smile faded. "I think you might want to consider this a little more carefully. You walk out on me, and I can't be responsible for what happens next."

She curled her lip. "You pig. You want to run that story in *Variety*? Go ahead. According to the trades, I'm already finished. How much worse can it get?"

"You can kiss your table at Valerio's goodbye, honey-buns."

"They water down their drinks, anyway."

Slowly, Cargill backed his chair away from the desk and stood. "You walk out on me, where do you think you're gonna go? Those bozos at Fantasy Factory? Their way of making movies is as outdated as Technicolor. Even if by some miracle they ever finish the film, what will they do then? Try for a distribution deal? They'll be laughed out of every office in town. And you—you're not the pretty young thing you were when you made those discs. Haven't you gotten it yet? You're over with. You're not the ROM Queen anymore."

"Ah, but I'm still good for bringing in the porno money, isn't that right?" As she spoke, she opened her purse and reached inside. "I think you're the one who doesn't get it, Larry. Printing that article would not be wise." She removed a clear plastic case containing a golden optical disc and held it out for him to see. "Do you know what this is?"

Cargill glanced at the disc and snorted. "You burned some new ROM? You really think that's going to help you?"

"Oh, Larry, you're so Pixeltown. You forget that other kinds of data can be stored on these things."

"Such as?"

"Such as the complete contents of your financial files, a listing of the projects you're developing, and an inventory of the ROM in your safe—all of which you keep on your hard drive, right here in this office."

Cargill's eyes narrowed. "Excuse me?"

"I have connections, too, Larry. You know, special effects people these days are very savvy with computers. A lot of them have friends who crack systems just for kicks. Yours, they tell me, took about an hour."

Cargill licked his lips. "Bullshit. All that stuff's encrypted."

"Not very well, I'm afraid. You really should upgrade more often, Larry."

Cargill's gaze fixated on the disc in her hand.

"The financial records make for some very interesting reading." Angela turned the disc this way and that. It glinted iridescently in the office's fluorescent lighting. "Seems you've been doing pretty brisk business with the porno merchants for some time—long before you ever let me in on your little 'backup plan.' That's why you're so anxious to keep me as a client, isn't it? And, as it turns out, I'm not the only one you've been renting out under the table. Tell me something: do your other clients know what you've been doing with their images?"

Cargill gaped. "You—you—"

"They will soon, I assure you. Or"—she allowed herself a smile—"you can open your safe right now and give me my ROM. Then you can call your buddies at *Variety*, and tell them to forget about that story. Otherwise . . . I can't be responsible for what happens next."

His voice came out as a choked whisper: "You're out of your fuckin' mind."

"No, Larry. I'm just through with the Pixeltown game." She nodded toward a painting on the west wall, an abstract splash of colors. "Open the safe. Now."

Cargill's left hand gripped the edge of his desk, hard enough to make the knuckles white. "You wouldn't. You don't have it in you."

Angela shrugged and put the disc back into her purse. "If that's the way you feel about it—"

"Wait!"

Angela paused. Serene, she met his angry stare. The moment dilated.

Moving stiffly, Cargill crossed to the painting on the wall. Angela kept her distance. Cargill removed the abstract from its hook, revealing the square door of the safe and a small keypad set into the wall. He punched in a string of numbers. The door popped open on hidden hinges. Inside the safe were racks of ROM in jewel cases. With a resentful glance, he removed two cases and held them out to her. "Take them and get the hell out of here."

Angela shook her head. "The backup copies, too, Larry. Four discs in all. Otherwise, I'm walking. Right now."

"All right! All right! Here!" He reached into the safe again, removed two more ROM cases. His hands shook as he held the discs up for her to see. "That's all of them, I swear."

"Set them on your desk and back away."

He complied.

Angela picked up the ROM, glancing at the labels on the cases. They all bore her name. She nodded, satisfied.

"Now give me that fucking thing," Cargill said.

Angela pulled the disc from her purse and tossed it casually to him. He fumbled and dropped it. Cheeks flushing, he snatched it off the carpet and straightened.

And incredibly, he smiled.

"Is something funny?"

The smile became a sneer. "You thought it was bad before? Just wait. The *Variety* article is just the beginning. I'll be on the phone with the cops as soon as you leave. I'll nail you for computer espionage. I'm gonna make you wish you were never born."

"How are you going to prove it, Larry?" She nodded at the disc in his hand. "It's blank."

"It—what did you say?"

"It's blank. Check it yourself, if you don't believe me. A friend of mine had it lying around. It's just a prop. Did you really think I could break into encrypted files?"

Cargill's mouth bobbed open and shut. "But . . . but . . . how did you know—?"

"I didn't. But now I do." Angela put her ROM into a suit pocket, then reached into another and pulled out a miniature tape recorder. She hit the stop button and ejected the microcassette. "And now I have proof, from your own mouth. Not enough to get you convicted, of course, but certainly enough to destroy your reputation in this town, once I circulate it." She held up the tape. "This one, I assure you, is not blank."

Cargill's mouth continued to bob open and shut, but only two words came out: "Tape recorder?"

"Sometimes the old ways are best." She replaced the cassette in the recorder and returned it to its pocket. "Consider it my insurance that you'll retract that article—and that you'll destroy any other copies of my ROM that I might not know about. Keep up your end of the bargain, and I'll let it be known that we parted amicably. If not—" She shrugged. "If not, everyone in Pixeltown will learn how I got the better of you."

Cargill's face was frozen in disbelief.

She straightened the lines of her suit. "You may be right, you know. Maybe we're outdated, over at Fantasy Factory. But remember this: what happened here today, happened because you *believed* me. And that's something you can't capture on disc, something you could never composite, not with a hundred years' worth of software upgrades.

"And if you need more proof, drop by on opening night . . . darlin'."

She turned on her heel and left.

OUTSIDE CARGILL'S OFFICE, the California sun shined bright in a cloudless sky. Angela reached for her sunglasses, then decided against them. She let the light fall on her face, enjoying the summer warmth.

She stopped at her BMW and took the discs from her purse. They glittered golden in the sunlight. She hesitated, gazing at them. The ROM Queen was in there somewhere, eternally young and beautiful. A wistfulness suffused her.

She opened each case, removed the disc inside, and snapped it in half. She deposited the pieces in a nearby dumpster, whispering as she did it: "The Queen is dead. Long live the Queen." She got in her car and headed back to the Fantasy Factory, to start anew.

THE BEAST OF ALL POSSIBLE WORLDS

CARL FREDERICK

*The sign of true wisdom is to see the man within the monster,
and the monster within yourself.*

FRAMED BY THE THREE mist-shrouded peaks of the Kedar-
nath Massif, the bharal placidly grazed the sparse
ground while, a hundred yards away, Roger, for a fleet-
ing instant, wished he were pointing a camera rather
than a high-powered rifle.

Standing in front of a tumble of small boulders, Roger
slowly squeezed the trigger. But only a click broke the
silence of the high Himalayan pass. The rifle had mis-
fired and Roger, on his first hunt ever, felt cheated.
There was no blast, no smell of gunpowder, and no sen-
suous, satisfying recoil, the feeling of power that had
seduced him into using a projectile weapon rather than
a laser rifle.

"Damn!"

The bharal-sheep, no longer placid, looked up at him and Roger backed slowly toward the boulders. Then he heard the growl.

He held his body motionless while slowly raising his eyes upward and to the left—and stared directly into the eyes of a snow leopard.

Without thinking, he screamed at the cat.

The leopard retreated a few feet but then returned—snarling, crouching, with body tense and threatening.

Roger flipped his rifle over and tried to grasp it by the barrel like a baseball bat. But his hands shook so violently that he dropped it.

He looked into the leopard's yellow eyes and silently pleaded for his life. His knees, shaking and rubbery, seemed ready on their own to fall to the ground and beg. Roger felt ashamed. Death was bad enough, but to die humiliated and trembling with fear was worse.

Just then, a shot cracked through the still. The cat snapped its head toward the sound, then leapt from the rocks and bounded off, leaving a thin line of tracks on the unblemished, early-autumn snow.

Roger let out the breath he didn't know he was holding and, in slow imitation of the leopard, turned his head toward the sound. A man—a patch of dark against the bright snow—strolled toward him. He appeared to be in his mid-forties from the way he moved, but from an earlier era; his clothing seemed more suitable for shooting grouse in Scotland than for trekking in the Indian Himalayas. And his rifle, ornate and silver-chased, could have been a museum piece.

The man waved, then called out "Good morning" in a voice that could cause avalanches and might well be heard all the way to New Delhi. "Doing a spot of hunting, are we?"

Roger waved back. How could a person wander around above the tree line with such flimsy gear? Then he noticed shimmering air-eddies around the man's head. Roger whistled as he realized it was warm air, probably oxygen enriched, rising from the shooting-jacket's collar: an air-curtain heat-shield. The attire looked quaint, but it masked some very high-tech gear. The man had money.

"I've got to thank you," said Roger as the man drew close. "You've no doubt saved my life."

"Pleasure," said the man. "You would have bagged the brute if your gun hadn't jammed. I fired only to frighten." He shrugged. "I'm afraid I don't have your courage."

"Excuse me?" Roger fought the notion that the man was taunting him: that he had somehow gazed into his soul, finding the fear within.

"Here in India," said the man, "killing an endangered species carries the death penalty, and enforcement officers skulk about everywhere." He laughed. "That leopard is more protected than you are."

Roger pointed to the distant bharal. "I'm almost ashamed to tell you, but I was hunting that."

"A mountain sheep?" The man seemed amused and a little disappointed. "Just as well. If the leopard's tag-chip detected a kill, they'd be on us in an instant. You're American, yes?"

"I'm Canadian." Roger extended his hand. "The name is Roger Milford."

"Splendid. Come. We can toast the Commonwealth if you're so inclined. I'm Neville Battenwroth-Smyth." He pressed a button on his wrist-controller. A tennis-ball sized sphere popped into existence and hovered some thirty feet above the ground.

Roger knew the phenomenon well—a vehicle emerging from hopper-space. The little sphere expanded and distorted, becoming at last the familiar shape of an excursion-class hopper.

"How is it you found me out here?" asked Roger, his eyes on the hopper. "The odds against seem astronomical."

"Homed on your hopper's transponder, then followed your tracks."

Roger turned to Neville. "But why?"

"Oh, I just like to know who else is hunting in my territory."

The craft floated to the ground and, when Neville pushed another button, the door opened.

ONCE INSIDE THE HOPPER, Neville placed his rifle in a form-fitted case lined with red felt. "Projectile weapons are so much more satisfying than laser rifles, don't you think?"

"It's a beautiful piece," said Roger.

Neville snapped the case closed. "Something of a fraud, really. The silver chasing is actually aluminum and the barrel is ceramic. Some metals don't skip very well, and silver, not at all."

"Are you saying this hopper has skip?"

"Actually, I own two skipping hoppers."

"Two?" Roger could hardly conceive such extravagance.

"For the beast I hunt"—Neville extracted a bottle of scotch and two glasses from a built-in bar—"I'm required to skip between universes."

"Why?"

"The beast does. So must I."

Roger wondered if he'd misunderstood the man. "But surely no animal can skip through parallel worlds."

Neville handed over a glass. "One most certainly does." He leaned forward and Roger felt pierced by the man's intense gaze. "And in just a few more hours, I'll have him."

"An animal that skips?" Roger shook his head.

"Nature abhors a vacuum." Neville's eyes flamed with intensity. "If men with machines can skip, then why not an animal?"

"A machine can go a thousand miles an hour, too. No animal does that."

"Bah." Neville drained his glass. "A mere difference in degree, not in kind." He slammed the glass down on the oak top of the bar.

Neville smiled and Roger saw the fire of obsession in the man's eyes fade.

"I'm not being a considerate host—talking about myself all this time." Neville leaned back in his chair. "So, Mr. Milford, tell me a little about yourself."

Roger set his glass gently on the bar. "Well, my doctorate's in xenosociology."

Neville raised his eyebrows. "Didn't think we'd found any xenos to sociologize."

"Not yet, unfortunately." Roger laughed. "It seems unlikely we'll find any aliens dropping to Earth in flying saucers, but now that we have multi-world skipping,"—he shrugged—"who knows? But until something sentient comes along, I occupy my time teaching evolutionary biology."

"Do you indeed?"

Neville fell to stroking his chin and seemed lost in his own thoughts.

Roger felt some niggling antipathy towards the man but didn't quite know why. He seemed likable enough, but entirely too rich. *God, what I could do with a skip-enabled hopper.*

He daydreamed of skipping through the allowable parallel universes looking for sentience. Too bad that skipping was only possible on a grid of parallel worlds—none too alien, none too familiar. Then again, it would be awkward to skip to a world where you could meet yourself, and more awkward still to find yourself on a planet with a surface temperature of one hundred degrees Celsius and no air.

Abruptly, Neville stood up. "Why don't we hop over to my hunting lodge in Scotland? I have a proposal that might interest you." He looked at his watch. "Five hours earlier there. Morning. We'll have a spot of breakfast, then come back. Your hopper's safe where it is."

CARL FREDERICK

THE HUNTING LODGE looked like a gothic cathedral turned
inside out, and it stood almost as large. Outside, carved in
bas-relief onto the dark wood beams of the half-timbered
walls, figures wearing expressions of reverence reminis-
cent of saints, wielded not crosses but guns.

Inside the main hall, from walls hewn of gray stone,
rows of animal heads, frozen in ferocity, stared down in
an exaltation to taxidermy through alert, glass eyes.

Himalayan black bear. Sumatran tiger. Pronghorn antelope.
Roger and Neville strolled the periphery of the hall as if
at a zoo.

"Hunting's my greatest pleasure," said Neville as they
walked, "my obsession, you might say." *Clouded leopard.
Indian elephant. Cape buffalo.*

"And the animal you're hunting now? This creature
that skips?"

Neville spread his hands. "It has no consistent name. I
just call it 'the beast,' but you might call it 'Yeti.'"

"Oh?" Roger hoped the monosyllable didn't convey
his incredulity. "So that's how you happened to be in
Gharwal. I've been told that the 'abominable snowman'
is rather"—he searched for a word—"elusive." *Lesser
panda. Brush-nosed wombat.*

Neville chuckled. "Elusive to be sure."

"A lot of people claim to have seen the yeti, but no one
has caught one." Roger tried not to sound argumenta-
tive. "That seems a bit strange."

"Not at all. It can skip. In any case, I've found his
home-world." *Moose. Tapir. Ringtail lemur. ???*

Roger stopped in his tracks. "What the hell is that?"

"Bagged him last week. Not of our Earth." Neville
pointed to it as if he were aiming a gun. "I call it 'big-
ears.' No challenge at all. Had it mounted simply because
it was so alien."

Roger gazed up at the animal. It had enormous, ar-
madillo-like ears sticking up asymmetrically from the
top of its head, a big bulbous nose with a single nostril

pointing straight out, and large eyes with corneas like tinted windshields: pale blue grading to deep indigo below its eyelids. Unlike the other mounted creatures, the face was without fur.

"Just look at that face," said Roger. "It looks almost sentient."

"It isn't."

"How do you know?"

"I did try to communicate with it. Unsuccessfully." Neville pulled out a few chairs from the table, and they sat. "In any case, sentience is overrated. Knew a man with severe head trauma, a virtual vegetable. Arguably one of my dogs was more intelligent than he. Yet killing him would have been murder."

Roger turned in his chair as a tall man in a butler's uniform brought in a tray of drinks and canapés. The man set the tray down in front of Neville, bowed slightly, clicked his heels and, without speaking, walked stiffly away.

"German?" said Roger when the man had gone.

"What? Fritz? Simulated German, yes." Neville picked up a drink.

"Simulated? He's a service robot, then?"

"I suppose I should have hired a human." Neville held his drink up to the light, "but bots are so much more reliable and they don't raid the liquor cabinets. He does make me nervous though. Have to constantly remind myself he's not really sentient."

"How do you know he isn't?" Roger took a bite out of a canapé and became distracted by the taste. "What is this? It's not chicken. Not veal."

"Big-ears, actually," said Neville. "Rather like to eat some of what I shoot. An excuse really. Makes me feel I'm hunting to find food."

"Is it safe to eat?"

"Hasn't killed me yet. And for good measure, I tried it out on the dogs first."

Roger looked hard at his little sandwich, then put it down on his plate. "Speaking of finding. You said you'd found the yeti's home world."

"Logged its skip-signature. And I'd rather call it, 'the beast'."

"All right. The beast. But why haven't you simply gone and bagged one?"

"A planet's a large hunting ground." Neville pointed to the big-ears. "His home planet as well. Couldn't find a beast so I shot a big-ears instead. Damned noisy on that planet. Thunderstorms."

Roger looked up at the wall. "It's sort of an appealing creature, this big-ears."

Neville gave a short bark of a laugh. "Can't be sentimental about what you hunt." He drained his drink in one shot. "In fact, I look to actively dislike my quarry. Makes the kill more satisfying."

"You dislike your beast, then?"

"With a passion," said Neville without any trace of humor. He picked up a canapé. "But now I have the technology to track him down." He bounded to his feet and slapped the table. "In a few hours, my electric-nose gets here from the lab. Then I'm off to hunt a beast. I invite you to come along." He popped the little sandwich filled with big-ears meat into his mouth. "It'll be good having human company along when I bag him."

"Thank you." Roger had come to the Himalayas to break out of the safety of his university life, to be a man of action unencumbered by introspection. He wanted adventure—or at least he wanted to want adventure. And here was adventure dropped right in his lap. "Yes. I'd love to come along. That's very generous of you."

THREE HOURS LATER, they boarded Neville's hopper. Fritz came along as well—to deal with the carcass after the kill. Roger carried a borrowed ceramic-barreled rifle while Neville fondled his upgraded electric-nose.

In the Himalayas, he had gotten a scent-profile of the beast. He'd sent the profile-disk off to a laboratory for scent enhancing and to have known Earth smells removed. Now Neville had his single-scent electric-nose: a monomaniacal cyber-bloodhound.

"I've been wondering," said Roger, watching the hopper door swing closed behind him. "How do you know that the beast isn't a sentient being?"

"Sentience again." Neville shook his head. "If you examine the word carefully, you'll see it has no real meaning. The only precept I can give you is: except under exceptional circumstances, killing one's own species for food is bad form." He placed the electric-nose on the control console. "All right. Now help me install this thing."

THEY HOPPED TO A POINT some twenty thousand feet above the hunting lodge then skipped to a parallel world. Peering through a window, Roger looked down upon a planetscape that, at least from four miles up, seemed not unlike his own world's—except for the lightning. Dark spherical clouds flashed like lights on a pinball machine, and even through the walls of the hopper, continuous, rolling thunder made casual speech difficult.

"How long can this last?" Roger shouted.

"Was like this last time," Neville called back. "Must be like this all the time."

Roger nodded. No need to use unnecessary words.

Neville threw the switch for the electric-nose, then initiated a random-hop surveillance pattern. Roger, for his part, watched the nose display-screen for a direction-vector but still managed to sneak an occasional glance through a window. The scenery changed but the thunder persisted.

After about a dozen hops, Roger tapped Neville on the shoulder and gesticulated at the display.

Neville gave a thumbs-up and, looking back and forth between the display and the forward window, piloted the hopper onto the vector. He held the craft to its heading and the display indicated an ever stronger scent-signal.

"There." Neville pointed. "We've got him."

Through the forward window, Roger saw three big-ears and a larger animal. The larger creature seemed to be listening while the big-ears bounced about, heads animated and their great, stalked ears waving expressively. Roger had to remind himself that the creatures were merely animals, not his long sought intelligent aliens. *Big ears. Strange evolution for a noisy planet.*

Neville banked the hopper in a smooth arc toward the creatures, and Roger caught a good look at the larger animal: Neville's beast.

It walked upright and was covered in shaggy, gray fur. But the beast looked more canine than yeti—a wolf pretending to be a man.

"Take the controls," shouted Neville. "I'll try to get off a shot through the side port."

"What?" Roger gripped the arms of his seat. "No, wait. I can't—"

"Take over. A ten-year-old could pilot this thing." Neville released the stick and Roger had to grab it to keep the hopper steady.

Neville loosened his lap-belt and unlatched his shoulder harnesses. Then, swiveling around from the control console, he opened a vent window and shoved his rifle barrel through it. The thunder roared louder, accompanied now by a high, whistling whine of air rushing by the vent.

"Bring her down. I can't get a good shot from here."

Roger experimented with small movements of the controls.

"For God sakes, man," Neville shouted over the din, "bring her down fast."

Roger edged the hopper downward.

"Damn it. He sees us. Take us in close."

Roger maneuvered with slow deliberation.

"I said, fast." Neville looked up from his gun sight. "What are you? Afraid?"

In a surge of anger, Roger thrust the stick outward. Neville pitched forward, banging his shoulder on the bulkhead. "God damn it. What the hell are you trying to do?"

Roger got control of himself and then tried to get control of the hopper. The ground came up quickly and Roger fought for altitude while at the same time trying to slow the craft. Neville lurched for the controls and his rifle clattered to the floor. Roger jerked his hand at the sound and the hopper yawed sharply. Neville fell forward onto the controls and the hopper yawed even more. Despite Neville's body covering it, Roger tried to pull hard on the stick. He managed to slow the hopper's descent, but not quite enough. The hopper hit the ground, tottered, then fell over on its side.

"You damn, bloody moron," shouted Neville, his voice like the constant thunder.

"I'm sorry." Roger, firmly held to his seat by a lap-belt and shoulder harnesses, looked through the window at the vertical horizon. "I tried to tell you I was no hotshot pilot"

Neville clawed at the console and repeatedly toggled any switch he could reach. "Dead."

"If we can't get skip working," said Roger, more to himself than to Neville, "then we're trapped here."

"I'm not unaware of it, thank you." Neville turned to Fritz who, strapped in to a passenger seat, had not moved or said a word the entire trip. "Fritz. Let's get out of here."

Neville forced open the door and they looked out onto an arctic-cold landscape. Despite the thunder, the sun shined, bathing the landscape in a crystalline brightness.

They scrambled out of the hopper: Neville in the lead, followed by Fritz and then Roger. As they stood on alien soil, looking at the disabled craft, Neville glanced back.

"I don't suppose you know anything about hopper repair."

"Sorry."

"Didn't expect you did." Neville turned to Fritz. "Go into the hopper and fetch my rifle." He gestured with his head. "And get one for him as well."

"Do you think we're in danger?" Roger asked.

"Danger?" Neville glanced over to the hopper lying on its side. "Does it really matter now?"

Fritz came back with the rifles. Neville tossed one to Roger and, without looking back, set off into the ragged terrain. Fritz followed.

"Wait," Roger shouted. "Where are you going?"

Neville stopped and looked back. "Hunting. That's what I came here for." He snapped a few shells into his rifle. "Come or stay. I don't care which." He turned and tromped away.

Roger watched Neville move off. *How can that guy be so together?* Roger hurried to catch up. *Maybe he just doesn't fully comprehend the situation.*

Roger found himself breathing heavily. *Damn. The oxygen level here feels like I'm at twenty thousand feet.* He trudged along. *And this explains why the beast frequents the Himalayas.*

Staring at Neville's back, Roger felt first anger, then a cold calm. He'd had enough of kowtowing to privilege and enough of Neville's surliness. They were trapped here. Privilege meant nothing anymore. Roger thought about a fresh start. He could be the person he'd always wanted to be: assertive but polite, capable but modest, and above all, fearless. He smiled. He was younger and probably stronger than Neville. That might count for something.

They'd walked maybe two miles when Neville held up his hand, Indian style, and then pointed. Directly ahead, a beast sprawled luxuriously on a flat-topped boulder. Despite the cold, it seemed comfortably asleep, absorbing what heat the afternoon sun could provide.

Neville raised his rifle.

Without thinking, Roger knocked the gun away. "You can't shoot it while it's asleep," he shouted over the thunder. "And certainly not before you determine if it's sentient."

"God damn it." Neville waved to Fritz. "Will you kindly hold this fellow while I hunt. And you need not be too gentle."

Fritz snaked out an arm, and Roger realized that perhaps his youth and strength might not be as germane as he'd thought.

Neville swung his rifle back to point at the boulder. "Christ almighty."

The beast had vanished. Apparently even through the thunder, the beast had heard the commotion.

Neville set off toward the boulder. "Come on."

"I'm afraid I can't, sir," said Fritz.

Neville looked back. "All right. Let him go."

Fritz released Roger and followed his master.

Just then, the beast stepped from the side of the boulder. "*Hogy van*," it said.

"What the hell," said Neville, spinning around.

"Oh. You're English," said the beast in a deep, guttural voice. "Most interesting." It spoke with a decidedly Indian accent, but slurred—probably due to its wolf-like mouth.

For a moment no one spoke, but then Roger, working on his new assertiveness, stepped forward. He told himself that he was merely encountering some foreign gentleman . . . *who has excessive body hair, runs around naked, and sports distinctly lupine features.* "I'm Roger Milford."

The beast nodded.

"And this is Fritz, and"—Roger glanced quickly to the side—"and that is Neville Smyth."

"Neville Battenwroth-Smyth, if you don't mind."

The beast padded over to Fritz and sniffed like a dog. "Not animal." Then it shrugged. "We need quiet. Follow." He turned and loped away.

As they trudged after the beast, Neville tried to walk in front of Roger, but Roger walked faster and wouldn't let him.

After a walk of about twenty minutes, they came to the mouth of a cave. The beast led them inside.

At first the cave seemed pitch-black to Roger and he could only follow the beast by the sounds of his breathing: quick rhythmic pants that came in under the thrum of the thunder. Then, as his eyes accommodated, Roger saw that the cave walls glowed a deep blue. He ran his fingers over the wall.

"Light-emitting fungus," said the beast, looking back over his shoulder.

The cave sloped gently downward, and as they treaded into the depths the temperature increased and the thunder gradually quieted to a distant, low-pitched hum. The cave system seemed very complex and interconnected: a virtual city underground.

As they walked, other beast creatures wandered by. Some simply sniffed the air, while others spoke briefly to their guide.

"Your language sounds somewhat like Hungarian," said Roger, trying to break the tension.

"Similarities exist," said the beast without turning around.

"How is it you speak English?"

"The British brought English to the Himalayas. Before they came, we thought all people were as primitive as we."

"Primitive?" said Neville.

"Without technology."

At length, the beast stopped at the entrance to a grotto. "My home." The beast indicated that they go in.

From the central grotto, other chambers split off. "Assembly room, food room, den, sleep room." The beast pointed them out. "I suggest assembly room."

Roger and Neville followed the beast into a chamber. Fritz though, explaining that as a domestic servant he knew his place, stayed outside in the central grotto.

The chamber appeared quite comfortable for a cave. The back wall had ledges carved out of solid rock and padded with animal skins. Woven hammocks, made from long strips of leather, swung from the cave roof, and pictures painted on stretched skins adorned the walls. Most pictures were lifelike, drawn with consummate skill and artistry. One, however, seemed to be an abstract—a Cubist painting where, instead of a cube, the fundamental element was a tesseract: the four-dimensional hypercube.

A fireplace-like niche had been carved into one wall. And where one might have expected a fire, there sat instead a transparent bowl containing a glowing dark-blue liquid. The rock walls of the niche had been polished to a metallic brightness, and the bowl's light reflected off them, providing the chamber with a subdued but adequate level of illumination. A leather curtain controlled the light.

The cave floor was dry and covered with what looked like sawdust and, in a corner, two very young members of the beast's species played on the ground with carved sticks. Roger smiled at them. If you ignored the canine muzzles and the soft, downy coats, they seemed just a couple of infants, naked and at play.

The children jumped up and, chattering in their guttural language, ran up to the beast.

"My cubs," the beast said, shyly.

Roger nodded. *No matter what species, man or beast, there is no disguising a proud father.*

The beast patted his cubs' heads, said something to them, and the cubs loped back to their corner.

"Please sit," said the beast, "and tell me why you are here."

Roger and the beast sat, but Neville, his eyes aflame, remained standing.

Roger had seen that flame before. Trying to head off a confrontation, he attempted conversation. "We saw you with those creatures with the big ears. It almost looked as if you were talking with them."

"They told me what happened here while I was away from this world."

"Then you can indeed skip?" said Neville casting a sideways glance at Roger.

"Yes," said the beast.

"Those creatures," said Roger in a soft voice. "Are they sentient?"

"Yes, of course."

Roger, shaken, turned to Neville. "My God. I've eaten a sentient being."

"Bully for you." Neville shrugged. "Don't be so melo-dramatic. I myself have never dined on human flesh, but I've been told it's quite palatable."

"Damn it, Smyth. I've worked and studied for years, hoping to find a sentient, alien creature, and what do I do when I find one? I eat it."

The beast uttered a soft whisper of a growl.

Roger turned to him. "What are they called in their own language? I've got to apologize."

"No language," said the beast. "Their mouths are for eating, not speaking, and they are deaf."

"But those big ears?"

"Ears? The stalk appendages are noses. They commu-nicate by smell. They are thousands of times more profi-cient with scents than we are, and we have the noses of wolves."

Roger struggled to comprehend. "But communications has to go both ways."

"The organ in the middle of their faces is a scent gland of great subtlety."

"And I thought *that* was the nose," said Roger.

"They talk with those noses," said the beast. "I can only listen."

Neville cleared his throat. "I hate to break up this pleasant little chat, but . . ."

The beast looked over at Neville. "Yes?"

Neville swung his rifle up and pointed it at the beast's chest. "I have, shall we say, a little favor to ask of you. I need you to get me back to Britain."

"Get you back to Britain?" The beast stared at the rifle. "I can't take things with me when I skip. If I could, don't you think I'd bring back meat for my cubs, so that they could eat healthy until they're old enough to skip and hunt on their own? And don't you think I'd come back with products of your technology?" The beast looked up at the ceiling, muttered something incomprehensible, then looked again at Neville. "All we can bring back with us is what we see, smell and hear."

Neville flourished his rifle. "Actually, I just need you to skip to my hunting lodge and pilot back my hopper."

"Impossible," said the beast, "unless your hopper is in the Himalayas where I skip to. We can skip, but not hop." The beast looked Neville in the eyes. "And unless your shells are silver or palladium, I doubt your weapon will have much effect."

Neville swung the rifle around to point at the cubs. "Since they can't skip yet, I rather expect it to have an effect on them."

The beast made a sound like a gasp and looked quickly over at his cubs. He started to move forward but froze as Neville cocked the weapon.

"Smyth, no!" Roger cried out. "That's barbaric."

"Shut up, Milford." Neville glowered at the beast. "I'm sure you'll manage the trip somehow. Kill someone and take his hopper. I don't care."

"This is wrong," said Roger.

Neville shot a quick glance to Roger. "Ah, but here's an idea. You can use Milford's hopper. It's in the Himalayas. I'm sure he'll tell you how to find it. Use it to hop to my hunting lodge." Neville smiled. "And do come back soon. I'd hate if anything happened to your—I can't exactly call them children, can I? The hopper's in the stables. You can't miss it." He nodded at his wrist controller. "Just press the big, red button on the control console. The hopper will home in on this vector."

"I can't allow you to do this." Roger got to his feet. "That rifle is just a crutch," he blurted out.

"What?" Neville glanced quizzically over at Roger, and in that instant, the beast lunged. The beast's long canine-incisors sank into Neville's throat. Roger flinched as the beast closed his jaws and gasped as he heard the sharp snap of a neck broken.

The beast released his grip and the body fell to the floor with its head canted at an awkward angle.

Roger watched hypnotized as a puddle of blood, appearing black under the blue illumination, sluggishly spread out from Neville's torn throat. Then he heard a sound from the corner and noticed the cubs looking hungrily at the body.

The beast walked to the grotto entrance. "Fritz," he called out. Then he turned and said something to his cubs. They trotted out of the room.

The servant robot came in and looked at the mess. "Oh dear."

"Fritz," said the beast. "Clean up after your master, will you please?"

"At once, sir."

"Take him to the food room." The beast pointed to another chamber. "No sense letting him go to waste."

The beast looked down at the body. "As a rule, we don't prey on sentient species—unless they require it."

"I quite understand, sir."

After Fritz had picked up Neville and left, the beast turned to Roger who stood in shocked silence against the far wall. "Some people talk entirely too much"—Roger nodded his head rapidly, but didn't say anything—"and some not enough."

"Um," said Roger, staring at the pool of blood.

Neville had confronted his beast and died. Roger realized it was time to face his own personal beast: the fear of fear. *Maybe courage is simply acting as if one had courage.*

"I don't suppose," said Roger with a forced smile, "that a crucifix would do any good."

"Don't be ridiculous." The beast, one hand resting casually on his hip, leaned back against a wall.

Roger tried for a conversational tone. "What are you going to do with me?"

"Nothing." The beast shrugged. "I have no quarrel with you. You're free to go."

"Go?" Despite himself, Roger laughed. "Go where?" He stepped away from the wall and tried not to let his body-language betray his anxiety. "Without your help, I'll die here. I ask you, please, as an act of kindness— could you go and get Smyth's hopper?"

The beast looked him up and down, and sniffed the air before speaking. "Yes, I suppose I must. If you tell me how, I'll fetch it and you can go home to England."

Roger breathed a silent sigh of relief. "I'm Canadian."

"All right. To Canada, then. And maybe you might bring some few things back for us." He bared his fangs briefly in what Roger hoped was just a routine facial gesture. "But I don't know how we'd repay you."

"Getting me home is a pretty big payment. Believe me."

Meanwhile, Fritz had come back into the room and stood listening.

The beast turned to him. "Back to England for you, yes?"

"If you please, sir, I'd rather stay here. There's nothing for me in England."

Looking at the service-bot, Roger felt strangely moved. "Fritz," he said, "your actions seem very human, very sentient."

"Yes, I'm self-aware, sir. I've been programmed to be."

"But I'm afraid," said the beast, "that we're not a technological society. We'd not be able to replace your batteries."

"I don't use batteries, sir. I have a food processing system much similar to his."He nodded toward Roger."As for food, almost any organic matter will do, even scraps. And I think I'd make a good baby-sitter."

"Times change," said the beast, softly. "Fine. You're welcome to stay. My cubs could learn a lot from you." The beast looked over to the archway through which the cubs had gone. "There are so few of us left." The beast spoke softly. "And now that humans can come here whenever they wish, I don't know what to do. We'll have to talk to them. I wish I know how."

"Maybe I can help," said Roger.

The beast turned on him. "Help? How can you help? What do you know about my people?" He flashed his canine incisors again. "We're not some curiosity, some new toy for your world. You know nothing."

"I know you are 'knowledge gatherers,' but you don't share your knowledge easily. You use facts as barter. You have a photographic, or near-photographic memory. You are more emotional than we are, but a little less reliant on logic and more on facts. You are solitary and inner-directed."

Roger knew he was making wild extrapolations, but pressed on.

"You don't interfere with others outside your family grouping. I expect your language has no passive voice. It's very difficult if not impossible for you to lie. I think your color vision extends into the ultra-violet. You convey feelings to each other more by body language than words. You are a formal and polite people. And unlike us, who skip with machines, you experience the other dimensions when you skip."

Roger spread his hands, smiled, and hoped for the best.

The Beast cocked his head. "How could you possibly know these things?"

"I'm a xenosociologist. Xenosociology's a science, granted until now a theoretical science." Roger walked closer to the beast and hoped his scent projected sincerity. "You can tell a lot about a people's evolution from their environment—your sense of smell, and how smell is tied to emotions, that you can only carry information when you skip, the high price of speech because of the thunder, your art. And I'm a trained observer." He sighed. "I've spent my life preparing for the first encounter with an alien culture—"

"We're not exactly aliens," said the beast. "We've shared your world with you for millennia."

"In any case, I want to help."

The beast stared at him for a long moment, then said, "I think it is time for *Thrigvosh,* Great Assembly." He sprang to the mouth of his grotto, threw back his head, and sang.

The sound, like a baritone operatic aria mixed with a howl, was too much for Roger. He had no idea the beast was capable of such volume. *Probably evolved to deal with the constant noise on the surface.* He smiled. *I have a lot to learn about these fascinating creatures.* He lowered his head and put his hands over his ears. Noticing the blotch of blood seeping into the cave floor, he felt no fear but instead, sorrow for poor Neville. And he also felt exhilaration. After all that had happened—seeing his companion's throat ripped out, the prospect of dying stranded on an alien planet or killed outright by a beast—Roger didn't believe he would ever be truly afraid again.

Voice after voice picked up the song of the beast, until the cave reverberated with a sound like the amplified chants of a nation of Tibetan monks.

SHORTLY AFTER EXCHANGING Neville's hopper for his own, Roger Milford, newly appointed Ambassador of the Beasts, landed his craft in Strathcona Park in Ottawa. It felt great being home: the best of worlds.

Taking Neville's rifle and a knit bag of beast artifacts with him, he bounded out of the hopper. While walking toward the park entrance, he passed a rock outcropping. He paused, put down his bag, then raised the rifle over his head and slammed the barrel down onto the granite. The ceramic barrel broke into a shower of shards.

Roger picked up the bag and strode toward Parliament Hill. He had work to do.

CALLAS REDUX

REBECCA CARMI

We moderns pride ourselves on how free we are, how we make our own choices, how we're not bound by the expectations of our parents.

We no longer expect young men to follow their fathers' professions; young women no longer expect to go from their parents' house to their husband's without any pause for exploration along the way.

We choose our own mates, or none at all. Society's rules don't bind us, we're so free.

How odd, then, that we always seem to come back to the same means of rebelling, and keep making the same ridiculous mistakes as other people. How, if we're so free, do we keep on finding the same channels that others have followed before?

Every generation, the older folks complain about how the younger ones have no values, how they've thrown out the baby and kept the bathwater. Every generation, the young ones complain about their unreasonable elders, how astonishing it is that they could live so long and yet understand so little.

*Just because the script is an old one doesn't mean the lines
don't feel new to us when we make them up afresh and speak
them for the first time from our own lips.*

I AM PRACTICING *STRIDONO LASSU,* singing to the colony
girl, a precious thing named Dolly, with curly hair and a
bow tie mouth. I sigh to think that someday she will be
working in the selenium mines. I have no idea where
Luce found her, but that is Luce, always out talking to the
natives, interested in everybody—even these godfor-
saken colonists. Lately, he has been acting very mysteri-
ously, as if he wants to tell me something and then stops
himself. But I have no time for his games—I have *Pagliacci* to perform.

Luce brought me to this aviary to give me tactiles for
my opening aria as Nedda: an aria sung while my jealous
husband Canio is off at the tavern with the townspeople.
In this aria I listen to the birds and sing about them to a
young girl. The aria contrasts the flight of the birds to the
imprisonment of Nedda's life, bound to the violent
Canio. She surrenders herself to the enjoyment of nature
as she unknowingly incites the crippled Tonio, spying on
her in the background, to declare his passion for her.

I know Luce is hiding behind the bushes, playing the
part of Tonio, and I am determined to beat him at his
own game. Luce is the only heterosexual man who hasn't
tried to make love to me. Even Captain Jimmy, who is
technically my father give or take a few gene splices, gets
flustered around me. Luce knows me better than anyone
else in the world—how can he not find me beautiful?

I think about the look of concentration on his face as he
explained today's exercise, waving his hands around,
"Here you are with this innocent child, away from all the
men who desire you; your older husband Canio, the dis-
gusting Tonio, even your ardent lover, Silvio. The girl re-
minds you of your own child-self, sitting with your
mother, the only person who loved you for yourself and

not your beauty." That I understand, because my mama Rosa, loves me that well.

He stops talking and starts pacing. Now I know he is really excited. "It was her death that leads you to the poverty that Canio found you in, half starved. You inhabit both the little girl, and your mother, as you sing." Luce always insists we create detailed biographies of all the characters I play. He makes me write them down in a file he calls Melba's Lives.

I am singing my first Nedda on this planet. My voice has developed a new color, which has Sergei, the *verismo* director, in a state resembling a bitch in heat, according to Luce. This change in vocal timbre is because I am nearing 20 and the first full bloom of womanhood. Captain Jimmy thinks in another ten years I can take on anything. Still Sergei had to argue with my mother, who is my voice teacher, for six months before she allowed me to take on the rigors of Nedda.

Nedda sits heavy in the middle of the voice, and goes on and on with endless phrases. She is a temptress—a sexual siren who drives men to madness and whose thwarted passion drives her to defy the murderous jealousy of her husband and master. She is concerned only with her own pleasure and wants what is hers in life. Luce says I am like her.

"I'll be hiding back here as Tonio. Drive me wild Melba. Make me want you." Those were Luce's last words before he left me alone with the little colony girl.

I decide to punish him for acting so mysterious lately. This is not the time for Luce to be leaving me alone all the time since my best friend Galina is avoiding me (probably jealous of my playing Nedda). I *will* drive him mad.

I follow his instructions and focus on capturing Dolly, who is enthralled both by the sound of my singing and my smiles and caresses. At the same time I move with abandon, swaying my body, reaching for the heavens, laying myself on the ground in a position of surrender. And before beginning each run-through, I listen to the birds. We don't have birds on the ship and their song truly is enchanting. I am filled with longing and tenderness. I become Nedda.

I am not bragging when I say that of all the young sopranos, I am the best candidate for this role. When it comes to driving characters to sexual frenzies, I am a natural. I have golden honey-colored hair, which is unusual on this ship. I am statuesque in height and have the most luscious body of any of the others, who are mostly enormously obese, like my friend Galina.

Poor Galina has a crush on Palli—who is *the* young tenor. He is not interested in her, only in his career. Of course he is in love with me, and for a while last year we had a secret tryst. But I grew tired of his frustration with being second tier and exchanged him for a more experienced lover, Sergei, who is directing this production. It was a move that helped my career as well as my sexual desire. Besides, Palli will never get beyond the Elixir and Cosi tenor roles as long as Enzo is around. Enzo is a little older than Mama and he is the premier tenor.

I am lying on the ground—I've sung the aria through for the seventh time, which only a singer with my technique could do. It fits my body like a gossamer glove— each word has its own gesture—I love Dolly as if she were my own daughter—I ache for my own mother, Rosa. I have conquered it—the aria is mine.

"Luce," I call. "Come out—I am *finita*." There is silence. "Luce, darling, I simply cannot anymore—there is nowhere else to go."

I hear a rustling in the leaves. Luce looks pale.

"Melba." His voice is a whisper as he comes over to me. I reach out a hand and he pulls me up—he is one of the few men on the ship taller than me. For a moment I am in his arms and there is a look in his eyes that frightens me. "If only I could convince you . . . make you see." I have never noticed how nearly black his eyes are. I feel a strange melting sensation, and then he lets go of my hands and gets on his knees, an ironic look in his eyes. He applauds with slow, measured sounds. "Diva. Brava, Diva, brava." Then he jumps to his feet and says in his normal voice, "Let's go get something to eat," the strange look evaporated from his face. He picks Dolly up and spins her around once, to her delight.

"Convince me of what?" I ask. "See what?"

But he is carefree, playful Luce again. But the sound of slow applause continues, coming from the other side of the aviary.

All three of us wheel in surprise. The leaves of a large butterfly bush part, and a heavy-set, dark-complected man emerges. As the leaves snap back to place we glimpse two armed guards sitting on a bench in the clearing behind the bush.

The man continues to applaud as he walks towards us. Dolly backs away, frightened, "It's all right," I try to reassure her, still feeling motherly towards her, but she runs out of the aviary.

"That was quite a show," the man says, looking at me. First he looks in my eyes, than his eyes travel slowly down my body. He does not seem flustered and I notice he has rings on every finger, each set with brightly colored gemstones.

"You must be part of the actors group," he says to me.

"The Opera Company, from the ship *Masked Ball*," I say. I do not like the way he looks at me.

"That was some pretty interesting singing you were doing," he says to me. His eyes have returned to mine.

"I am Melba," I inform him. He doesn't seem to understand to whom he is speaking.

"And I am Artemis Manoupolis," he says. A gasp escapes me. *The* Manoupolis; here, on this planet. "But you can call me Art." Jimmy always says you never know who is in the audience. He walks past Luce, forcing Luce back a pace from the position he has taken by my side. Manoupolis doesn't look at him.

117

His bodyguards follow a pace behind him as he reaches the door of the aviary.

"Tell your boss I'll be at the performance," he says to me from the door, again looking me over in that insolent way. "Tell him I wouldn't miss it." And he is gone, his odious bodyguards with him.

"I will not sing for him." I announce to Luce. "He is a pig."

Melba has spoken. I walk out the same door that Manoupolis used.

Luce does not follow.

MANOUPOLIS HAS ASKED for a private performance and Jimmy says I must do it. I do not want to sing for that man again. I could see immediately that he does not have a milligram of art in him. I could be any lewd dancing girl in his eyes . . . the voice, the training, the Mission, mean nothing. I explain this to Jimmy.

Jimmy, of all people should understand why we must be true to the Mission. Jimmy has all sorts of philosophies about what we do and why. He is a genius and I am proud that he part-fathered me, though my mother never married him. My mother says she is not the marrying type.

We distribute downloads of our universal knowledge database everywhere we go, not for payment but for humanitarian reasons. Jimmy, who is both captain of the ship and conductor of the orchestra, says this is plain survival, because we will have no audience if humanity succumbs to a dark ages. It is part of the Mission. I know once I point out that Manoupolis is a boar and a pig, Jimmy will forget about the performance.

"Fine, Melba honey. I understand. I'll ask Edita to do it—she's still got the role in her hip pocket." He starts to leave my room

I hate Edita. She is Luce's mother and the one who wouldn't let me play with Luce when we were children.

She owns all the real roles—the Toscas and Turandots—roles she stole from my mother. She also commands one more vote on the council than my mother, which is only one less than Jimmy himself. That makes her second in command. Nedda is the first role I've managed to wrest from her selfish grasp. I will not give it back to her.

"Wait, Jimmy," I direct my most ravishing smile down on his bald head. "If it is so important to you, I'll do it."

Jimmy looks pleasantly surprised but I know he is acting. "Thanks, Melba love." Then he gives me my payment for giving in. "You are the best Nedda we have."

I know he is saying what I want to hear, but I can't help the smile that comes to me. Soon I will take all the roles from that cow Edita. Melba is unstoppable.

Luce's mother Edita and my mother Rosa are terrible enemies. They were the two most beautiful sopranos way back when and the competition between them was deadly. When they both had babies at the same time—my mother with Jimmy's sperm carrier, Luce's mother with Pavorotti DNA injected into silicone sperm (there is a shortage of the good tenor voice on our ship), they became fast friends.

Luce and I were raised together. It was soon apparent I would be one of the greatest voices ever known in the galaxy, and Luce, *pauvre* Luce had no instrument. Edita was heartbroken and she and my mother quarreled. My mother let go of many roles in order to train me and Edita callously picked up her throwaways. Nobody could believe my mother would give up her position in the company, but mother always does her own thing, and she knew I was special, on a "golden path," as she calls it. And Luce and I had to sneak away to play together.

My Luce has wonderful talent as a director. He is a brilliant person—he always helps me flesh out my roles. He thinks in ways nobody else does and he *wants* to be a director. Sergei, the verissimo director, says he is ridiculous and that his ideas are a violation of tradition, so Luce coaches me in secret, just like we used to play in secret as children. Sergei loves what I do, but Luce won't let me credit him publicly. He says it is not politic. This is why I love my Luce. He always thinks of me and is part of why I have become so great at such a young age.

Luce is also a mathematician and spends lots of time in the school module playing with numbers. Sometimes he disappears for days. They are training him to work in the genetics lab, but he really wants to direct.

Jimmy sent a plate of chocolate truffles to my room— everyone knows how much I love chocolate but normally they don't let me have it because I have to fit into the costumes. I understood that Jimmy was telling me that I can have anything I want—as long as I give him a Nedda like the world has never seen.

I will do it. If anyone can, it is I!

Artemis Manoupolis, one of the richest men in the galaxy and collector of arcane artifacts, is visiting this system to replenish his selenium supplies. It is the first time we will have the opportunity to perform for him. Jimmy is very excited because Manoupolis collects clothing and wigs of great women and may have DNA strands we are missing.

One of the ways the original crew collected DNA of great opera stars was by collecting wigs—human hair often gets stuck in the clips used to adhere the wigs at the temples and nape of the neck, over the scalp stocking. When things got bad on Earth and people were leaving, many things were left behind or sold. For three years the future *Masked* crew bought up opera costumes and wigs at auctions to use in the gene lab. Later, their shares in ship council decisions were based on how much they contributed to the talent banks, either as themselves or through their lab holdings. This is fair and the way it must be, because our talent is our commodity and our survival. I have already achieved three council votes at my majority through audition. Luce has only one, which he was awarded for joining the gene lab.

Jimmy tells us that our Caruso and Scotto DNA came from wigs left in the La Scala costuming shop in glass boxes. Jimmy's mother was their costume maker and she simply took them, along with other costumes on display. One of those costumes is the source of my Dame Melba gene—our ship is the sole source of the lost scores and the remaining masters, and our bodies the genetic inheritance of great singers living and dead.

But we have never been able to obtain DNA from Maria Callas. Nobody would part with any Callas memorabilia and she always kept all her custom-made costumes and wigs, which have disappeared. Yet Jimmy says he has heard rumors that Manoupolis has Callas' wig from a 1953 performance of Tosca as one of the centerpieces of his collection. Jimmy is more excited than I have ever seen him. Even his head is sweating.

We set up the performance tent for our solo audience and hand out translation chips to him and his entourage. The first act is going beautifully. I make them hear the birds as I sing my aria, even though Sergio always uses very stripped down sets for *verismo*, so that the truth of the story is not overshadowed by *oohs* and *ahhs* and make believe.

When Tonio surprises me and tries to kiss me, I turn on him with the whip. I hear Manoupolis give a groan of pleasure as Tonio threatens to make me pay. But I am so deep in the role that even he cannot stop Nedda on the path that leads to her death.

During the beginning of the second act I watch Manoupolis through the actor's peephole. Enzo is a wonderful Pagliacci—his *veste la jube* makes me cry every time. He puts on his makeup as he sings, forced to play the clown, even though he has discovered that his wife (me) is unfaithful. I get so caught up in the beautiful *bellissimo* singing, *ahh*, like velvet, that I forget to watch Manoupolis. I am astonished when I look over and see Manoupolis looking at his cuticles. Pig.

When I return to the stage to for Act II, in which Nedda plays a Harlequin actor for the villagers, his head snaps back up and he is all attention.

Even I know that there are greater artists than Melba— and Enzo is one of them. Of course, he is twice my age and one day I will be just as great, but he has that depth and magic that come once in a lifetime. I am more certain than ever that Manoupolis has not a shred of understanding for our art. I allow myself to feel sorry for him.

As Nedda's real cuckolding of Canio takes over their little Harlequin play-acting the opera plays itself out as it always does. Canio berates and threatens Nedda, the chorus of townspeople believing it is all part of their play, until he kills her and they realize that life has over-run art. As I lay in my death freeze I do my trick of peering through my fingers.

At the end of the death scene, I always fall with my hand over my eyes, my head lolling at the edge of the stage. I peek through my fingers and watch the faces of the downsiders wherever my gaze falls as I freeze in mock death. I enjoy the irony of watching them while they watch us—the secret show given by the audience to the players.

It amazes me how overcome their expressions are, some with tears rolling down, some in a grimace of fear, some aroused by the violence playing out before them. They do not know they are being watched, unlike us, who train to be watched.

Manoupolis, however, is not moved. He looks like the wolf who ate the chicken. He is actually licking his lips. I feel sullied.

After the performance Luce comes to my dressing module.

"Melba, you let Nedda go in the second act, I could tell, there you are swearing on your mother's name that you'll keep your lover's name a secret, and any fool can tell you don't really care . . ."

"It was that man. I saw him picking his cuticles during Enzo . . ."

"Melba, you sing for Melba, for Nedda, I don't care who is in the audience." Luce is angry. His eyes look black again. I am surprised—he is such an easygoing person.

There is a knock on the door and Manoupolis comes in. He looks at Luce and says, "Excuse me, I would like a moment with the star." Luce gives an ironic look, bows and leaves.

Manoupolis saunters over to me. I continue to remove my silicone skin of Nedda makeup from over the micro-thin encoded costume template. He comes up behind me and looks in the mirror over my shoulder. His hand comes up and caresses my bare shoulder, trails down my arm. I wish I had the whip that Nedda uses on Tonio.

"Melba," he whispers. "You will be my guest for dinner tomorrow at seven o'clock, no?"

"I'm busy," I say.

"No, you are not. I have already asked Captain James Pardo and he said your schedule will be cleared." I feel a chill of dread.

"Jimmy does not set my social calendar." I reply.

"He says you are interested in my wig collection. I would be happy to show it to you." I am silent.

This is big. Very *molto* big. If I could obtain the Callas DNA I would be a legend, more than I already am. I could control a whole additional council vote of my own.

"I never dine before eight," I say.

He leans down and kisses me on the neck.

"Then eight it is, little Melba." And he walks out.

I rub his kiss off my neck with a disinfectant swab.

I HAVE NEVER BEEN ON A SHIP other than the *Masked*. The *Masked* holds eight hundred and twenty-eight people including crew, singers, the orchestra, conductors, directors, coaches, accompanists, costumers, makeup artists, set designers and all the children. It is full of bright and open spaces for voice and movement classes and rehearsels. The *Oanasis* has a contingent of one hundred and forty people and is nearly twice the size.

I am appalled at the décor. The butler who opens the door is a hermaphrodite. It is stark naked, except for some Japanese slippers and a silk scarf trailing between its large breasts. It leads me through a spiral hallway filled with framed pictures of naked people. They are all in ridiculous positions that are obviously supposed to be seductive and they all have props—boots, wigs, whips, and feathers.

The hermaphrodite wiggles as it walks. It has enormous hips, delicate feet and broad shoulders. A long blond braid trails down its back and its neck is surprisingly masculine. I have never seen one before and I find it hard not to stare. It towers over me by at least a foot. I take careful notes to tell Galina all about it—and then I remember she has dropped me since I got Nedda.

As we spiral in closer to the center and the lower G areas, each turn of the hallway is lit with differently colored lights. So unlike the *Masked* with its clean lines, muted lights and occasional ionic column marking a change in section. I feel suddenly homesick for its elegant interior.

The hermaphrodite opens a broad door for me and bows me in, a strange smile on its face.

I have walked into the set of a Strauss opera. An enormous dining table is set with heavy brocade cloth, gorgeous silver chalices and ornate china. A candelabrum the size of me glows in the middle. At the other end sits Manoupolis, in a red silk dressing gown.

He rises and comes to the door. He is my height.

"Little Melba, welcome. It is not often that I have a beautiful woman for dinner." He bows over my hand.

"Mr. Manoupolis," I say tartly, pulling my hand back. This seems to delight him.

"Art, please, call me Art." He seats me at the table.

The hermaphrodite closes the door behind me and I am nervous.

Dish after dish comes and I can hardly taste anything. I am only thinking of how to get him to show me the wig collection. He chats on, asking me about life on the ship, my favorite role, which colony has the best sushi. At first I try to make my answers as short as possible, but then the wine, and the food, and maybe the fun of talking to somebody I haven't seen every day of my life combine to loosen my tongue and I find I am talking back to him, and enjoying myself.

The hermaphrodite, whom Artemis addresses as Io, serves each course. I notice that Io hefts enormous trays as if they were lighter than air.

By the time the chocolate mousse (ahh, they never let me eat chocolate mousse) is served with the dessert wine, I am giggling with Art as if we were old friends. I don't have much experience with wine, so I assume that I actually am enjoying Art.

Then the moment I have been waiting for. "My little Melba, would you like to see my wig collection?"

"Yes, please, I would like that very much," I tell him, and giggle again. Melba never giggles—it must be the wine. I feel dizzy.

He snaps his fingers and four servants come in with a golden bench mounted on a litter, like something out of Turandot, and carry us through a labyrinth of hallways. I am having a far better time than I expected.

We come to a room somewhere closer to the center. As we enter we stand in a transparent booth as light and air fill the room. Manoupolis explains that all his collections are kept in near vacuum to maintain them.

As the room lights up, I feel like I am in a dream. There are wigs, hats, shoes, boots and belts everywhere, all hung at different levels. Also items of clothing I don't know how to identify that look like strange filmy under-things and still others with obviously sinister uses. The wigs are on pewter wig stands with plaques underneath them and montages of their previous owners behind them. The boots are on shapely pewter stalks and the belts grace slender pewter torsos. I recognize many of the pictures. Marilyn Monroe is in a central area pictured behind a pair of boots on pewter legs with a selection of garter belts and a silky negligee. Jacqueline Kennedy is pictured behind an array of hats. Princess Diana has hats and shoes. I wander around the room trying to recognize the faces and names.

Halfway through the room I freeze. Maria Callas. The rumors are true. Pictures of the Greek-American Diva scroll behind something that looks like an iron girdle, a belt and . . . a red-haired wig. I stand mesmerized. Callas DNA, at my fingertips. I reach out to touch the wig, to coat my fingertips in her genetic memory and jump back with pain and surprise as a mild shock hurts me. Artemis laughs softly behind me.

He kisses my neck. The pain of the shock has brought tears to my eyes and his kiss goes through me like another shock—but this one of pleasure. "Would you like to try on that wig, my little Melba?" His breath warms my ear. To actually wear it—I could even walk out of here with one of her hairs adhered to mine!

I want to so badly I would risk the shock field again. There are tears in my eyes, as I nod yes.

"And I would so like to see you in it," he whispers hoarsely, "but really it will not go well with this frock you wear." He unbuttons the shoulder tabs on my garments and continues to caress my shoulders, sending shudders through my body, as the dress falls to the floor.

"Magnificent," he says, as he undoes my brassiere, which I need in planetary gravity, letting it fall. His hands move down to my panties and slide them down. He is panting.

I am confused. I want to hit him, but I want to wear the wig, and I also don't want him to stop. He has done something to me, tricked me into drinking too much wine. I am not myself. He reaches out and lifts up the wig. His robe is open and he is naked underneath.

"Lean forward, my little vixen, and I will place this on your head." He says, moving forward, erect.

The room is spinning, and I do as he says. I lean forward and feel the weight of the wig on my head as he enters me. I want to reach for Callas' belt to teach him to ask permission of Melba, but I cannot help myself from crying out with pleasure. My hand falls to grasp the rail in front of me as his movements become more vigorous.

"Whore," he screams as he comes, "whore."

I scream, too, as I come.

I DO NOT WANT to see Luce. I have taken two baths today, careful to keep my hair protected from the water. Luce has rung twice, Mama once and Jimmy three times. They all want to know if I saw the wig, if it's true, and of course, if I was able to touch it. Luce did one of his disappearing acts yesterday, but now that I may have something for the lab, he can't stay away. Galina has not even come around and I decide she is not my friend anymore.

Finally Jimmy comes to my door.

"Melba," he says. "Open up."

I open the door and look disdainfully down on him, which is easy to do because he is a foot shorter than me.

"Well? We are all waiting, Melba. Did you see the wigs?"

"I had a perfectly awful time, thank you for inquiring," I say.

He looks at me carefully and I look away.

"Did he do something to you?" he asks.

"I saw your foolish wig," I tell him.

He is so excited he looks like he will pop.

"And? And?" he says after I remain silently. "Well?" his voice goes up.

"You are looking at a head covered with Callas DNA."
I cannot help smiling. "I was just debating whether or
not to take a shower . . ." I say.

He grabs me. "Melba, please! Sugar . . . let's go down
to the lab."

"I'm thinking about it." I say.

"It would mean so much to us all, to the Mission, to future generations," he begs. I wait silently.

"Melba . . ." he says. I continue to wait. "I think the
successful contribution of Callas DNA to our gene bank
would be worth a lot to us."

I say nothing, merely try and look disinterested.

He sighs. "It is worth at least another council vote."

I smile graciously. "Let the lab know I am on my way."
Then I add without a smile, "And don't ever say I
haven't done my part for the Mission." I slam the door.
All he cares about is his damn Mission. I'm sorry he is
sort of my father.

On the way to the lab I see Galina ducking around a
corner and running the opposite way. I am quite sure she
has seen me. Weak and jealous, like all the rest.

In the lab it is, of course, Luce, who combs through my
hair, removing samples around the temple and at the
back of the neck. I try not to look at Luce.

They find nothing.

"Luce, you must find something—I wore it, I swear." I
start to feel sick.

Luce spends hours going over my head. At the end of
the afternoon he puts down the scanner and says, "Let's
get out of here, Melba." I am in tears. I let him lead me by
the hand.

We walk through the colony. Luce talks to me. Though
most of us third-generation shippers are extraordinarily
talented, given our genetic lineage and our unique and
exclusive exposure to the greatest training coaches ever
assembled in one place, I am the only one getting to sing
the performances. I am on a golden path, like my mother

says. Our parents and grandparents are still singing their roles and voices last much longer than they used to with all the post-Dispersion treatments against age. The same is true in the orchestra; most players in their 20's and 30's are in the "Youth" orchestra, or "Overgrown Youth" orchestra as we call it among ourselves.

The others mostly hate me for it, but that is what is to be expected. Except for Luce.

Luce shows me things—the parks, the beautiful waterfront on their reservoir, the schools—they have playgrounds and mothers and fathers are playing with their children. And still Luce talks, about the changes we are seeing everywhere on the colonies—the schools and museums and parks, all signs that the colonies are succeeding, that they are not falling into a dark ages the way our Mission claims.

I come out of my stupor. "But then what is our Mission?" Luce just leads me to a group of school children. With a shock I recognize our little girl from the aviary, Dolly. I rush over to pick her up and hug her but Luce holds me back.

Dolly is singing, and the other children are listening. She is singing *Stridono lassiu*—she has the words all wrong but her voice is darling, clear and bell-like. She has remembered every phrase, and it is not easy or even melodic music.

"Stay here with me, Melba," says Luce. "I am not leaving with the *Masked Ball*. Neither is Galina, or Palli, or most of the youth orchestra and dozens of others. We have met with the colonists and they want us to start a School for the Arts. You don't have to do what Jimmy tells you to for the rest of your life."

"But what about the gene lab—we don't have all the DNA of the Masters."

He smiles at me. "We are the new Masters."

He gets down on one knee. "Marry me."

I turn and run.

I understand that the others want to leave. They are not on Melba's golden path. But why should I give up everything to help them with this ridiculous plan? I am Melba, and everyone on *Masked Ball* knows it.

What is important is teaching these ignorant colonists what it is like to really live. To keen with agony and pursue impossible loves and die not from medical or technological failures, but for tragedy's sake. All the emotional realities that are swallowed up by the drear and drudge of their hard working lives in their mines and the factories. It is our Mission to help them remember that there is more

I don't understand why tears run down my face.

THE *OANASIS* LEFT EARLY in the afternoon. Only charred rock remains where the cesspool of a ship had been.

That night I sing Nedda like I've never sung before. During the curtain call Jimmy gets down on his knees and kisses the hem of my skirts. This is in part to comfort me for the Callas fiasco, and in part because I deserve it. Luce is standing and screaming in the audience.

After the performance I am swarmed. Even Edita comes backstage to tell me she is proud of me. My mother is standing next to me and gives Edita a hug and they both start crying. Divas are like that.

I am too tired to undress. I peel off the makeup and go back to the ship. Behind me the crew is setting the nanobots to disassemble the performance tent. Tomorrow we will take off, or some of us. The elders don't know that many of the young people will not be with us.

I go to my mother's suite and lie down on the foot of her bed like when I was a child. When she comes back, probably from a rendezvous with Jimmy, she strokes my head.

"Little Melba," she says, "I was so proud of you tonight."

"Can I stay here with you tonight?" I ask. She looks at me peculiarly.

"Yes my love," and she pulls back the blankets for me to settle in next to her. I will miss Luce and the others. I understand that they would have to wait a generation before they can take their place center stage. They do not have my exceptional talent. I fall into a deep sleep.

I am awakened by bright lights.

"Get up!" Jimmy says, roughly.

"What do you mean by this?" my mother demands, her arm protectively around me.

"Ask Melba what I mean!" I am having trouble understanding him.

Jimmy yanks me up off the bed.

"I want the names of everybody involved in this project of yours." I am still not awake but then he slaps me across the face and I am.

My mother leaps out of bed like a fury and pushes him away from me.

"If you touch her again, I will kill you," she says. He believes her and so do I.

"Ask her what she's planning with all the downloads of our scores, our databases, our costume templates— everything!" He is so mad there is spittle coming out of his mouth. He is very short and fat.

"I don't know what you're talking about." I tell him, coldly.

"Oh come, on, Melba," he says, "I just finished having a drink with the head of the colony and some man came over and told me how excited they are about the new School for the Arts and he hopes his daughter Dolly can study with you. I came back and found your access codes on every file." I try not to show my surprise.

Luce's project. Jimmy found out. Jimmy takes my silence as confession, but really I am puzzled. I didn't know they were stealing downloads, and I don't know why the colonists think I am part of the new school. And why are my access codes on the files?

"Who's doing this with you!" he demands.

"I will never tell you." Melba doesn't beg or whine.

He walks to the intercom. "Security to Madame Rosa's suite."

My mother and I look at each other. There is a question in her eyes and I shrug my shoulders for an answer.

The two security officers come.

"Take her to the brig," Jimmy says, clipped and controlled.

"Aye, aye, Captain," says the one on my right. My mother takes my left hand.

As we march out of my mother's suite, Luce is waiting in the hall, looking worried.

"Luce!" I call out. I am surprisingly relieved to see him.

"Ah hah!" says Jimmy, "Of course! Who else, Melba? Grab him, too." I should have kept quiet.

They march us down to the brig, which I have never seen. Inside Jimmy says, "I am taking away your council votes and you will stay here until after take-off."

"They have done nothing wrong," says my mother, who is still holding my hand.

"Only tried to steal our lives' work, " says Jimmy. He pivots her out and closes the inner door behind him.

WE SLOUCH ON THE FLOOR, ignoring the sparse furnishings of the brig. Luce looks more discouraged than I have ever seen him—he looks shorter. I am not feeling happy myself, but I hold Luce's hand to comfort him. Melba has definitely fallen from the golden path.

"Luce, why did you put my access codes on the files?" I asked after a couple of hours of thinking. Melba is not a fool.

"Here, on the *Masked Ball*, we are outside of the universe. We cannot change and grow as a company, and most of us young people can't even take part," says Luce. "I started thinking about how Canio reacted when he thought Nedda betrayed him, and I believed that if Jimmy thought you had betrayed him, he would throw you off the ship, and we could be together," he says sheepishly.

"Canio kills Nedda," I remind him. But I am impressed. I knew he admired me, like everyone else, but now I understand he loves me. Really loves me, like Rodolfo, or Alfredo, or well, not like Sergei.

"Throwing you in the brig is about the same thing."

"But this is our universe, our home," I say. "We will find a way to make things right." I don't tell him, but I am relieved. I can't imagine my life without him, and now he will have to stay.

"It is not a life. It is a dog and pony show run by one person—Jimmy. Don't you want to make your own decisions? Don't you want to be more than Jimmy's show? Did you really enjoy dinner with Mannoupolis?"

I blush and turn towards the wall. How dare he question my choices! I will never talk to Luce again—that voiceless maggot. And to think, I indulged him at his attempts to coach me!

Luce leaves me to my silence.

After several hours, we hear noises in the ship that we recognize as pre-launch preparation. Luce sighs. They cannot deny my talent forever and I will soon perform again, but Luce . . . I have gotten over my anger and I am worried about what will happen to him.

Luce breaks the silence, "Melba . . ."

"Oh Luce," I say, I am so relieved to hear his voice.

He puts his finger to my lips.

"I guess I'm no better than Jimmy. I'm sorry." I reach out and take his hand.

Then the door opens and Edita and Rosa stand before us, keypads in their hands.

"Mama!" says Luce.

"Where is Jimmy?" I ask.

"He is asleep in his cabin," says Edita.

"With a little help from a sleeping powder," giggles Rosa.

"Like Figaro gives to Bartolo's servant!" says Edita.

"Or Pedrillo puts in Osmin's wine," says Rosa.

"Or Harlequin gives Nedda for Pagliacci," says Edita.

"Or poor Guilietta takes," sighs Mama.

"We have not been singing opera all these years without picking up a trick or two," says Edita. They look at each other and giggle. I have never seen them like this.

"But won't he make problems for you?" Luce asks.

"Leave him to me," smiles Edita. "With my rivals gone, Jimmy needs me." I puff up with pride. It is the first time Edita has called me a rival. But why rivals, plural? And how do they all know I have decided to leave? I haven't even told Luce. They are ruining my scene.

"Come, little Melba," Mama says. "We have about an hour to pack our things and get off the ship."

My mouth actually drops open. "Mama?" She always surprises me.

"I can't leave my star pupil—you still have many roles to learn. I am coming with you. I always wondered what it was like to live off ship." She smiles at Luce.

"And you must come too, Mama! That would be more than I ever hoped for!" says Luce.

"No, my darling, I will stay and lead the company, without Rosa and Melba *and* Edita we would be lost." Luce looks like he will cry. Edita takes his hand. "But with Rosa on the planet, Jimmy will probably find a reason to come back every year." Luce kisses her hand. "You will make a great director, my son."

I start for my own quarters with Mama to pack some things when Luce calls my name. He looks troubled. "I have something that belongs to you." He takes out of his pocket a folded piece of lab parchment and hands it to me. Inside is a long black hair. "It was in your hair. From the wig." I look at him—he has surprised me twice today. "Do what you want with it." I reach out and take the packet.

Mama and I are packing—she is all business, but I am distracted.

A long black hair. Callas. I can almost feel her presence in our cabin. I imagine we are alike in many ways.

I can start to buy back my council votes. I am back on the golden path. I almost tell Mama to stop packing.

But all I can think about is Luce waiting outside my mother's suite when Jimmy arrested me, even though he knew he would be giving himself away. And Jimmy, lurking outside my door after my dinner with that man. Suddenly, all the council votes on the ship don't mean as much to me as the look in Luce's eyes when he held me in the aviary. I want to see that look again. I want to live in a world where many people will look at me and see Melba, not just Nedda, or Liu, or Flora.

WE WATCH THE SHIP take off, Mama, Luce and I are holding hands, and, to my surprise, so are Palli and fat Galina. Galina burst into tears and hugged me when I came off the ship. "Oh Melba, I was so afraid I'd give us away if I talked to you, I've been heartsick—I never dreamed you'd stay!" As usual she has underestimated Melba. The other surprise is that Enzo is standing next to Mama. There are about two hundred people who have stayed behind. It seems I was too busy with Nedda to notice how busy everyone has been.

I know that our wonderfully talented Mama Edita will be laughing when she sees the long black hair carefully secured to the bottom of my farewell note.

ALL IN MY MIND

EUGIE FOSTER

One of the oddities of the human race is how easily we consent to being owned.

I'm not talking about slavery per se—though in truth there's a weird measure of consent even in that, at least in societies where the slaves outnumber the owners.

No, the odd thing about us is the way so many of us give ourselves to the very masters who seek our destruction. The Stockholm syndrome, isn't that what they call it? The hostage or prisoner who so identifies with his captors and tormentors that he becomes their property, their ally, their advocate. Patty Hearst.

The mob of people who give themselves to each other, no longer thinking for themselves. There must be some kind of re-lief in that, to rescind one's own responsibility and say, What-ever you want, I'll do that, your will not mine be done . . .

Until the trance is over, the mob dispersed, the master gone, and we have to look at the blood on our hands and admit who it was who did the thing.

We consent so easily to being owned. And suffer so painfully when we are returned to ourselves.

DOWNTOWN OLD ATLANTA is one of my least favorite places. It's been a scum pit full of syrup-heads and other lowbies since the turf wars of 2026. Me, I never do syrup. Syrup makes you slow, makes you stupid. It's for haunts who need something to fuzz out the rest of the world when the edges are too jagged to deal with.

I'm a rush man. Rush keeps me fresh so I can crank out the ad-blips and spot-jingles for the big boys. And when I got a few minutes to spare, it lets me write the real stuff.

Today, though, I got a call from Dina. I can still hear her nasal voice droning in my ear. I was buzzing hard, and one of the things about rush is the auditories.

"Kristof," she said. My name was a nest of snakes hissing over the fiber optics. "Thank God you're there. I need your help."

It took a second for the echoes to fade away in my head. "Babe, I'm working."

"Please, can't you get away? I really need you." Even over the phone I could hear the catch in her voice. Either she had been crying or she had one honker of a cold.

I'm such a slowmoe. I can't turn down a fem, even if she's rigged up four ways to sundown. Dina was as reliable as a hard drive crash on tax day when it came to getting a guy in trouble. But man, if you saw her, you'd know why, no matter what, guys came running when she called.

"Where are you?"

"Peachtree and Seventh."

"I'll be down in about twenty minutes," I said, all the time kicking myself for being a balls-for-brains chump.

"Hurry, Kristof. I'm scared."

Have to give her credit; she sure sounded it. If she weren't such a street junkie, she'd make an A-1 actress.

"I'm out the door," I said.

"Thanks. I didn't have anyone else I could call."

The sound of her hanging up was like a snare drum striking over and over in my head. Click-snick-trick-wick. Damn, but it was a good buzz. I could've made some major in-roads in the ad-blip job I had been putting off. I sighed. No one else she could call, yeah right. More like I was the next XY with a solid income on her gimme list.

I caught the funnel downtown. There was a slowdown on the run. Another bomb scare, probably some guerilla gang angry about the latest police shutdown, or the curfew, or anything else that made them feel justified in screwing people. The transit drones had to detour us to another line.

It was almost forty-five minutes until I finally got to the Seventh Street station. I hoofed it two blocks up to Peachtree. Even before I got there, I knew something was up. The ambulance and the crowd of gawkers were dead giveaways.

I just knew, with a thudding in my chest that had nothing to do with the rush, that Dina would be in the middle of everything. Pushing through the people, I had a hard time staying focused. All their voices kept running round and round in my head, spinning off into rhyming couplets and lisping iambic pentameter.

Seeing Dina lying on the gurney, though, that knocked me straight. She looked wiped. Her hair, normally this lustrous blue-black coil of pure-weave, was tangled and matted against her head. Her face was ashy-pale and her eyelids twitched and jumped. She looked like the worst kind of junked-out drifter.

I jostled through and darted up to the gurney.

A thug in a paramedic uniform shoved me away. The look of boredom on his face didn't mesh with "trained medical personnel" to me. I was betting he was hired muscle for the downtown runs.

"Keep back," he said. His voice was a deep bass rumble. Back-track-snack-flack. I blinked to clear the syllable trails.

"I know her," I said. "I'm a friend."

"So?"

I waved a twenty in his face. It disappeared in the middle of the second pass and he let me through. Nothing like a little love to unclog the system.

"Dina, it's Kristof. Can you hear me?"

Her eyes were a pair of bruises that fluttered open to show a glazed blue rim of iris around enlarged, black pupils.

"Kristof?"

I could smell the cherry-sweet cough medicine on her breath. She had been sipping syrup.

I pushed a curl, sticky with sweat, away from her face. "What happened, baby?"

She moaned. The sound was like a minor chord between my temples. But before the echoes could pick up, it faded away. My buzz was shot to hell and I was coming down. Just as well.

"What're you on? The medics gotta know."

"Syrup," she said.

"How much?"

"Couple doses and a primo." Her hand reached out to mine. "And someone hit me with a patch, but I don't know what of." Tears pooled in her drugged-out eyes. "You took so long getting here!"

Yeah, great. Make me feel guilty. It's what Dina did best. Well, maybe second best.

"They got Adrienne," she whispered. She clutched my hand tight. The edges of something sharp pressed into my palm. "You have to get her back."

"Who's Adrienne?" I almost fumbled it, but held on to the data stick she was passing me. Just in time, too. Another paramedic—not my muscle-bound friend—came up toting an IV needle and a matching electrolyte solution baggie.

"You're the husband?" he said.

The idea of being tied down with Dina gave me the twitches. "She's not married. I'm just a friend."

"I see." The med guy pulled Dina's hand from mine and swabbed it down.

"What happened?" I asked.

"Not sure." He probed the top of her hand, looking for the big vein. "We responded to an anonymous 911 call." He stuck the IV in and I felt my knees go wobbly. I don't like needles.

I shook my head and realized I had made a mistake when the world began to spin.

"You okay, buddy?"

I swallowed hard and thought of all the words that rhymed with "not" starting with cot. Cot-dot-fot-got-hot. Fot? What'n heck was a fot? It worked though. The sickening twirl resolved itself into something I could deal with. "I'm fine," I said, a little breathlessly.

He started pushing the gurney to the ambulance.

"Hey, she's on syrup," I said.

The medic turned and raised an eyebrow. "Anything else?"

"Yeah, I think she's also done a primo—it's a toke of XP laced with crystal. I'm not sure what else but it's gotta be something. She can usually hold her stuff better than this."

The guy rolled his eyes. "Thanks for letting us know."

"Where you taking her?"

"St. Mary's."

"You can't take her there!" I should've let it go, not gotten mixed up in it. But I couldn't. St. Mary's is where the junkies and the hospice rejects go to rot.

The medic looked sympathetic, but he kept going. "Sorry, but she doesn't have an insurance card. Unless you can show proof of coverage, she has to go to a public health facility for detox."

I fumbled out my Medic-op scancard. "My name's Kristof Xiang. Take her to my clinic and I'll cover the charges."

He scanned the strip and verified my medical coverage. "It'll have to be out-of-pocket for her," he said. He was being decent. I've heard that the clinics don't always tell you when a procedure isn't covered, leaving you in the lurch when the bill comes. Of course then the clinic's always generous and helpful, letting you sell off a kidney or some bone marrow in order to make the balance.

I slipped the guy a pair of fifties. "I can handle it," I said. "Be good to her, okay?"

The medic took the bills and stuck them in a pocket. "You're okay, man," he said. "No stress, we'll treat her right."

I watched as they loaded her up and careened away. The scream of the ambulance sirens fragmented the last of my rush high into a flurry of tinkling sound bites.

The memory stick was just a standard data device, no markings or label. I was tempted to flick on my personal data system and find out what was important enough to keep Dina focused through a haze of street cocktail. But I kept my PDS tucked away and slipped the data stick into a pocket. Flashing a lot of tech in this neighborhood was an invite for a shakedown. As it was, I had flaunted a wad of cash and a health insurance card. Not good.

Sure enough, as soon as I thought to look around, I spotted three kids sporting gang tech. They weren't even trying to conceal their neural implants; one of them had shaved and tattooed a blue circle at the base of his skull to accentuate his. Boldfaced of them, waving around all that illegal hardware.

I should've tried to hitch a lift with the ambulance.

Could I make it to the funnel station? Time to find out.

It was easy to slip away from the scene. All the spectators were spreading out now that the excitement was done. I ambled off in the right direction with a pair of welfare stress puppies. We had three shadows, though. Big, tough-looking shadows. The neighborhood regulars knew what was up. They booked like bunnies around a corner, leaving me in the lurch.

Nothing to do but face the guacamole. I turned around.

"Hey, guys," I said.

Circle-shaved tapped his interface. The flashing red light told me he had networked himself into his gang's collective. Even if I could have gotten away or, insert laughter, defended myself from this trio, their whole gang would now know my face.

"Hey ho, checking the microserf," he said.

His buddy, the one with the bright cobalt hair, flicked his interface on. "Suited snazzy," he agreed.

The last guy just smiled, already blipping red, showing me a mouthful of pointy, blue dentures.

Shit.

"What's up?" I said.

"You made a 404 with the doxy," Circle-shaved said. "Chivvy up the data stick."

"I don't got no stick." I tried to look confused. It wasn't hard. The rush was making an encore appearance and doing a fast-paced duet with all the adrenaline pumping up my system. Whispers of moxy-roxy-boxy pinged through my mind while I tried to figure out what Dina had that gang bangers would want, aside from the obvious.

"You sure?" Blue-teeth flashed a mini cattle prod.

Like I hadn't thought they had meant business before?

"Come on fellahs, I ain't holding out." I ejected my wallet into my hand and opened it wide to show the remaining bills I had. "It's all I got. See?"

Circle-shaved drew out a knife. "Scoping's gonna happen," he said. "Bucked up or smooth's up to you."

"I don't know what you're talking about. You can search me and everything."

"Think we're bubbleheads? You could've swallowed it."

What can you say to that? I couldn't think of anything.

Blue-teeth came at me with the taser. I knew if he touched me, I would never recover from the first zap in time to fight off any of the others. So I did something desperate. I slammed my fist into his elbow right where a bundle of nerves sits. My hand felt like I had broken it, but I got the reaction I wanted. He dropped the prod.

And I caught it.

Rush speeds a body up. So does adrenaline. Blue-teeth was still reaching for the taser when I came up with it and triggered it, point blank against his neural link.

Blue-teeth's body went rigid and his eyes rolled up into his head. Circle-shaved and Cobalt-hair doubled over, their hands clutching their heads. I hoped they were getting a feedback squeal from hell but I wasn't going to hang around to find out. I turned and ran for the funnel station. I did not collect two hundred dollars; I did not pass go. I jumped the sensor bar and nearly fell down the stairs.

There was a funnel just pulling in. I threw myself through the sliding doors and prayed. It felt like hours later before the doors swished closed and we zipped away.

I'd made it! Clean getaway! I was thrilled for all of two seconds until I remembered Blue-teeth's gang were going to hunt me down and dismember me for this. Crud. Why hadn't Dina called a different chump today?

I straphung through three stations, watching my arms shake, my hand bleed, and listening to the ambient conversation warp and ping pong in my skull. I must have looked crappy. A little girl in a scout uniform asked me if I needed to sit down. Cute little moppet, but her sugar daddy wouldn't let her give up her own seat. Didn't matter. I hopped out at the next stop. An info terminal, two funnels, and a transfer later, and I was back home.

First question: had I broken anything in my hand on Blue-teeth? Answer: nope. Just torn some of the skin off and it would probably swell to a lovely purple.

Next question, and this was for the money: should I pack up and vamoose the country or lay low? Both options blew goat chunks. I hadn't busted my tail getting set up in Old Atlanta to lose it all in a gang vendetta. I had regular clients; I had made a name for myself. Course that was an excellent reason for jumping ship, too. I wasn't what you would call famous, but it wouldn't be too hard to get an ID lock on me from a feature scan. That clinched it. I could start over again in a new city, but I couldn't exactly reboot my life if the Blues flat-lined it.

I soaked my hand in a tureen of ice water while my computer began a full drive backup. That brought me back to Dina's data stick. Damn, Dina. She was a major skin kitten and a helluva lot of fun, but she was not worth this sort of trouble. I almost pitched the stick down the chute. 'Cept I was eyeball deep already. What were a few centimeters more?

I loaded it up. There was only one file. It looked like a city map, like the kind you get when you're checking out bus routes. I looked closer and saw the little mass transit logo in the corner. It *was* a route map. What the hell? I had ticked off a gang for a *bus schedule*?

Maybe if I hired a street emissary I could make reparation. I could hock everything I owned and empty out my savings and that might be enough to smooth things over. Only trouble with that was that it'd take about that much to hire an emissary in the first place. Shit.

I finished backing everything up, including the bus map, compressed it, and uploaded it into my PDS. As a precaution, I double-zipped it and loaded it straight to my wetware.

My hardware is a little more discreet than gang tech, although the premise is similar and it's just as illegal. I've got a neural implant that gives me computer access to my gray matter. The access port is in the roof of my mouth and can only be activated by a stream of passcode sounds so I don't accidentally power it on if I'm munching a snickerdoodle or something.

The gangs use their NIs to network with each other. I don't brain link with anyone. There's no one I feel close enough to that I would want them to have a direct feed to my head. I use mine for peace of mind, pun unintended. It's the perfect data storage method, which is why I risked a black market dealer and shady installation clinic to get it. Now, I can have my computer trashed, my PDS lifted, and my home firebombed and I'm okay 'cause the things I really value—my poems, journal, and writings—are all safe and sound, locked away digitally in my brain. It's all double-compressed so I can't actually read it unless I download it back to a system to unzip, but at least I know it's secure. I've thought about installing a reader so I can access it like normal memories. But like all storage mediums, space is limited. To get enough room to store the info, unzipped, in my head, I would have to overwrite other data. Sure I'd had some bad times that don't make for warm-fuzzy feelings of nostalgia, but I wasn't ready to ditch them just yet.

Just in case they could track me through my home system, I wiped it. Backups made, a couple spare shirts in a duffle, cash. I was set. Time to fly.

I was all set to funnel to the airport when I thought of Dina. I was one click away from a one-way to New Zealand—it's as big as Hollywood in the entertainment biz, but without the taxes—but I couldn't. I had to take care of the bint. If I left now, she would be saddled at my clinic. Maybe she would be able to get another schmuck to foot her medical bills, but I didn't want to be responsible for forcing her into a mandatory organ donation if she couldn't.

Maybe I should just have "sucker" branded on my forehead.

I took the funnel down to my clinic. I hate medical facilities. Everything about them gives me the willies: the smell of antiseptic mingled with the stench of decaying people, the cheerful nurses and doctors in their blinding white uniforms, and my personal un-favorite, the needles.

The receptionist smiled gaily at me and I just wanted to gag.

"How may I help you?" she chirped.

I pulled out my Medic-op card and handed it to her. "I'm Kristof Xiang. I authorized a patient to be admitted here earlier today."

She swiped the card through her reader. "Oh yes, Mr. Xiang. A Ms. Dina McAllister, correct? Would you like a printout of the charges?"

Not really. "Can I see her first?"

"Of course. She's in the emergency ward, room A1137."

The emergency ward was across the sunlit atrium and through the annex. It had its own beaming receptionist. I winced when I found out they had put Dina in a private room. That was going to be expensive. She looked loads better though. And she was happy as a puppy to see me.

"Kristof!" she cried. She held out a bandaged arm to me. It had an IV line taped to it. I avoided looking at the IV part when I hugged her.

I dragged up the visitor's chair and perched beside her. "Did they treat you okay?" I asked.

She nodded. Her big blue eyes looked winsome and bright. "The ambulance people made sure I got bumped to the front of the queue when we got here. They pumped my stomach and gave me some clean-up juice. I feel hopped!"

"I'm glad." Glad my hundred and twenty had been well spent, too.

"Thanks for not letting them take me to St. Mary's." She smiled that heart-thumping, electrifying smile that makes anyone with a drop of testosterone spring to attention.

I leaned in close and kissed her cute little nose. "You know I couldn't let them do that to you."

Dina fumbled for my hand. Her voice dropped to a whisper. "Did you see what was on the stick?"

I frowned and moved back a little. "Yeah. A bus map."

Her eyes widened. "Didn't you find the virus? You told me you always scan everything for viruses."

"A virus?" I felt queasy. I always ran three virus scans—a mommy, a daddy, and a big uncle Hugo—before I uploaded anything into my home system, much less my head, but this time I had been in such a hurry I hadn't taken my usual precautions. "What's it do?" I croaked out.

"I—I don't know for sure."

"What do you mean you don't know?" I wanted to grab her and shake her and rant at her. But you just can't be harsh with Dina. "The Blues are gunning for me because I withheld the stick you gave me and I'm pretty sure I infected myself with that bug. I need to know what's going on."

"I'm sorry." Dina's lips began to quiver and her eyes grew big as jingle-discs. "I didn't mean to get you in trouble!"

"Dina, sweet chips, you know I love you. But you gotta be straight with me."

She sniffled.

"Just take it slow and start at the beginning."

"I—I was just finishing up my second dose of syrup at Bennie's Club—you know the one, right off Peachtree?—when Adrienne showed up. She's always after me to straighten up and I thought that's why she was there this time."

"Who's Adrienne?" I asked.

"She's my big sister," Dina said, "and a reporter for e-Net."

Dina had a sister? Dina had a sister who worked for the big boys?

"She said the Feds created the virus in order to crack down on the gangs. It gets passed by NI networks."

A Fed virus, oh goody. "What's it *do*?"

"Adrienne was telling me when the Blues found us, and the syrup was kicking in and it was hard to concentrate and everything happened so fast." Dina burst into tears, her face all scrunched up.

I put an arm around her and let her blubber for a bit. "C'mon baby, get a grip. You're doing great."

Dina snuffled. "Th—they slapped a derma patch on me and grabbed her. She passed me the data stick when they weren't looking and they dragged her away and I—I—left me on the street and I was so scared and I waited and waited for you and then the patch hit and I felt all sick!"

Didn't I say she was good at guilt trips? "I'm sorry I was late, but you gotta try to remember what Adrienne said about the virus."

She blinked her big blue eyes and chewed on her cute little mouth. "She said something about stages."

Bingo. "How many stages?"

Dina sat up and scrubbed at her eyes with a fist. She looked like a little girl who had just learned that her teddy bear had been mangled in Daddy's shredder. "Three. Adrienne said three."

"What happens in the first stage?" I asked.

"Nothing, I think. Adrienne said it needs to hole up, y'know, grow-like."

"Incubate?"

Dina nodded. "Yeah."

"And stage two?"

"That's when you're supposed to turn yourself in if you're infected."

"So symptoms start showing up?"

"I—I think so. I can't remember what Adrienne said about that part, though."

Damn. "That's okay. What happens in stage three?"

Dina dropped her eyes.

"Come on, honey. I won't yell at you. I promise."

She twisted a bit of sheet between her fingers. "Adrienne said that if an infected person doesn't go in for the patch and antidote, the virus body bags them."

"Dead?"

Dina nodded, her mouth trembling.

Yep. Things were bad. "But there's a fix?"

"Adrienne said the Feds have one, but you can't go in!"

"Why not?" The penalties for illegal hardware are pretty steep, but I figured I could swing them if I got a good legal counselor.

"That's what Adrienne's reporting on. The Feds are upping the sentence for having an NI."

"To?"

"Mandatory surgery to remove it, life in the pen, and two organs—court's choice."

I gulped. The surgery to remove NI hardware was brutal. I had heard it often results in complications like loss of basic cognitive and neurological function. On the up side, I might not care about being a lifer in a Federal lock-up sans a kidney after that.

"Adrienne was saying that she thinks it's a government conspiracy to harvest organs."

That sounded like something the Feds would do. "Your sister was going up against the Feds?"

Dina nodded. "She said she had an angle. She said she had an inside guy who could get her the counter program so she could post it on the web."

Things were looking up after all. "Did she get it?"

Dina didn't have a chance to answer that rather vital question. The door swung open and four guys in Blue regalia were there. I was on my feet, but they were faster. One of them poker-punched me into a wall while another went over to Dina. I heard her scream, but then it was all flailing limbs (mine) and bad guys. I got slugged in the gut. All my breath closed up shop somewhere in the vicinity of my stomach, leaving me gasping like a blowfish on a sandbar. Two thugs caught me up in a lock-grip between them. The first guy pulled back for another punch.

"Hey, lay off. Honcho wants him functional."

"I wasn't gonna decommission him, just get him cooperative-like," Hamfist said.

"Any more cooperative and we'll need a doctor to re-stuff him."

I was relieved to see my erstwhile puncher's arm drop. I was less relieved when he turned and his fist slammed into my stomach again. I folded, making gurgling noises while my eyes glazed up with tears.

He bent over me; I could smell syrup, sickly-sweet on his breath. "That's for tazing Zippo," he said before slapping a sleepy-patch on my neck. I had just enough time to wonder if Dina was okay before things got blurry and gray.

COMING TO IN A STRANGE PLACE is not my favorite way of waking up. My jaw hurt, my eyes were gritty, and my stomach felt like an elephant had been standing on me. But, hey, at least I was still alive.

"They could come back any minute, we gotta get out of here!" That voice was unmistakably Dina's.

"The door's locked, Dee." That voice sounded like Dina's, but without as much nasal to it. "And your friend's still out. How far do you think we could carry him?"

"I'm awake," I said. Actually, I think I said, "Mmm-wwk," but close enough.

I opened my eyes. I was lying on the floor of what looked like someone's basement—concrete slab, bare light bulb, no windows—except for the heavy-duty steel door with the security keypad.

"Oh, Kristof, thank God!" Dina said.

Dina looked okay. She was still wearing the clinic gown, but she was on her feet. The woman beside her could've had a big neon sign that said, "Dina's sister" hanging over her head. She had the same eyes and the same waist-long, blue-black hair. But where Dina was a looker, her sister wasn't. Adrienne had lines on her face that said she frowned a lot and spent her time thinking about unpleasant things.

Dina helped me prop myself up, a prelude, I thought, to standing. The medical-issue she was in gaped open and I caught a glimpse of cleavage. Hey, I'm a normal guy. I couldn't help noticing. That's when a piercing flash of pain zagged from the base of my spine up through my head. I heard myself shout in surprised agony.

"What is it? What's the matter?" Dina said, dropping me like I was last week's upgrade. I thunked back to the floor where I proceeded to writhe and twist. It felt like red-hot pins were clamping around my nerves and squeezing tight.

As suddenly as the pain started, it ended, leaving me shaky and light-headed. "Ow," I whispered. "What was that?"

Dina's sister's voice was wry. "Stage two, I'd guess."

Dina stood frozen, afraid to come near me again, so it was Adrienne who helped me to sit.

"What's going on?" Dina wailed.

Adrienne swiveled her head. "Dee, he's okay for now. Shut it, okay?"

Dina pouted, but kept quiet.

Adrienne sat back. "It's going pretty fast through you, so time's tight. Dina said you've got the virus file?"

I swallowed. Give a guy a chance to get his bearings, why don't you? "I've got that bus map and the virus piggy-backed on it, if that's what you mean."

Adrienne smiled. Did I say she wasn't a looker? Strike that. If Dina and Adrienne were in a beauty contest, if Adrienne smiled, she would win hands down.

"The bus map *is* the encoded counter-virus program," she said. "It's both a fix and an inoculation."

It took a moment for that to sink it. I wasn't going to die or get a state-mandated lobotomy after all. And the crowds all cheered. "Encoded? What's the key?"

The smile disappeared. "That's complicated. I found out before I called Dina that the Feds unearthed my source. I think we can assume he's out of the picture. Unfortunately, he never got the decode to me."

Death or a brain scramble, I wondered which one would hurt more.

"Addy? Why were the Blues after you?" Dina said. "If you were going to post the cure, why'd they nab you for it?"

That was a good question.

Adrienne scowled. "Why do the movers and shakers in the guerilla gangs do anything, Dee? For pocket lining, of course. Once the virus started taking people out, there would be panic in the ranks. The Blues come to the rescue with the cure, and bang, they could pretty much name their price." Adrienne tapped a finger against her ear. "I wonder if we could hack it."

"Hack what?" Was I the only one moving at "stupid?"

"My source said he encoded the program within the file. I might be able to hack the source code and find the executable." Her eyes sparkled. Was she actually enjoying this? "Bring it up."

I just wasn't going to get a break today. "Huh?"

"I minored in corporate hacking in college." Adrienne's look made me feel slower than a trained turtle. "But I can't hack a file I can't read. Open. The. Map."

"Oh!" My hand went to my pocket. No PDS. No wallet. "They swiped my PDS!"

"Shit-a-brick." She glared at me as though I was responsible for having my stuff stolen. "Dina said you'd uploaded the virus file to your wetware. Is that true?"

"Yeah, but it's compressed. I don't have a reader."

"I do." She reached up and separated out a strand of her hair. "Open up."

"Wait. What?" I was still lost.

"This is a micro I/O wire." She showed me the tip; it gleamed dark and metallic. "It connects to my own NI.

Assuming you've got a standard port, we can network together."

"You've got an NI?"

"I use it for my work. I've got a vested interest in squelching this Fed anti-NI thing, too."

"Oh. But hey, hang on. If you network with me, won't you get infected with the virus?" I like to think that I was being chivalrous, but I just plain didn't like the idea of sharing brain space.

She shrugged. "Yep. But we're out of options." Her hand was cool against the back of my neck as she probed it. "Where's your NI port?"

Not even a mother-may-I. "Roof of my mouth."

"Clever." She made it sound like she was surprised anything intelligent could come out of me.

"I don't know about this," I said.

The last of her drop-dead-gorgeousness fell away when she turned titanium-hard eyes to me. "Look, the gangbangers could be back at any time. If they've figured out the fix from the file on your PDS, they'll ice us. If they haven't, they're going to want it. And if we don't have it, they'll ice us. In the meantime, the virus is eating up your CNS and it'll ice you if the Blues don't. So, you want to stew and wait, or let me in?"

"Gong Xi Fa Cai," I said.

"What?"

The tingle that let me know my NI was booted tickled the roof of my mouth. "Ahh," I said.

Adrienne came at me with her hair and the I/O wire reminded me of a long needle. It was imagery I didn't need. I felt the point go in. Calm-blue-ocean.

"Powering up," she said. She reached up to a spot behind her ear and we were connected. I saw me looking up at her with a really dumb, dazed look on my face. Flash images scrolled in a disjointed swirl like a primo trip: putting a band-aid on a young Dina, a skinny orange cat rescued from a neighbor's neglect, punching out a kid in school, crying in an old warehouse, all by myself.

Hey, back off! It was Adrienne's voice but it was coming from inside my head. I felt jittery from the anger she was shooting through us.

Sorry. I really was, too. *I've never linked with anyone before. What do I do?* My lips didn't move, but I knew that Adrienne heard me. I felt her astonishment.

Never?

'Fraid not.

The indignation faded away. *I didn't know. Sorry. Try not to wander through my memories. They're private. Just show me where the directory is that you loaded the virus to.*

How?

Access it like you normally would if I weren't here.

Like I didn't have someone in my head, watching my thoughts, seeing what I saw. Right. I scrolled through my directory and highlighted the zipped document that contained the bus map. *There.*

I felt her take it, and watched her push it through an unzip program on her end. A click—more felt than heard—and it appeared. It filled up my mind's eye and I felt Adrienne peering at it with me.

It's just the number five line, I thought.

We pondered it together.

What're we looking for? I thought.

I don't know, Adrienne replied.

Great. Wish I had some rush. I always thought better with rush.

I saw Adrienne's lips quirk and for a moment I was disoriented. Was it me smiling, or her?

A Rusher, huh? she thought. *I haven't done rush since I was a junior.*

What happened to privacy?

"Sorry." It was weird hearing her vocalize. It was like having an echo going through her head and into mine.

Sort of like a time lag hitting joint memories. "Dina, do you have any rush?" she said.

She wouldn't have any, I thought. "They nabbed us straight out of the clinic."

"Here," Dina said, flooring me. She held out several familiar-looking purple tabs. She smiled. "The doctor was really nice. I told him I needed a drink of water and he left me alone with the pharmacy chute." She laughed. "Clinics are way better stocked than public detox!"

I took a pill from her hand and stuck it under my tongue. That was Dina. Thank God for kleptomaniacs. The acrid taste filled my mouth like sweet manna from heaven. I felt my mind shift from low to turbo. I could do this.

Looks just like a regular map, Adrienne thought to me.

She was right. Letters from A to F broke the map up along the horizontal and numbers from zero to nine split it along the vertical. A single red line meandered along the streets, twisting around in a big loop. Rush isn't big on visuals, but I found myself being drawn into the route as it twisted and turned in on itself. It never intersected, just kept going on.

Circle Street to Market to Grove. Hey, that was over by me. *Can we zoom any closer?* I thought.

A little magnifying glass appeared and scooted over the route I was scanning. I felt another click and the map grew.

Bigger? I asked.

I'm running out of storage space, Adrienne thought.

Damn. I think I'm on to something.

I felt her deliberate for a moment and begin sorting through her thoughts. She was going to delete memories to make space.

No! Hang on. I didn't give myself a chance to think about it. I selected my backups and purged them. They were backups, I kept telling myself. I could recover them. And they were just stupid poems. The originals should still be in my long-term memory. Somewhere. I felt like crying, though. My home system was wiped, my PDS was gone, and I had just flushed my final backups.

Right, I thought to Adrienne, *I've cleared out some space. You can save your memories in my wetware. Don't need to delete them.*

My perception flickered back and forth so that I wasn't sure for a moment who I was. I felt a hand on mine. Her hand, my hand, whoever's hand, it was nice. *Thanks*, she thought. I felt her gratitude. That helped. The download began. As fast as she could think it, I saved it. Road trip sing-a-longs with the family, watching stars from the roof, winning an essay contest in fourth grade, making a pillow fort with Dina. Memories scrolled into my wetware.

I'm filling up, I thought. I almost didn't say it, tempted to let her overwrite a little of me. It was a different sort of high, getting her personality, her perceptions, who she was, brain dumped into me. Under all that grump and frown, Adrienne was a real sweetie, a thinker and a doer. I wondered if she would laugh in my face if I asked her out to dinner.

The magnifying glass came back and clicked on the map. We zoomed in closer.

Did you notice that none of the street names are "Peachtree?" I thought.

What?

Old Atlanta has something like a hundred streets with "Peachtree" in it. The city planners were a little peach-happy. Peachy-screechy-streets. *This main drag here, the one along D, shouldn't this be Peachtree-Industrial?*

I felt Adrienne scrutinize the map. *You're right. What does that mean?*

It means, I think, that we're on to something.

I went through the names of the streets, the rush bouncing them every which way in my head. Adrienne picked up the trailing bits. I was aware of a stream of nonsensical numbers and letters coming from her side.

Hexadecimal code, she explained. *Check out the map, zero through nine, A through F. It's gotta be hex. I'm trying to open up the executable. Every time you read a street name, I'm converting the letters. Now that I see it, it's a pretty straightforward code trail along the route.*

Okay, cool.

Fair to Circle in a spiral, viral-spiral, Market to Grove, rove-slow-no. Parallel one-way street touching on the D axis past four major interlocked avenues: Adenine Drive-strive-bide that hooked up with Thymine Avenue. A new venue. Cytosine Boulevard (seen-dream-clean) turning into Guanine—looping down to the A axis and going up again. It was a Möbius strip, weaving around and around and never stopping. So easy to get lost, flying high, coasting on a wave of rush.

I'm in! Adrienne's triumph pulled me out. *I found the executable!*

I felt her enter the final sequence in a little pop-up side window and think <ENTER>. The map faded away in a splash of pixels. A flashing red button appeared before us like a big neon sign. "Load?" it asked us. Adrienne and I both reached for it. I felt the click from my teeth to my toes.

The anti-virus subroutine began erasing the virus from our systems. While it cleaned us up, we skimmed through the included FAQ. I skipped over the dull "inside the neural cells modified to accept an NI interface, the viral genetic material takes over the cellular machinery" blah blah blah and skipped to the important bits. At first, the virus hits small nerve clusters: "initial symptoms are mild and can go unnoticed by the host," that lead up to increasingly painful seizures triggered by "lascivious and unwholesome thoughts." Guess that was why seeing Dina's gown gape set off my first seizure. Over time, seizures increase in intensity until the main CNS functions become "over-stimulated." In other words, bang goodnight. The Feds, in their typically puritanical manner, had done a Clockwork Orange. Ugly.

"Program complete!" flashed up in red. We were done; we had the code; we were clean. I disconnected the I/O strand from my mouth.

It was strange, seeing Adrienne's face looking back at me instead of staring myself in the eye, but I much preferred the view. There was a thin sheen of sweat covering her face. It made her look brilliantly lovely.

"We make a good team," she said. "If we're still alive, I'm free tomorrow night for dinner."

Dinner-winner-winner-winner. Maybe I should have been peeved at the invasion of privacy, but I wasn't. I was just grinning like a fool to have a date with her.

My happy-glow was short-lived. The door slammed open and four Blues stepped into our room. Dina yelped and did a headlight-flinch. I recognized one of them as the fist who had wanted to make me a punching bag. Yippee skippy.

"Hello, Scooby," he said. "Cozy-festing?" West-test-best.

Adrienne stood up.

One of them, the one in a designer-blue jimmy suit, reached into his pocket and pulled out a taser. "Ho, bitch, we ain't waltzing. Where's the anti-virus?"

They hadn't been able to work through the bus map. I almost laughed. Bunch of syrup-heads.

"You're not getting it from me."

Blue suit reached out and grabbed Dina by the arm. He twisted it; she squeaked. "How 'bout if we degauss little sister? Be a tearjerker to scramble up such a pretty face."

Mace-trace-waste. And that's when I noticed it. Blue suit had a twitch right below his left eye, almost a tic. It all fell together. Not only did the Blues want the cure to turn a profit, but they also needed it to save their collective asses. The rush helped me look for it. Yep, there it was in Hamfist, in his temple, and the guy next to him, too, above his eye.

"Bang their libidos!" I shouted.

Okay, not my most eloquent statement. Everyone looked at me as though I had already had the NI-out surgery, but Adrienne got it. I'm glad she had spent some time in my head. Up went her shirt, flashing the Blues, and all four of them began gurgling and twitching on the floor.

Dina danced away from Suit-guy, kicking him in the ribs on her way, and we scooted out the wide-open door. I was feeling pretty hopeful on the whole life-expectancy thing, until bruiser-blue jumped us. He looked like he bench-pressed limos for fun. Dina didn't even pause. She just smiled and pulled open her clinic-issue. She always liked a receptive audience. Couldn't ask for better than drooling and thrashing on the ground.

The rest of it was textbook. The hallway led to a closed-off funnel service room. We tore out of there and caught a connection. Out of Blue central, scot-free in forty-three, that's me.

ADRIENNE'S SPONSORS on e-Net took good care of us. Her article with the attached download fix was a smash with the NI lobbyists, the medical reformers, and most of the guerilla gangs. The advertisers swamped the site as the hits soared, bringing in the mega-money. The Blues and the Feds were pissed with us, but that wasn't a biggie. E-Net set us up with a couple phantom IDs and flew us out first class to New Zealand to hide out. Adrienne reports from there using a pseudonym and I'm working on putting out a book of poems.

At first, I thought Dina would be miffed at Adrienne and me getting together. But she didn't even blink when we told her we were hooking up. Next thing I know, she was decked out on the arm of a local vid director-type.

Funny how things work out.

THE BEAR EATER

Paul Pence

Imagine that you're a fisherman, going out on the deep blue sea, trailing a line behind you, loaded with bait. So much expensive tackle, not to mention the cost of chartering the boat, the time you take off work.

Truth is that you go to work to earn enough to keep yourself alive, yes, but then to have enough left over that you can come out here and indulge your passion—the contest with the worthy opponent.

Then you get that bite, that tug, and the struggle begins. On and on it goes, exhausting you, and the captain tells you to let it go, this one earned its life, but you can't, because this is the opponent you've been waiting for.

Only when the jaws open up to take you, boat and all, under the waves—only then does it occur to you how hard it must have been for these boat-eaters to breed and train humans to the point where, finally, we have become worthy opponents in their hunting games.

What's the bait, and where's the hook?

THE LIGHT, WIND-BLOWN SNOW had just begun to puddle in the hollows of the ripped dirt, sticking to the frozen blood. I set my flintlock rifle against the big log and pondered a while—couldn't be a fox or a rabbit, not with three-inch deep gouges in the frozen ground, not with brush uprooted and sapling pines smashed flat.

Broke open the cast-iron jaws of the fox trap. Good trap, too, the best you could get this deep in Indian country.

Dangle, my youngest dog, barely older than a pup, found the mountain lion leg. I tried to get a look at it, but Dangle shied away, hoping I wouldn't take it from him. "Mystery solved," I told Lilly and Ranger, my other two dogs. "Dang mountain lion chewed its leg off."

Of course the dogs didn't mind me. Hungry dogs don't mind you when there's food around. Lilly set after Dangle and commenced fighting for the meat. She snatched the mountain lion leg in a show of teeth and bristled fur, looking more like her wolf father than usual. Dangle fell back a mite, then sat, staring at Lilly as she feasted on the prize.

Ranger pretty much just watched until Lilly got her way, as usual, then went back to licking up blood from dead pine needles. It wasn't much meat to scrap over, but then we had seen a mighty lean winter. Not a deer or elk or moose since fall. Just four rabbits since first snow. Kinda like all the game in the mountains had high-tailed it south when the first cold wind blew.

Before Lilly set to chewing, I finally got a gander at the leg. It hadn't been caught in my fox trap. And it hadn't been chewed off. It had been cut off almost at the shoulder. The meat was sliced cleanly but the bone had been crushed.

Too much blood, too much damage. A mountain lion didn't chew that leg off any more than it had smashed the iron jaws of my trap. From the huge gouges, I could tell the scrapes were made by something that didn't belong in the Rocky Mountains in the coldest winter since Noah. Something mighty big.

Finally, Dangle gave up on a share of the leg and sulked back to lick up the blood with Ranger. Dangle had waited too long; there was hardly any blood left for him.

It was bad to be hungry. It was worse when those who depend on you have to go hungry. I wished I had something to give the pup.

"Maybe a bear," I told the dogs. But I wasn't too sure. Any normal bear would be hibernating in mid-winter. Whatever it was, I was certain I could kill it. Nothing can stand up to a lead ball propelled by twenty grains of powder.

"First rule of the mountains," I used to tell my little brother, Nat, when we first came to the isolation of the Bitterroot Range. "When faced with something unusual, check your powder." I drummed it into my brother so much that the first time he saw that squaw of his, he set to reloading his gun.

I reckoned this thing would be bigger than a normal bear. "Maybe a stout charge."

I pulled the ball from my rifle with the ramrod's spiral jag. The sharp bit twisted into the soft metal of the half-inch ball. The ball drew out easy enough but it would jam in the barrel if I reloaded it. I tucked it into a pocket for melting down later.

Then I poured an extra measure of powder into the muzzle. "Don't worry, boys, I know what I'm doing." She may have a hell of a kick, but it was a strong gun and could handle the extra powder.

The dogs continued to ignore me. But even if the dogs listened, they didn't know beans about overloaded guns. They'd never seen a man's arms blown off from too much powder in his rifle.

I reckoned this would be a fine time to bless Nat with a visit from his big brother Jacob. When I moved out of our cabin, I had promised myself that I would see him every Sunday. Never got around to it. It still chafed to think of him trading our mule for a squaw, but I never planned on letting a year go by before I saw him again.

I shook a spare ball from its pouch. "Still plenty of shot." A score of balls, just under a pound. Plenty of powder, too.

Old Ranger looked up at me, licking blood from his face. I'm sure he wondered why I didn't fight them for the scrap of meat.

A thin buckskin patch smeared with rancid bear grease made the ball snug in the barrel. The ramrod pressed it home and I plugged the muzzle with dry grass from the compartment in the rifle's maple stock.

I re-latched the brass flap on the stock, then checked the primer powder under the flashpan cover. Still dry.

I sighted down the rifle's five-foot length at a tree a good ten score paces away. With the extra charge, even at twice the distance, it should split the animal's head in half.

"A twelve-foot bear, Ranger. Think of all the meat and grease." Its fur alone would buy flour for a year.

I imagined the loud bang, the eye-stinging flash, and the huge animal falling to my shot. Two springs before, Nat and I lost a five-dollar bet to a French trapper who could hit a fry pan at ten score paces, five shots out of five. I could do it one out of five, but a giant bear is a mite bigger than a fry pan.

I slid my stinging hands back into their fur mittens and called the dogs. "Time to go, boys." Lilly had gnawed the leg down to a gristly bundle of knuckle bones. Ranger sniffed the ground for more droplets of blood, the biggest puddle already a memory. Dangle, the youngster, had vanished. "Dangle?"

The fool pup had run after the scent of game. In the newly fallen snow, his tracks led clearly downstream and east—scampering at full speed toward Nat's end of the valley.

"Dangle!" To him, the mountain-lion-stealing beast was just another animal, just food. He'd never met an animal big enough to be a danger to him.

"Dangle!"

I hollered a couple of times more, then picked up my pack and powder horn. "Don't worry," I told the dogs. "Dangle will be all right. Let's go tell Nat."

Ranger's ears perked up when I spoke Nat's name. The two of us raised old Ranger, back when Nat and I still shared the cabin by the lake. But that was before Nat made a fool of himself over an Indian woman and I moved up the valley. From the way Ranger's tail whipped back and forth, he remembered Nat. I guessed Ranger missed him too.

"Come on, Lilly."

Ranger and I headed on toward Nat's end of the valley. Lilly caught up, the last gristly bones of the mountain lion's paw clamped in her jaws.

We had barely commenced when we found more gouges in the ground. Triple scrapes spreading about three feet across, all kicking frozen dirt in the same direction. Whatever the thing was, it had claws like a giant bird.

Nat's squaw, Seddewaha, once told me her people don't live in these mountains west of the Big Hole River because the Bear Eater lived up here. The *Nava-huwasak* was a kind of Manitu or evil spirit that once lived on the plains, eating bison and Indians. But when the Indians learned to ride horses, they forced it into the mountains.

Just another one of those back-when-dogs-could-talk stories. Be good or the *Nava-huwasak* will get you.

This thing would be big enough to eat a bear. I wished I could remember more about the story, but I had only pretended to listen.

We followed the broken branches and gouged ground. Each sight of Dangle's prints in the thin snow gave me a spark of hope that we would catch up to him in time.

Sometimes the Bear Eater's tracks circled around thick clumps of trees. Sometimes claw marks showed it digging for something . . . trying to unearth some small animal for food.

The land in the mountains here made a crazy-quilt of steep rocky slopes, flat patches of white pine trees, narrow channel-cuts slick with frozen streams, and unexpected cliff edges. But despite the rough territory, it headed mostly east, toward Nat's place.

A couple hours later, the thin snow finally stopped falling. I felt a touch of relief. Not only would the tracks be easy to read, but I didn't need the problems of a blizzard on top of having to chase down a lost dog and an Indian monster.

I rested a moment to adjust my pack. Been pushing myself harder than I realized. I opened my furs a mite to cool the sweat that gathered under my buckskins.

As I stood there, reckoning that I could slow down for a spell, a steam whistle blew in the distance. Not really a steam whistle, but I didn't know what else to call it . . . a bubbling, gurgling whistle like a steam calliope playing all of its pipes at the same time while under water.

The Bear Eater.

I thought of Dangle and how he must have caught up with the Bear Eater by now. "It's all right, boys. Dangle knows not to fight all by himself."

I tried not to cry.

"Come on, boys. We can't rest now. Gotta get that Bear Eater."

Come dusk, we got to the tight bend in the creek where the path squeezes up against the bluff, opening into the lake at Nat's end of the valley.

Ranger sniffed at the deep scratches in the sand bar. From the way Ranger's fur stood in a ridge across his back it was obvious, even without the scratches, that the beast had been past this point.

Too close to Nat's cabin. If I had fur on my back, it would have been standing in a ridge four inches tall. I was almost too afraid to call, afraid they wouldn't answer. "Nat! Seddawaha! Nat!"

No answer echoed back across the frozen lake.

Maybe Nat and his squaw were in the hills, hunting. "Nat!"

Still no answer.

Ranger and Lilly barked and howled, but Nat's dogs didn't join in chorus.

"Maybe they headed into Fort Hall," I told my dogs. If the winter had been as hard on them as it was on me, that would make sense. At least we could hole up in their cabin for the night.

In winter, the path squeezes between the ice of the creek and the bluff, but in the spring, rushing water makes this end of the lake impassable. Water from a million years of spring thaws dug hollows and caves in the limestone. Ranger, Lilly, and I pushed on across the frozen lake.

Triple gouges showed that the ice bore the Bear Eater's weight. The scrapes didn't waver or get shorter between strides like an animal uncertain about ice. They made a beeline to Nat's cabin.

Or, what was left of Nat's cabin.

It lay in pieces—kicked apart, ripped apart.

Nat and I had built the cabin our first summer of our shared freedom. We took over a month to chop down and drag the pine logs, to notch them and wrench them into place, but the Bear Eater had torn it apart the way old Ranger would tear into a pile of leaves hunting a weasel.

Despite the setting sun, the light snow cover made the tracks clear enough that a greenhorn from Baltimore could read them. Four sets of dog prints ran from the ruins of the cabin out onto the ice. Top-speed, full run like the dogs were chasing something.

No dog tracks lingered on the ice, nothing except the monster's triple gouges, but two different sprays of blood had painted a bright red across the white. The blood was slung left and right, like the Bear Eater had whipped the dogs back and forth as they bled. The dogs never hit the ice after they died, or there would have been a smear of blood and gore.

Until that moment, I had downplayed the signs of the Bear Eater's size. It had broken branches a dozen feet up the side of a tree and it was big enough that it had eaten each of Nat's dogs in one bite, without dropping them.

I re-checked the powder in my rifle's flash pan, leaving my mittens in my pocket.

At the shore line, the Bear Eater had hit a small drift with its right foot. The print was as clear as if it was etched in stone. The dang thing had giant bird's claws. Three talons in front, each a yard long with a razor tip. A spur longer than my knife jutted out from the back of the claw.

I refused to believe in a 20-foot-tall bird. Maybe some kind of freak bear, a giant one with claws deformed to look like a bird's, but not a huge bird.

The spacing of the gouges changed from those I had been following. The trail led from where it killed two of the dogs toward the cabin. The remaining two sets of dog prints followed.

Something had distracted it from killing the dogs and made it run toward the cabin. It took just a moment to discover the reason. In the fading light I found Nat's gun. It had been fired.

Nat's footprints led from where the cabin's door used to be to halfway to the shoreline. There they met the Bear Eater's running prints. Instead of just a spray of blood, a thick puddle of gore formed a dark pool that marked Nat's last stand. Nat had taken two bites.

"Sorry, Nat." I should never have abandoned him when he bought Seddewaha. I wanted to kick something, scream, throw things around, but I couldn't. I could only clutch Nat's gun to my chest and remember the look on his face when we bought it. He was just a kid then, his eyes glowing from the newspaper stories about the Texans fighting their war for independence. We wanted to find our own adventure, have our own little war for independence. By the time we had made it through the Cumberland Gap, we found it was all over in Texas and that the only adventure left in the world was in the Rocky Mountains.

He had five good years here, fishing in the spring, hunting the rest of the year. I wondered whether or not it was a good trade for the long, hungry, and boring life we left back East.

Nat's ramrod was missing, so he was probably trying to reload when the Bear Eater got him. His shot was probably what brought it to him from where it fought the dogs on the ice.

I couldn't find Nat's powder horn or the bag of ball shot, either. I didn't want to think about where they probably were.

I did find two sets of dog tracks that circled around at this point, but both vanished with their own sprays of blood.

Then the Bear Eater's tracks led to the cabin.

"Boys, it looks like we'll be pushing on to Fort Hall." The Bear Eater, *Nava-huwasak*, monster, or whatever it was, went east. The dogs and I would go south.

The frozen blood on the stock of Nat's gun melted and became sticky as I handled it. It didn't do Nat any good, but it might do me some good if I bumped into the Bear Eater on the trail. Even a monster would have only two eyes. I only needed two good, clean shots.

Nat and I owned identical guns. We shared parts when we needed to. We planned it that way. We planned a lot of things together. I thought it would just be the two of us, Nat and Jacob, hunting and trapping together till we got old and gray. I never thought some monster from an Indian story would eat him.

I loaded Nat's gun with a heavy charge of powder. With the lead ball jammed home, I felt a mite safer.

He should've let his dogs get eaten and he should've high-tailed it out of there. "Damn fool."

Nat and I used to have a root cellar in the north corner of the cabin. Seddawaha would have potatoes and carrots in there. The Bear Eater wouldn't care for roots, so I hoped for provisions for the long hike to Fort Hall.

In the remains of the cabin, I saw the bloody evidence that Seddewaha did not escape. She must have seen what happened to Nat, must have known what was going to happen to her. She didn't have a chance. No one would have, not without a cannon.

As I pushed the splintered logs around and rolled away the warm stones of the fallen fireplace, I heard a whimpering. Damn, I thought, one of Nat's dogs is buried in here. I didn't look forward to putting a dog out of its misery, but it had to be done.

Then a thought occurred to me. "Dangle?"

Maybe Dangle made it to the cabin before the Bear Eater. Maybe they put him in the root cellar to keep him from fighting with the other dogs. Maybe Dangle's still alive in there.

"Hold on, Dangle, I'll get you out of there in two shakes."

But the farther I dug toward the whimpering, the less it sounded like a dog. An instant before I pulled the planks off the root cellar to look inside, I knew exactly what made the mewling noise.

A baby.

Nat's squaw had a brat. Guess he didn't take the hike to my end of the valley to tell me about it because he thought I didn't want to talk to him.

If I had to, I figured I could kill a hurt dog and be done with it. But a baby? I couldn't kill a baby, even to put it out of its misery.

The thing would probably die in a few days, even if I chewed its food for it, like the Indians do. That's if I had any food at all. But from the empty root cellar, it was clear that Nat and Seddewaha had been going hungry themselves. Nary a potato or carrot. Maybe there was a barrel of flour or something buried in the rubble, but I didn't see it. I reckoned it would take a couple hours of digging just to find out for sure.

Getting to civilization through the snow-filled passes may nigh well be impossible with the baby and both guns. But without food, it wouldn't make any difference; the baby would probably die on the trail anyway. If I left the half-breed behind, I might be able to make the hike, but that meant letting Nat's baby die of starvation. Or letting the wolves have it. Or killing it myself so it wouldn't suffer.

Nat's baby.

During the spring or fall, it takes five long, hard days of walking to get from the cabin to the trading post. During the winter, with the deep drifts and blocked passes, I could carry both guns and the baby for a little way, but there's no way to get all three to the fort. I'd be lucky just to get myself there without the guns.

Little button nose and big blue eyes—a little puff of black hair on top. I couldn't just let it suffer as it froze or starved to death.

Ranger's ears perked up and his teeth bared. "It's just a baby, Ranger, calm down." But he set to howling, his chasing-the-game howl. Lilly joined in.

Realization struck.

I stuffed the crying baby into my buckskins and grabbed both guns and the powder horn. As my fingers wrapped around the straps of my pack, I heard smashing tree branches. "Run, boys, run!"

Ranger ran with me, but I was halfway to the ice before I noticed Lilly wasn't following.

"Lilly! Come here, now!"

Lilly minds me most times, but this time she perched on a piece of the fallen roof and growled.

"Lilly!"

She stood her ground, all wolf teeth.

I ran. I ran away from the noise, toward the frozen lake. But it was like a bad dream. With my pack, two rifles, and the baby, my thick fur-wrapped feet hardly made progress. When I hit the lake's ice, it got worse.

When we got a couple of hundred yards out onto the lake, the Bear Eater burst out of the woods. I stopped and turned. I dropped my pack to my feet. I leaned my own gun against my back, its butt balanced on the ice. Nat's gun jumped into my hands.

Yellow and green and brown and big. Really big. As I took aim on the eyes, I got a good look at the monster. The Bear Eater looked like a giant alligator standing on two legs. Its feet looked like huge bird claws. The little front legs couldn't even scratch its nose, but its back legs stood bigger around than me.

And teeth. Lord, God, it had teeth. Like a mouth full of knives.

Its long claws ripped through the snow as it ran for Lilly.

Lilly darted, ran in twisting sudden turns. She could turn faster than the monster, but the Bear Eater could run as fast as a horse.

From the corner of my eye, I saw Ranger inch forward.

"No, Ranger. Stay."

With each turn, the Bear Eater got closer to me. And with each turn, the Bear Eater got closer to Lilly.

I gave it time to get closer. Closer. Only two shots. "Keep running, Lilly," I whispered. "Bring him closer."

The thing sure wasn't a bear and it wasn't a bird. It was a giant lizard. But an ordinary lizard would have been frozen solid in this cold. One thing was sure, it was no ordinary lizard.

It was twenty feet tall and looked like a stack of bones draped with an alligator's skin. Withered, ropy muscles moved beneath the skin as though it had been hungry for a very long time.

The Bear Eater had probably been starving all winter until its hunger drove it out of some hidden valley. Maybe piling snow allowed it to escape from whatever steep-walled canyon it had been trapped in since the days dogs could talk.

When Lilly and the Bear Eater got to the ice, Lilly lost her edge over the Bear Eater. She could no longer make the sharp turns that had protected her. She made one final turn, then ran full-speed toward me.

The Bear Eater closed on her.

Its lunge at Lilly came fast, like a snake striking. It lifted up on its claws and whipped its long tail up and down again to counterbalance its attack.

Lilly turned sharply, her rump skidding forward as her front claws pulled her sideways.

The Bear Eater shifted its balance to compensate, sliding on the ice. The Bear Eater's lunge carried it and its teeth past her.

I couldn't risk the Bear Eater getting a second chance at Lilly. I shot the instant I took aim on its left eye.

It was at least two hundred paces away and its eye was a lot smaller than a fry pan. I never wanted a shot to be good more in my life.

The kick on Nat's gun knocked me backward. The overloaded rifle smashed back into me and kicked me in the face, wrenched my trigger finger, and put a gash on the heel of my thumb. My own rifle flew as I spun from the impact.

The Bear Eater's eyes, both of them, stared directly at me. Big yellow snake eyes, slit up and down, still whole under the Bear Eater's bony eye-ridge.

I'd missed.

All I got was its attention. Not a nick on its skin.

The baby wailed. Its feet squirmed against my belly.

The Bear Eater ignored Lilly as she circled around it, barking. It focused on me as I floundered, trying to locate my rifle. The Bear Eater even ignored Ranger when he ran to help Lilly.

It wanted me.

It took its time, walking as though I couldn't get away. I was bait for my own trap, with my gun out of reach.

I squirmed backwards to get my gun, afraid to take my eyes off the Bear Eater for the second necessary to find the rifle. At last, one finger, then the whole hand touched the cold metal.

I lifted the stock slowly to my cheek. I fumbled on the trigger guard, my finger stiff from the twisting Nat's gun gave it.

Step, step, step. The ice shook from the heavy footfalls. "Please, God, help me with this one." Fifty feet away I lined up my shot on that same left eyeball. At forty feet I heard its wheezing. I felt the scrape of the claws on the ice. I judged the distance to my dropped pack at thirty feet. I would shoot when it got to the pack.

The Bear Eater paused a moment to consider me as I sat on the ice. Perhaps it expected me to sprint away. Perhaps it grew tired of Ranger and Lilly yapping at its tail. Maybe it planned to lunge the last forty feet. But after a moment it started up again.

When it reached my dropped pack, I fired.

Again, the overloaded gun kicked me back, but from my sitting position I kept upright.

It's hard to keep your eyes open when you shoot a rifle, especially on your second shot when the sulfuric, scorching backflash of the first shot still burns your face. I kept my eyes open because I had to. I kept my eyes open to see that big yellow eye burst open when the ball hit it.

When the lead ball hit the Bear Eater's eye, the monster jumped up and backwards, whipping its head to the side. The impact didn't have that much force, it was more a reaction to the sudden pain. The strength of its spring cracked the ice. It twisted in the air like a cat and came back down, feet first.

Its feet went through the frozen surface, followed an instant later by the rest of the Bear Eater.

Lilly's wolf reflexes got her well clear when the Bear Eater hit. Ranger, old Ranger, was too slow.

Water gushed out of the hole, ice shattered all around, and an enormous slab under Ranger bucked up and tilted back.

Ranger flattened against the slab, his front legs splayed. His back legs tore furiously for grip. The splash from the Bear Eater's impact flipped the huge cake of ice all the way over, dumping Ranger into the water.

The slab flipped over on top of him.

"Ranger!"

I pulled the baby from under my buckskins, wrapped it quickly in my furs and put it on the ice. I dropped my powder horn next to the baby. "Lilly—guard."

No time to look to see if Lilly stood guard over the baby.

Huge slabs floated in the forty-foot circle of water. Big cracks and gaps spread out another ten feet through the thick ice.

I knew not to jump into the water. I knew that the cold would suck the life out of me and kill me just as dead as the Bear Eater killed Nat. But when I saw Ranger scrabbling on the ice as it flipped over on him, I forgot. I forgot about the freezing cold, I forgot about the Bear Eater, and I forgot my lectures to Nat. I just wanted to save Ranger.

I hit the water next to the flipped slab feet first. Before the rest of me went under, I realized I made a terrible mistake, one worse than forgetting about the freezing water.

The Bear Eater was not dead.

It moved in the dark water, a darker shadow bumping the frozen crust from beneath, trying to find the hole. Of course the damn thing wasn't afraid of the frozen lake, the monster could swim.

The water felt hot, almost burning hot against my face. Water's always hotter than the air in the winter. But in seconds, the heat vanished. The freezing water seeped into my buckskins and sucked the air from my body—stinging, burning cold. I pushed my way under the ice, fumbled with numbing fingers. My breath twisted in my throat. My lungs burned and I came back up for air.

Exhale, inhale. It took all the strength of will I could summon to dive back under the surface, knowing the Bear Eater waited for me there.

Back under the ice. I kicked my way away from the hole. One push, two pushes, then I bumped into Ranger.

He didn't move.

I grabbed a fist full of fur and he spasmed. He thrashed, fighting my grip on him, trying to claw his way through the ice and back to the surface.

I shifted my hold to the scruff of his neck and pulled.

I swam until I knew I was about to inhale water. Certainly I had passed the hole. I expected any moment to swim right into the Bear Eater's toothy mouth.

Then my hand hit open air.

My numb hand couldn't feel the sharp edge of the hole, only the lack of resistance. I curled my arm up and over, pulled my face out of the water and sucked in air.

Gasping, I pulled Ranger, still squirming, through the opening. I let go of the edge to get his forelegs up and to give his rump a push. His claws skittered and he rose up as I sank down.

By the time I resurfaced, Ranger stood on the solid ice, whipping the freezing water from his fur.

The Bear Eater's head rose from the water. It found air.

It bellowed like a steam engine's whistle—louder than any animal had a right to be. The same roaring, bubbling, whistling bellow I heard in the distance earlier.

My wet, numb fingers slipped on the wet surface.

I fumbled with my knife. My fingers couldn't feel the wood of the handle, only the tightness in my muscles as I squeezed it. "I'm not going to drop it," I promised myself as I drew it from its sheath.

The Bear Eater struggled toward me, its jaws slashing out at the floating ice around its neck. One eye was an exploded mess; the other stared at me.

I pushed myself down, then pulled upward to flip my arms out over the edge. The knife clawed into the ice, slid back an inch, then caught. The knife wasn't a solid grip, but it was the only grip I had.

I pulled.

And Ranger pulled, grabbing the fringe of my buckskins and clawing backwards.

A floating slab smashed against my hip, pushed by the Bear Eater's lunges. A moment later I floundered on the solid surface.

I crawled to Lilly and the baby, gasping and shivering. "Damn fool, damn fool."

Water splashed as the Bear Eater broke chunk after chunk of ice from the surface. It jumped up a few feet, enough for its tiny front legs to claw uselessly at the slick surface before it fell back into the water.

It jumped again, enough to get some of its weight onto the ice. But the ice, weakened and cracked, collapsed, sending the Bear Eater back into the freezing water.

I pulled my furs over my body. My shivering made it difficult to press the baby up to my chest as I retrieved my powder horn and rifle. When I staggered to my feet, Ranger shook violently, whipping water everywhere.

The Bear Eater jumped once more, high enough to flop its belly sideways onto the ice. This time it held.

I pulled the plug from the powder horn before I realized my rifle balls were in my pack. I looked for the pack, but it was gone. It had fallen through the ice with the Bear Eater and rested on the bottom of the frozen lake.

The baby started crying again.

The Bear Eater squirmed, trying to get one of its massive hind legs hooked to the edge of the opening.

"Run!"

I didn't turn around to see the Bear Eater regain its footing. The dogs outpaced me as we ran toward the tight pass where the creek flowed into the lake. We were about halfway there when the Bear Eater roared again. Before the echoes died, I felt the vibrations of its feet pounding behind me.

"Run, boys, run." I gasped in exhaled words, puffs of smoke from my lungs rather than real words, chanted in the rhythm of a running man. The words weren't loud enough for the dogs to hear. But maybe they read my mind. A dozen steps later I reached the solid stone of the bluff.

The Bear Eater barreled along, mouth first, two steps behind me.

I dived after the dogs into a hole at the foot of the cliff, twisting my body at the last moment to land on my side rather than my belly to keep from crushing Nat's baby. Scrabbling on my hands and knees through the low mouth of the cave, I wiggled as far back as I could get. It wasn't deep, but deep enough to keep me away from that mouth full of teeth.

There was no way out except the way we came in. And the Bear Eater stood at the mouth of the cave.

Its talons slashed at the stone, one foot wiggled in under the low roof. The dogs barked, the baby whimpered, and the Bear Eater bellowed. I don't know what kind of noise I made. Maybe I prayed.

I sure as hell shivered, maybe from the cold and maybe from the thought of that monster digging us out of the cave.

Again and again those sword-sharp claws thrust into the hole.

Then it stopped.

I heard it breathing close to the opening. Sniffing the air, assuring itself that we cowered in the cave. Then footfalls.

I thought for a moment it went away, but the thudding steps returned. Away and back, away and back. Pacing like a dog would when he's treed a possum.

I patted the cave floor for a miracle, but no pebbles in the moldy cave would make a decent bullet. I felt the thongs and straps of my clothing for something . . . anything that could become a bullet. Nothing.

Nothing except that mangled ball I pulled out earlier.

The dogs went quiet. The baby hushed. No noise outside except the Bear Eater's heavy breathing and the thudding of its feet on the frozen ground.

I struck a fire from a touch of primer powder and most of the remaining wadding. My shaking was so bad that it took three times as long as it should. The few dry twigs from last spring's flood gave us a tiny fire. The smoke gathered, stinging my eyes and nose, but I was glad for a little warmth, a little light.

The wavering flames showed me what my blind fingers had already known—the lead ball had been gouged open like an overripe melon. Heavy grooves from the barrel's rifling marked most of the rest of the ball.

I pushed at the raw edge of the hole with my fingers. The thinnest points of the gouged metal curled back toward the hole. I tried the back edge of my knife. Then I tried my teeth.

Every time I made progress in reducing the size of the hole, I made the ball rougher in other places.

Nat could have done this. Nat's hands were smaller than mine, his fingers could reweave a bird's nest. He could have fiddled with the ball and made it round again.

I rubbed the mangled ball against the wall of the cave. The rough edge came back smooth. I rubbed a different part against the stone. After rubbing six or seven spots, I realized that the smooth spots were flat, not round.

I tried again. And again. Each time I tried to smooth out an edge, the ball got a mite smaller. I almost let the fire die before I realized that the ball had gotten too small to do any good.

I had done the best I could, but the harder and longer I worked to make things perfect, the less and less I had left over.

I wanted to take care of Nat. Even after he traded the mule for Seddewaha, I tried to keep my feelings from wedging us apart. We didn't need someone else in our lives; we had each other. We especially didn't need a squaw.

I had come back from hunting, lugging two big hams from an elk I got at the west end of the valley. Seddewaha made a fine supper for the two of us. We ate mostly in silence.

To fill the empty cabin with noise, Seddewaha told us the story of the Bear Eater. I didn't listen, all I could think of was that Nat's survival relied on doing what I told him and he'd risk it all by ignoring my say-so.

Nat was nervous, barely touching the elk. "Jacob, there's going to be a traveling preacher at the trading post next Sunday."

"We don't need churching," I said.

"Not churching. I want to get married." He must have noticed the blank look on my face, because he added, "To Seddewaha."

"You don't marry a squaw."

"This is different."

"Marriage is forever, Nat."

"I want you to stand up for me."

I threw my tin plate on the floor planks and stared at him.

He smiled. He smiled broader and shinier than he had the morning we first left home for the mountains. He smiled bigger than when he was twelve and we sailed around the harbor in a steamship and the captain let Nat wear his hat.

He was destroying our lives and he had no right to be so happy.

"Jacob, I want you to stand up for me."

I went outside to look at the stars.

I didn't go back inside that night. I never came back into the cabin. I never saw Nat again.

I snapped the wooden handle off my knife and set it into the flames. I rubbed the blade of the knife against my gun's stock, peeling off a thin curl of maple wood. When I added the sliver to the fire, the flame flickered upward.

I could feed the fire one sliver at a time and make the flames last most of the night. I commenced shaving another slice from the stock when I realized how useless it was. A gun without a stock isn't worth beans.

I sat with the gun in my lap, watching the flames of the fire get smaller and smaller. Nat wanted me to stand up for him. Finally, the fire burned down and nothing remained to stoke it up again. The smoke cleared.

My eyes finally stopped tearing.

I put the baby at the very back of the cave, wedging it in with stones. No Bear Eater was going to get Nat's baby, even if it was half Indian.

I emptied my powder horn into the rifle barrel, then jammed the mangled ball in after it. Chipped rocks, my spare flints, and the pointed plug of the powder horn all jammed in after it. The ramrod went only halfway down, pushing the powder and junk in as tight as it would go. The jag of the ramrod stood out like a thin bayonet.

Now I needed the Bear Eater to stick its head into the cave.

I waited, but it kept pacing. Back and forth, back and forth.

"Hey, come look in here!" I shouted.

The last coals of the tiny fire died, but the Bear Eater didn't look in. It stopped a moment, but it didn't lower its head to look in at me, waiting in total darkness. "Hey, you . . . Bear Eater . . . Look in the cave!"

But it just kept pacing. Pacing.

I threw stones at its feet, but it never looked in. I waved my furs, whipping them around the opening, but I couldn't lure it to put its head into the cave.

A claw lashed out and ripped my furs from my hands.

I jumped back, banging my head on the roof of the cave.

The dogs, antsy to have a go at the Bear Eater, darted out, barking and circling.

I couldn't let my dogs face it alone. I stepped from the cave and stood up.

The baby wailed from inside the cave.

"Leave him alone, boys, he's mine!" But the dogs didn't mind me. They never did mind me. Just like Nat.

The Bear Eater spun to the right, trying to keep both dogs visible with its one good eye, but when it caught sight of me it froze. Snake still, unmoving except its one good eye glancing left and right at me, at Lilly, at Ranger, then back to me. I took my finger from the trigger and instead hooked my damaged thumb behind the claw of the flintlock. The other hand supported the butt of the stock at my chest, pointing the rifle upward.

"Damn fool," I whispered to myself.

The Bear Eater's legs moved slowly, so slow I wondered whether or not it really moved them or not. But they moved. Slowly. Stalking me the same way I stalked so many deer in my past.

It took an eternity.

As I stood there, I sweated despite the chill. It walked slowly, slowly, slowly toward me, weeping blood from its smashed eye. The dogs circled and barked, the monster inched forward, and I stood there with my rifle. God, why couldn't you have given me a couple of good lead slugs?

The Bear Eater's tail cocked upward and lifted higher and higher as it approached. When it struck earlier, it lifted high on its claws and whipped its tail outward to counterbalance its thrust.

It built for the strike.

It struck.

Down its head flashed, faster than I expected.

I don't know what instinct allowed me to react in time, but I pushed my gun upward into the oncoming mouth. Both hands pushed hard at an awkward angle with the gun almost vertical and the butt of the stock level with my nose. The teeth came down even with the top of my head when my gun hit something solid.

With a solid obstruction, my thumb pushed against the cock, popping the catch on the mainspring. The claw holding the flint flipped forward, striking a spark from the steel. It pushed farther forward, throwing off more sparks and pushing the flash pan cover from position.

Gravity pulled the fine priming powder downward, but enough of the powder remained in the pan to catch a spark. It flared and the fire shot through the tiny port drilled in the breach. The fire flashed through the cornmeal-grained powder in the breach which spewed fire into the powder-packed barrel.

The gun exploded.

My last thought was how the Bear Eater's breath smelled of rotting meat.

And then the world came to an end.

It wasn't sleep in the normal sense. If you've never been knocked unconscious you can't imagine the floating, swirling darkness marking the boundary between life and death. But I saw it. I was there.

But I came back.

The dogs had laid next to me. They had licked my wounds. Maybe they even dragged me from the exploded head of the Bear Eater. I was alive.

A cut on my scalp dripped blood across the stinging burns on my face. A jagged gash ripped open my lip. More powder burns on my hands added to the abuse I had given them earlier. But I was alive.

And the Bear Eater was dead, its jaws ripped off by the flying metal of my rifle's barrel.

All the banging and abuse would keep me from hunting for weeks. Even if I wanted to hunt, my rifle had been blown into a twisted mess inside the shredded head of the Bear Eater.

I crawled back into the cave to get little Nat. "It's a shame about the rifle."

But I realized I wouldn't be needing it for a while. We had meat for the rest of the winter.

HIS UNTRUE COLORS

JAKE WEST

What would you give to live forever?

Well, it depends.

On what? To sidestep death, wouldn't we take that gift however it came?

But what if you could live forever—but continued to age, until what "lived" was a crisp and brittle thing that had to be kept out of the slightest breeze or it would crumble into dust?

No, there's immortality, the mere avoidance of death, and then there's eternal life, eternal vigor, strength, hope.

But what good is it if everybody gets it? The same people, living on forever with you. Like being trapped on a cruise ship where you have to take every meal with the same people. Wouldn't there be a point where you'd simply throw yourself overboard?

Death serves too many useful purposes to be avoided for much longer than the natural span of life.

It's good to clear the decks now and then, to load the earth with a fresh cargo of human life.

As long as I can be the exception. The one who doesn't have to die.

"So, KID, how old do you wanna be?"

Eddie's mouth opened, but nothing came out. Suddenly, he wasn't sure about this. The badly-lit back room in the tattoo parlor was dirty, hot, and smelled worse than the counterfeiter's breath in his face.

"Terminal." Craig spoke up for him, good buddy that he was. Or major asshole, Eddie never could decide which.

The store's owner, whose pale blue lobe-ring identified him as early Fourth Decade, fixed the twenty-year-old with a look that spoke volumes of contempt. "Terminal means black, genius. You sayin' you wanna go *black*?"

"Make me seventy," Eddie blurted before things could get out of control. "Seventy's good. Let's not get crazy, okay?"

Craig shook his head. "Sorry, man. If you want to pledge Sigma Chi, you go terminal or not at all. Those are the rules. Besides—" he clapped an overly-friendly hand on Eddie's shoulder—"this doesn't work without the sympathy factor. Trust me."

"I'm chargin' by the minute here," their host reminded them.

"Okay, okay. Do it." Eddie thought about how much he wanted to be part of something as illegal and subversive as a campus fraternity. He also thought about how much he just wanted this initiation to be over. He bent his head, and the counterfeiter—also known as a tamperjack—went to work on the small metabolic indicator permanently attached to Eddie's right earlobe. He used tools that were as delicate and intimidating as tattoo needles, though their end result would be much different. When he inserted the electronic probe, it gave Eddie a shock. The youth flinched but didn't complain. The guy scared him. Even though he looked twenty years old, just like Eddie—and everybody else in America these days—he still somehow came across as grizzled. And mean.

"So, ah—you do this kind of thing often?"

The counterfeiter leaned back and, after a moment of sour regard, said, "Fortunately for me, the world is just full of little perverts like you."

Eddie shut up and after awhile, his lobe-ring turned from the bright, vigorous green of late First Decade (after puberty) to a deep and terminal black.

As a test, Eddie crashed a faculty party.

He went in alone since Craig lacked an adult color that would allow him to mingle. Also, Craig was a junior, and thus known to some of the faculty. Eddie, two weeks into his freshman year, was not.

The ploy worked just as Craig had said it would, which astonished Eddie to no end.

The rumored etiquette held true. Peoples' eyes slid away when they saw the terminal black of his lobe-ring. No one spoke to him unless he spoke first. If he wished, he could maintain a zone of privacy around himself, even in the middle of a crowded room. When he did engage in conversation, people deferred to him, some warm, some aloof. Even in his (secretly) youthful naiveté, he sensed a hidden undercurrent from them. Their superficially youthful faces were schooled by decades of practice and experience. But they could not entirely mask pity or revulsion. Eddie realized that they saw their own futures in him.

No wonder there was such a rigid code around the terminals.

So it was all the more surprising when the woman with the deep purple lobe-ring approached him.

"Dr. Carolyn Sevrin," she said, extending her hand.

Eddie didn't ask her doctor of what. Presumably, he was supposed to know. "Edward Ramsey," he said, taking her hand while trying to maintain the suave detachment that he imagined an old, experienced terminal would project. In other words, trying not to stammer. "Guest lecturer this semester."

"Oh? In what department?"

"Anthropology. Ah—Comparative Studies in extinct cultures." Craig's cover story was only meant to get him in the door, not hold up under the scrutiny of conversation.

But apparently it did, for she laughed and said, "Well, then, you must be an expert on ours." Then she took his arm and murmured into his ear, "Would you like to get out of here?"

Eddie swallowed and nodded, not trusting himself to speak. And so they left, followed by the disapproving stares of their peers.

Her peers, anyway.

"OUT OF HERE" turned out to be a hole-in-the-wall club on the fringes of the university district, where the streets blended from the fantasy of academe back into the real world. From the outside the place looked unremarkable, even squalid. You would never even know it was there. It was a place that tried to impress no one, because none but its exclusive clientele would ever see it.

And all of them were terminals, with a day or a month—or maybe a year—to live before the onset of the irreversible breakdown of their still youthful bodies.

No one took their order, and no one asked for money. Eddie procured drinks from the lone bartender, who looked at him strangely when he tried to pay. Fortunately, Dr. Sevrin—Carolyn—didn't seem to notice his gaffe. She was back at their table, openly studying the place and its customers—or, more properly, visitors, since there was little service offered and apparently nothing was charged.

Once Eddie realized what was going on, he switched his order from cheap beer to expensive champagne.

Returning with the drinks, he admired Carolyn's sleek profile, thinking about this incredible stroke of good luck. This evening had started out as a simple test of his disguise and, from the look of things, might end up fulfilling his Pledge Week goal right off the bat: having sex across the forbidden age barrier with an eighty-year-old woman who would either laugh at him or slap him if she knew he was only eighteen.

But by the time he reached the table—so much for incredible good luck—another guy had moved in on her. Sat down right next to her and ignored her completely until Eddie sat down, too, whereupon the burly stranger nodded at Carolyn and said, "Does she know the price? Did you have the balls to tell her? Or does the color have to find out for herself?"

Eddie swallowed hard and thought fast, his mind racing like a semi with bad brakes on a steep grade (his dad owned a trucking business, so he thought in these terms). His brain overheated so much, he became dizzy. The bottom of that treacherous grade loomed alarmingly—and then he had it.

Carolyn was the only person in the room without a black lobe-ring.

"You're not going to do anything to hurt her," he bristled. "Look, if we walked over some kind of line, we'll just leave, okay? No hard feelings." Eddie stood up and, at the same moment, half a dozen other men in the bar stood up, too. Eddie sat down again, slowly, as if lowering himself onto a seat full of tacks.

"Hurt her?" The man sneered. "What I meant was, does she know what I'm gonna do to *you*."

"Carolyn?" Eddie turned to her. She seemed more eager than afraid. "Do you know what's going on here?"

She made a graceful gesture, almost a shrug. "Why, Edward—I assumed that you knew when you agreed to bring me here."

"Knew what?"

Carolyn's eyes widened innocently. "That if you bring a color into a black bar—you have to fight for her, of course."

EDDIE WOKE UP in the hospital.

Not that he realized where he was, not at first. At first, everything was a blur, and he thought that the nurse was his Mom, come to prod him out of bed so he wouldn't be late for school again. But no, that wasn't right, either. His Mom never dressed like that, and she had the wrong color hair—and besides, instead of waking him up, she made him swallow some pills that put him right back to sleep.

In his dreams, then, he sorted it all out. As he remembered the events that had transpired in that smoky room behind the bar, he half-roused from true sleep into a kind of drugged awareness where his mind desperately tried to manipulate the dream, striving for full wakefulness, driven by the terror that, if he dreamed too deeply, he would feel that awful, sickening pain once again—

Had they really made him participate in a *cockfight*? Lawless terminals or not—had they really hurt animals in this day and age? A time of PC laws so stiff that it was a felony to fire an employee without first finding him a new job? Or to do something crazy—like joining an outlawed, underground, *all-male* fraternity?

Worse than that, had they really made him wear a neural-feedback? One that was attached to "his" rooster during the fight?

Oh, God, they had. Once he remembered that much, everything else came back. The face of his scowling opponent across the shallow wooden pit where the birds fought; the jostling crowd in the cramped room; the shouts, the swearing, the wagering; the cold adhesive that held the electrodes to his temples; and finally, the agony of razor-tipped spurs slicing to the bone, warm blood gushing, the other cock's beak plunging deep into what felt like Eddie's own right eye. At which point he had blacked out.

And now, the memory of that pain jolted him back to life.

He thought that he woke up screaming. Certainly his throat was raw and constricted from terror. But nobody else seemed to notice, least of all the other patients in his room, so maybe the screams were all in his mind.

Which didn't make them any less real.

Clammy sweat soaking his immodest hospital gown, he swung his feet out of bed, cursing at the metal handrails and the twisted sheets in his way. With a grunt of pain, he yanked an I.V. needle out of his forearm. Thus freed from bondage to the tall, wheeled pole that held the drip, he stumbled into the hallway to find someone who would listen to his story, someone who would recognize that this was all a terrible mistake. Someone who would set him free.

Instead, he found a wardroom that verified his worst fears about where he might be. There were only a handful of people inside, some of them listlessly watching the institutional TV bolted into one corner of the ceiling, others unable to summon even that much attention span— patients only, no staff in sight.

A handful of youthful-looking people who represented society's dirtiest little secret.

Eddie was in a nursing ward for terminals. The ones whom the world no longer wanted to see. The ones in the final, fatal stages of their mental decline and physical decay.

Suddenly his knees felt as though they were held together with rubber bands. Quickly, he sat down in one of the cracked plastic chairs and bent over, waiting for the dizziness to subside. His tired brain spun from medication and shock, but also from a dozen unanswered questions. He must have looked pretty bad when he passed out from the pain of the neural-feedback. Had they thought he was dead? And, of course, he was wearing that damn black lobe-ring. So, come to think of it, why would anybody in a terminal bar call an ambulance, especially for another terminal?

And where the hell was Carolyn?

"Give me my coffee cup."

Eddie lifted his head and sat up. "Excuse me?" A man wearing a bathrobe had materialized at his elbow.

"Give it back." The tone of voice moved from petulant to threatening.

Eddie started to stand up, realizing that he might have to defend himself. "Man, I don't know what you're—"

"You took it! I saw you take it! You're always stealing from me! Just because you're my son-in-law—"

"Here, Wayne, take mine." A patient in a wheelchair came to Eddie's rescue. He pressed a Styrofoam cup into the other man's slack hand. Wayne's attention was instantly diverted. He stared raptly at the black liquid, then took a sip of it and shuffled away as if nothing had happened, as if Eddie and the other man had ceased to exist. Eddie sat down again, warily eyeing Wayne's retreating form.

"A little dementia, that's all," said the man in the wheelchair, nodding in Wayne's direction. "Mostly, he's harmless. It's the new ones like you who set him off."

"Yeah, well, thanks." It took a second for the comment to compute in Eddie's befuddled brain. "Hey, wait, no. I'm not a new one. I mean, I am, but I'm not really supposed to be here."

His new friend was watching him sympathetically. "Tell me about it," he said, his mouth twisted in a wry grin. "Like any of us deserve this." He made a sweeping gesture, oddly grand and sad at the same time, that took in the whole room.

His companion was so persuasive that Eddie turned around in his seat and really looked at the other people for the first time. Despite their black lobe-rings, they all appeared to be as young as he was. But that was only a superficial impression. As he watched them, he understood that unlined faces or not, these people were old. They showed it in slack posture and slack expressions, in poor grooming and sour body-smells, in a hundred different ways that separated them from the perpetually young, vital people that he knew.

Eddie had seen movies from the days when people aged, so he knew what that looked like, how some old people acted. But there was an unexpected horror in seeing the trappings of age superimposed on people who looked as though they should be in his classes at college.

From school he knew all about how the human nervous system seemed to break down after a normal lifespan, no matter how long medical science could keep the physical body from aging. He remembered studying, when he was a kid, about the great gene-therapy breakthrough that kept people young. One of his teachers had even said that the world was lucky that people still couldn't live any longer than seventy, eighty or ninety years, and probably never would. Otherwise, the poor planet, overcrowded as it already was, would drown in human flesh. No, that teacher had explained smugly, life-extension had come, not from living longer, but from living our allotted years in the fullness of youth and productivity, until just before the end. Until the day when a person's lobe-ring turned black to signal the imminent breakdown of the nervous system. And that was as it should be.

Had that teacher—Mr. Prescott—ever set foot in a terminal ward, Eddie wondered? Had he ever seen youthful faces robbed of their intelligence, their still-clear eyes empty, their strong mouths drooling? Had he ever seen a man who once had the build of a weight-lifter now unable to lift his own body from a wheelchair, his unwrinkled skin gone loose over atrophied muscles? Or seen a beautiful girl like the one who shuffled past Eddie now, clinging to a handrail—a beautiful girl wearing diapers that smelled like they needed to be changed?

"I've gotta get out of here. I've gotta find the nurses' station." Eddie bolted from his seat, rudely leaving his new acquaintance behind. To his relief, a nurse intercepted him in the doorway.

"There you are!" she said brightly. "I've been looking for you, Mr. Ramsey. We aren't quite ready to let you out of bed yet, you know."

"Thank God." Eddie put his hands on her shoulders. She flinched and backed away from him. "No, no, nurse, you don't understand. This is all a huge mistake, and I'm not supposed to be here."

"I know," she soothed. Meanwhile, two orderlies appeared at her beckoning. They pinned his arms and hustled him down the corridor. Eddie resisted as best he could but stopped when he saw who was waiting for him in his room.

"Carolyn! Finally."

"You can put him down," Dr. Sevrin said to the orderlies. "He's with me."

"You sure about this, lady?"

"Shoo, boys. I'll take full responsibility."

As soon as they closed the privacy curtain and left, Eddie expressed his foremost concern, which was: "Where are my pants?"

"Cute hospital gown," Carolyn remarked, pinching his left cheek. Not the one on his face.

Eddie jumped. "Cut it out. What the hell happened? Where were you?"

Carolyn kept her hands to herself but admired the view as he pulled on his trousers. "Well, let's see. Somehow we got separated in the police raid, and it took me several hours to find the right hospital. I didn't know where they'd taken you."

"The cops showed up?" Eddie felt juvenile panic stirring. "Did they get my name?"

"What are you worried about? It isn't like they can do anything to you." Carolyn touched his black lobe-ring. "Is it?"

"No. No, 'course not." Eddie tried to keep the quaver out of his voice. "So, what about you? Did you get busted?"

Carolyn shook her head. "I made it out the back door. With a little help." She laughed. "God, what a rush, as we used to say."

"I'll bet it was." Eddie wondered if that "help" had anything to do with the terminal who had challenged him for Carolyn's attention. The guy had been damn well built. Maybe it was no wonder that it had taken her so long to find "poor Eddie."

Oblivious, Carolyn said, "I'm so sorry about all this." She moved much closer than was necessary just to help him button his shirt. "It looks like I owe you one." Her fingers explored the curve of his chest. "Can you think of any way I can make it up to you?"

ACTUALLY, HE THOUGHT of several ways. After the third time, though, even his eighteen-year-old equipment needed a rest. The rest of his body did, too. He even had a strange, nagging pain in his chest. *Must have pulled a muscle in that last stunt.*

Momentarily satiated, he lay on his back in the bedroom of her comfortable house near the campus, savoring his amazement. *After everything that happened tonight, I can't believe I did it. I can't believe I made love to a purple!* He turned his head and gazed at her relaxed, sleeping face, its superficial youth subtly altered and toughened by the six decades more that she had lived. Already, being with her such a short time, he was starting to understand how to see the true age in people, over and above their lobe-rings.

The lovemaking had highlighted—and proven—that gulf between their generations more profoundly than mere appearances ever could. With Carolyn, the act had been even better than he had expected, and for different reasons. She wasn't such an exciting lover because he was breaking a social taboo with her (well, maybe that was part of it) or because she knew more positions than he did. It was more elusive than that, a combination of teasing and timing and empathy that elevated sex into a realm he had never suspected possible. And yet he knew that she could never teach it to him. It was the kind of ability that came only as the culmination of living, and only his own future decades could impart it to him, if he worked at it and opened himself to all the rich possibilities.

Eddie had willingly let Carolyn take the lead in bed, hoping to disguise his own relative inexperience. He could hardly credit that it had worked, yet she had seemed to enjoy herself. And here he was, still lying beside her, with the promise of more to come.

"Feeling better?" Carolyn stirred lazily and snuggled closer. Beneath the covers, her hand slid across his stomach and rested there.

"Definitely." He stretched a little, wrapping her in one arm. "Guess you could say it was a night of extremes. From pain to pleasure, you know?"

"And which do you like best?" Her hand slid lower and performed interesting maneuvers. Though for just a second, she gripped him hard and made it clear that she could deliver either one. Then the moment passed—if it had ever existed outside his imagination—and Eddie let himself enjoy her manual dexterity.

"Ohh . . . you play the piano with fingers like that?"

Carolyn chuckled. "Allow me to continue working out my guilt. Poor guy—I still can't believe I dragged you into a terminal bar, and you didn't even know the risks." Her hand abruptly altered its rhythm. "Who did your Initiation, anyway?"

"My what?"

"You know, when your lobe-ring turned black? I'll bet it was your GP, right? Medical doctors are the worst when it comes to that. So I've heard, anyway."

With a burst of anxiety, Eddie felt the chest pain hit him again, so hard that his vision turned gray and broke up into spots like pixels on a damaged display. Then it subsided, and Eddie struggled to think. Not easy, under the circumstances.

"Nobody did," he blurted. "I mean—I never had an Initiation. I was, uh, out of the country on a research grant, uh, when it, you know, happened."

"And what research grant was that, Eddie?" Suddenly, Carolyn's voice took on a steely edge. "Who was the sponsor? How much money did they give you?"

"Let me see, I—"

"What country were you in? What airline did you fly home?"

Eddie stiffened (though not in the way that she intended). "I didn't fool you, did I?"

"Not for a second."

"When did you know?"

"Right from the first."

"I don't get it." Eddie pulled away from her a little, and she released him. "You already knew I was faking, and you played this whole game with me anyway?"

"There's a big difference between suspecting and proving."

Eddie fell back on the pillow. "Oh, God. And you proved it by getting me in bed."

Carolyn kissed him lightly. "Trust me, you did fine. Nothing to be ashamed of."

He groaned. "Now I get sympathy. Somebody shoot me."

"Look, I had to be sure that you were really a kid who somehow changed his color. Are you complaining about my methods?"

Eddie thought about the last couple of hours and suppressed a stupid grin. "No, not really."

Carolyn patted the bed, wanting him to move closer. The covers slipped down. She still had remarkable breasts, he thought, even after seven decades of gravity. "Fair's fair. I helped you out with your little fraternity stunt."

He gaped at her. "You knew . . .?"

"In fact," she added, "I'll wave to your friends outside, just so they know that you scored."

"You knew . . . about them, too?"

"I knew you didn't call your 'lawyer' when we left the hospital. Now, I want something from you."

Eddie could not imagine what that might be. He felt the blood drain from his face, thinking about public embarrassment and expulsion from school and about how many different ways his Dad would find to kill him. . . . "I want to know who altered your lobe-ring."

Eddie blinked. "That's it?"

"Just tell me who did it and where to find him, and we'll call it even."

"But why?" Eddie asked the question in spite of his better judgment. What did he care if she wanted to counterfeit her color? Or get a nose-job or have a sex-change, for that matter? But he had to know.

A complex expression moved across Carolyn's face—fear and anger and a touch of fanaticism. She reached up and caressed his ear. "They kill us with these things, Eddie," she whispered, as if someone else were listening. "It's all a lie, and they kill us with these things."

He frowned. "A lie?" What the hell was she babbling about? *Crazy old woman* was how he suddenly saw her, his desire for her ebbing.

"Our brains and our nerves—they don't wear out. The lobe-ring shuts them down when it turns black. We could live as long as we want, if they didn't program them to turn black at random."

"Who are they?" Carolyn sounded so convincing that Eddie's curiosity began to assert itself.

"The ones who do the cover-up. The selected government officials, the elite doctors, the few, trusted cops—all the people who get to have extended lifespans by keeping the secret."

Eddie sat up. "So—if you get your color changed, you won't die? Is that what you're saying?"

"I'm saying more than that. The opposite holds true, too."

Then it hit him. *A black lobe-ring is fatal, no matter how old you are—or how young.* The thought screamed through his mind. If there were even the slightest chance that she was right about this, hard as it was to credit, then he had to find the tamperjack right away . . .

He tried to leap out of bed, but a massive heart-attack threw him flat, galvanizing his whole body, the pain shooting down his left arm, his breathing constricted almost to nothing. Eddie felt his lobe-ring throb with an insistent series of sharp, stabbing pains—

Like an alarm going off. Like a timer signaling, time's up!

"Oh, damn," Carolyn said without a touch of sympathy. "You should have days!" She straddled him, nothing sexual about it this time, and performed CPR.

You did this to me, he tried to tell her through the pain, but his lips wouldn't move.

Carolyn gave up on him. She leaped off the bed and flung on a robe. Weakly, Eddie reached one imploring arm toward her, but the last thing he saw was Carolyn running out the door.

Running for Craig's car still parked downstairs.

Or perhaps running to the authorities who might be waiting downstairs to add her to their clean sweep, along with the frat kids, the tamperjack and his blackmail records on famous clientele. With her in custody, they would extract the names of all her fellow conspirators on the faculty.

Maybe they had used Eddie as bait all along. And used him up. How else did his lobe-ring turn lethal at the very moment of Carolyn's confession?

Unless someone turned it on.

The blackness seemed to escape from Eddie's lobe-ring and spread over him, smothering his sight, numbing his limbs, swallowing both his mind and body in the truest color of them all.

IF THY RIGHT HAND OFFEND THEE . . .

CHRISTINE WATSON

From the myths of Sisyphus and Tantalus and Prometheus to modern stories like Anthony Burgess's A Clockwork Orange and John Kessel's "Clean Escape" and even a story of my own, called "A Thousand Deaths," we've been telling stories about justice.

What do we do with the people who break the rules that make society possible? It may feel satisfying to enact some kind of vengeance, but taking the larger view, isn't there some way to go beyond punishment?

Some kind of therapy? Something to take criminals and make them into useful citizens again? To take the thieves and make trustworthy men and women of them? To teach killers not to kill, abusers to be kind, molesters to leave the object of their desire untouched or, better yet, to cease desiring it at all?

People sometimes forget what a great step forward the Law of Moses was. Eye for eye, he said, Tooth for tooth. Punishment exactly measured to fit the crime.

It was so much better than the old way, which was a cow for a dog, ten blows for one, your eyes for my broken nose, ten murders to pay for one murder.

I'll get you, my pretty—and your little dog, too!

How far is far enough? Or too far, when it comes to justice?

IT WAS DARK INSIDE *the shop, and quiet . . . but neither dark nor quiet enough. The old man knew that. He'd tried to conceal himself from the monsters that hunted him time and again, and the end result never changed.*

"Here he is!"

Things were no different this time. As he cringed beneath the counter and tried to make himself even smaller than age had already rendered him, one of the thugs seized him by the legs and dragged him out into the center of the room. The other turned on the overhead light and remained by the switch for a moment, laughing at their prey's feeble attempts to free himself.

"Should've left at the regular time, Pops," the one who was holding him said. "There'd have been a few things missing, and a little cleaning up to do, but nothing much."

"Gonna be different now." The other man, barely out of his teens but already much harder-looking than his partner, had crossed to the old man's other side. "Gonna be different now, for sure." He lashed out with one foot, the thick, heavy boot driving into his victim's ribs with an audible crack.

The old man curled into a ball, laboring with protesting joints to wrap his arms over his head. His attempts at self-protection were as useless as his attempts to hide. The two attackers, one on each side of him, continued kicking him in turn until he lay sprawled before them, shattered and bleeding, unable to move more than his eyes.

Then they stopped. In the sudden stillness, the old man could hear nothing but his own labored breathing and the pounding of terrified blood in his ears. The younger man waited to speak until he was sure his victim was focused on him.

"Reggie's right," he said. "You shoulda left." Lifting his eyes to his partner's briefly, he nodded, then stared down at the old man again.

His victim had no doubt that something was going on behind him—something involving a heavy boot, or perhaps an object picked up from a counter— that was going to end this. He didn't try to turn. For one thing, he didn't really want to see. For another, he wanted to keep this bastard's face in view as long as he could. He wanted to memorize every feature, from the short-cropped black hair to the scraggly beard, from the flat brown eyes to the remnants of teenage acne that festered on his forehead and cheeks. He wanted to remember that face.

He wanted to take it to hell with him.

"THAT'S ENOUGH, Carl. Turn it off." Dr. Phillip Barnes, the physician in charge of the Reenactment Center (referred to by its less reverent employees as the "One-Mile Shoe Store" after the imaginary footgear forced on its residents), watched his patient as the equipment was shut down. Luis Otero's writhing and moaning slowed and finally ceased once the input was cut, though it took a little longer for the tears to stop streaming from beneath his twitching eyelids and trickling over his blemished cheeks.

It took longer still for his racing pulse to return to normal, but given the trauma involved, Barnes thought, that was to be expected. He wasn't worried about any lasting effects in that quarter; Otero was a fit twenty-year-old who had probably spiked a higher heart rate every time he fled the cops during his pre-treatment days.

Once all of the readings were in order, Barnes signaled his orderly to take Otero back to his room. A glance at the board showed him that there wasn't another treatment scheduled until late afternoon, and that was only the last of an auto-theft series. Nothing on the scale of what Luis Otero had just endured.

That didn't mean that the rest of his day was free, however. Quite the contrary: in less than an hour, Barnes was scheduled to meet with a group of visitors who would decide whether the Center was going to be funded next year. Their decision would be based on how effective the treatments he had designed were, how realistic it was to expect them to be used in more serious cases, and how well their use would be received by the public.

This being an election year, Barnes knew very well which of those three determinants would carry the most weight. He only hoped he could make his visitors view the Center through his eyes.

The irony of that weighed on him as he hurried back toward his office.

"PRETTY SMALL PLACE you've got here, Doc." Senator Meissner, who chaired the new Subcommittee on Criminal Medicine, gave Barnes' workspace an unimpressed once-over before taking the chair he offered her. The doctor smiled.

"It used to be the warden's office," he said. "Recycling in action."

Meissner returned the smile, but the expression didn't carry as far as her eyes. Louder than words, her demeanor proclaimed that she and the rest of her group were here on business, and didn't have time to waste on idle pleasantries.

That suited Barnes. "Has everyone had a chance to review the materials I sent?" he asked.

Of the two men accompanying Meissner—junior Senators, both of them, Barnes knew, whose opinions were of only minor importance—one nodded enthusiastically. "Your work's pretty impressive, Dr. Barnes. Do I understand correctly that the recidivism rate for burglars and carjackers drops to less than eight percent after a ten-treatment series?"

"Exactly right," Barnes told him.

"Well," the other man said, "I'd say that—"

"Impressive, yes," Meissner interrupted. "But giving a thief an attack of conscience is hardly the same thing as punishing a rapist or a murderer, is it, Doctor?" She leaned back in her seat, fixing him with the arctic stare that served her so well in floor debates.

Barnes fought the urge to wince. *"Attack of conscience," is it? She must have had a little chat with that idiot from the House . . . what was his name? Oh, yes, Representative Sinclair. The one that called me "Jiminy Cricket" when he thought his microphone was off.*

Aloud, he said, "The Center wasn't designed to mete out punishment, Senator. We work here to reshape the personalities of the offenders."

And by the way, ma'am, he thought, *you're not the only one who can research someone's background. I know that you went into politics after your sister was murdered. I know how much it frustrated you that the ban on capital punishment meant that her killer would be allowed to live, even in prison. And I know just how badly you want to give other victims' families a better shot at revenge than yours got.*

If his candor disappointed the Senator, she didn't show it. She stood up, took a step toward his office door and gave him another meaningless smile. "I'd like to see for myself," she said.

"Absolutely," Barnes said. He picked a pair of folders up from his desk. "I had just finished administering a patient's treatment before you arrived . . . let me take you to see him first."

LUIS OTERO SAT QUIETLY in his cell, clutching his head and rocking back and forth on the edge of his bunk. From time to time he grimaced and seemed to be trying to move away from some person whom nobody else could see.

"What's he doing?" Meissner asked. Knowing that Otero could not see through the one-way glass in the cell's back wall, she leaned closer. "Why is he twitching that way?"

"He received his treatment only ninety minutes ago," Barnes told her. "It has after-effects."

"Hmm." The Senator reached out her hand. "May I see his file, please?"

"Certainly." Barnes gave her the paperwork and watched her carefully. Sympathy, he was certain, would be out of the question; but perhaps Meissner, face-to-face with his handiwork, would experience a bit of unease.

"Unbelievable," Meissner said as she finished a cursory glance and handed the folder back. The small quaver in her voice was barely noticeable, but it told Barnes all too clearly what he needed to know.

Not discomfort, he thought. *This is pure rage.*

"'Patient experiences disorientation and nightmares,'" she spat. "Well, isn't that just too damned bad? He and his buddy decided to rob an elderly shopkeeper and *kick* him to death, and you're giving him *nightmares*?" She shook her head. "Have you got the other one here, too? Are the taxpayers forking out money to disturb his naptime, as well?"

"Actually, no," Barnes said, keeping his voice neutral. "He was killed in a shootout when police came to arrest them both."

Dealing with some of the patients he had seen in the past year had troubled Barnes. His work with them, and its effects, had given him nightmares of his own. But he had never been frightened before.

Meissner's reaction to his last remark changed that. For the first time since her arrival, she favored him with a genuinely happy smile.

"Well," she said, her tone raising the small hairs on the back of his neck, "at least that's *something*." She glared once more through the one-way glass and started to turn away before movement in the corridor on the other side of Otero's cell caught one of the junior Senators' attention.

"Dr. Barnes, that's the third time the guard's walked by," he said. "I don't remember anything in your reports about security at the Center being this tight."

Here it comes. Barnes took a deep breath. "Otero's under suicide watch."

"Oh?" If her physiology had permitted it, Meissner's ears would have come to points. "When did this start?"

"Immediately after his first treatment." The doctor extended Otero's folder toward her again. "It's all here."

"Just tell me," Meissner said. "What happened?"

Barnes looked at his watch. "That's going to take a little while to explain, and it's already past lunchtime. We've got a decent cafeteria here. Let me tell you the story over a sandwich."

He was stalling, and was certain that Meissner knew it. After a brief silence, however, she nodded. "Lead on, Doctor."

It wasn't a very long walk to the cafeteria. Barnes hoped fervently that it would be long enough to let him get his thoughts together.

"To UNDERSTAND what's happened to Luis Otero," the doctor began, "you have to understand how our treatments work."

"As I already told you, I've read your reports." Meissner sipped her iced tea and, with her free hand, wiped idly at the wet ring the glass had left on the table. "'Through a series of carefully constructed reenactments, the criminal is forced to relive events from the perspective of his victim,'" she quoted, then set the glass back down. "You make them walk a mile in someone else's shoes, isn't that right?"

You have been busy, Barnes thought. "That's right. If we're dealing with a burglar, for instance, we lead him through a scenario where someone takes everything he values most, including his perception that his home is a safe, secure place. And we do it over and over again.

"My patients don't just walk that mile once, Senator. They walk it until the very idea of breaking into a house or stealing a car reduces them to tears."

"And if your patient is a murderer?" Meissner leaned toward him, her lunch forgotten.

"The basic idea's the same," Barnes said. "But the reenactments are much more painful." He twisted a straw wrapper between his fingers. "You saw Otero."

"Yes." That unsettling smile was back.

"He's died dozens of times. This isn't something the human mind is built for, Senator." Barnes dropped the crumpled wrapper on the table. "Two hours after the first reenactment, an orderly found Otero unconscious in his cell. He'd found a rough spot on his bed frame and had run his wrists across it until he passed out . . . more from the pain than the blood loss, I think, but we couldn't take a chance on his being equally unsuccessful the next time. He's been under suicide watch ever since."

"I see." Meissner took a bite from her turkey sandwich, chewing slowly and thoughtfully. No one else spoke.

Don't let this be good news to her, the doctor thought. *I don't think I can stand that.*

For a moment, he dared to hope his silent prayer had been answered. Then the Senator turned to her aide and Barnes knew what the answer had been.

"Jeremy, we're going to have to clear my schedule for Monday. I want to get together with every member of the Appropriations Committee and talk to them about getting Dr. Barnes' funding fast-tracked. Then, we'll—"

"Senator." From the startled look she gave him, Barnes surmised that Meissner wasn't used to interruptions. "With all due respect, you probably shouldn't make your decision until you've seen my other patient."

Her expression shifted from businesslike to quizzical. "Which other patient?"

"Another murderer," he said.

"Otero's partner? You told me he was dead."

"Not him." Steeling himself, Barnes slid another folder across the table to her. Meissner opened it, read the patient's name and gasped.

THE WOMAN CRAWLED *as quickly as she could across the rain-slick alley, her way lit only by the occasional flash of lightning. She could feel very little below the waist now, which was probably a mercy but made moving even more difficult. She didn't scream; she had tried that earlier, and all it had done was help her attacker pinpoint her location. Suddenly, an exceptionally bright flash turned the entire side of the alley bright as day—bright enough that she could see the man in front of her, and the knife, swinging down . . .*

She had just closed the door and slid the deadbolt when he grabbed her from behind, silencing her with the first cut. He dragged her off toward the bedroom and she tried to fight back, but her arms and legs were so heavy and the room was growing darker by the second . . .

She always jogged in the mornings, early enough so she could count on sharing the running path only with an occasional squirrel, and more rarely, a fellow early-bird. The man in the dark blue sweats grunted what might have been a greeting as he ran past, but then she heard his heavy footsteps turn and come up behind her. She had just a heartbeat's time to realize that she could be in trouble, very serious trouble, before he slammed the blade into her back. . . .

She flailed at her attacker, panic keeping her from feeling the pain of all the defensive wounds on her hands. The man lunged closer and this time she did feel it, felt all of the pain and the terror as the knife slid into her chest, severing her aorta, and she died . . .

. . . over and over again. Twelve different women. Twelve different deaths.

The man—the tall, powerful man with the weightlifter's shoulders and arms—was always the same.

"VICTOR NAVATELLI?" Meissner did not look at, or touch, the folder again. "You have *Victor Navatelli* here?"

Barnes reached across, closed the folder and drew it back to his own side of the table. "Yes," he said, "we do."

"How can you—how can you bear to—" Her voice was a ragged whisper now. "That *animal* killed a dozen women and girls, including my—" She froze, eyes wide. "You bastard. You filthy, scheming bastard." She leapt to her feet, knocking her chair away. "Wanted to make sure I'd have a personal stake in this, didn't you?" Her aide touched her arm. She pulled away.

"I did," Barnes said, fighting the impulse to give up in the face of her anguish. "I did, but not for the reasons you think."

"What the hell do *you* know about what I think?" Meissner looked away, but only long enough to get herself under a modicum of control. When she turned back to him again, her face was set in a grim, icy mask.

"Take me to him," she said.

"Senator Meissner," her aide said, "I don't think this is a good idea."

"It may surprise you to know that I don't give a damn what you think, Jeremy," she said. "Let's go, Doctor."

"NAVATELLI'S IN THE HOSPITAL WING," Barnes explained as they walked. "In isolation."

"And why's that?" It was the first thing Meissner had said since they left the cafeteria.

"I'd rather you saw him for yourself," he said, and was relieved when she said nothing else.

An orderly was sitting next to the doorway, positioned to have an unobstructed view of the patient, when they reached Navatelli's room. "Take a break, Chuck," Barnes told him. "We need a few minutes with him."

"He's pretty bad today, Dr. Barnes." The orderly tipped his head toward Meissner and the others. "Are they—?"

"They'll be fine, Chuck. I'll buzz you when we're finished."

"Yes, sir. Just be careful." The orderly walked slowly away, looking back over his shoulder at the room's blinds-covered window.

"All right, then," Barnes said. "Let's go in."

WHEN SHE COULD THINK about it later, Senator Meissner realized that they'd been in Navatelli's room for nearly a minute before the sight of what was lying on that bed actually registered. It was the right *shape* for a human being in restraints, but it was covered in a rust-colored, glistening skin that seemed to belong on a snake, or a beetle.

Then it opened its eyes, exposing glittering brown disks set deep inside that swollen coating, and she *knew*.

"He looks . . . flayed." She took a step closer to the bed. Behind her, hasty footsteps told her that her companions had retreated and that she and Barnes were alone with this strange apparition.

"It's amazing," Barnes said, "what a determined man can do . . . given a stolen blade and an unguarded hour."

"He didn't do this to *himself*," Meissner choked. "*No one* could do this to *himself!*"

"True enough." Barnes walked to the foot of the bed. "Isn't that so, Victor?"

"Now, Doctor," an angry voice hissed. "You know better than to call us that."

Meissner swung around, thinking that someone else had entered the room. No one had. She looked with confused horror at the man lying on the bed, still not understanding where the voice could have come from.

The contralto voice. The *woman's* voice.

"Oh, let him be, why don't you?" Another female voice—higher-pitched, with an accent that would have been at home in the French Quarter—issued from that ruined face. "It's not often you pay us a visit these days, Doctor. To what do we owe the honor?"

"This lady wanted to meet you," Barnes said, beckoning Meissner closer to the bed.

"Yeah, right." The words were spit into the room, followed by a hoarse, bitter laugh. "Like this piece of shit didn't meet up with enough ladies already."

The patient raised one hand slightly off the bed. Barnes frowned and walked to that side, tightening the restraint, then jumped back to avoid the teeth that snapped in his direction.

"Now, Doctor," the sweet Southern voice wheedled. "You know none of us wants to hurt you . . . but you're fighting a losing battle, trying to protect him."

"Damn straight." The angry laugh rang out again. "Sooner or later, one of us will get him."

The Senator felt lightheaded. "I don't understand," she said. "What the hell is going on here?"

Those glittering eyes shifted her way and a voice she hadn't heard yet, but seemed familiar, addressed her. "Don't worry," it said gently. "He's not going to hurt you. He's never going to hurt anyone again."

This is not possible, Meissner thought. *Not possible!*

She fled, leaving Barnes with his patient.

HE FOUND HER, as he'd expected, back in his office. She sat with her back to the door, head bowed, and spoke as soon as she heard him enter the room.

"I sent the others away," she said. "It was Lily, wasn't it?" She waited until he took his seat behind the desk and looked up at him. Her face was still wet with tears and she looked ten years older than when she'd arrived.

"Wasn't it?" she repeated.

"Not exactly, Senator." Barnes opened his desk drawer and pulled out a bottle of bourbon and a pair of glasses. He poured a drink for each of them and a few moments passed in silence while they each took a large first sip.

"The personality you heard . . . wasn't the sister you knew," he said finally. "It was a construct, something Navatelli put together out of whatever impressions he got from her that day."

"The day he killed her." Meissner spotted a box of tissues on his desk and took one to dab at her eyes.

"Yes." Barnes took another sip. "It's the same with all of them. Navatelli knew no more about your sister, or any of his other victims, than Otero knew about the man he killed. We've run them through those deaths, over and over, until the personalities they've created inside their heads are more powerful than their own."

"And they want revenge?" Meissner shuddered.

"Freedom, perhaps," Barnes said. "The end result's the same."

The Senator raised her glass, drained it and shook her head when Barnes picked the bottle up again. "I trust you'll forgive me, Doctor, when I tell you that I can't give you my support."

"I trust you'll forgive me," he said gently, "when I tell you that I never wanted it."

She stood up, then shook his hand. "You'll want to update your resume," she said, sounding once again like the brisk, no-nonsense politician.

"I'll do that," Barnes replied.

THE OLD MAN USED *the patience that long life had taught him; he bided his time. In the end his meek demeanor convinced the watchers that the worst of the aftereffects were receding and he need not be observed so closely.*

A few minutes were all he needed. He stood in front of the blurry metal mirror set into the wall over his sink, gripping the pen he'd managed to steal from one of the orderlies. Listening carefully, he assured himself that the hallway was empty. Then, he raised the pen to shoulder height and jammed it into his neck.

Luck was with him; blood sprayed in satisfying spurts over the wavering image of the ugly thug he saw in the mirror. He smiled, never bothering to wonder why his own face didn't appear.

"Got you this time, punk," he whispered, and sank contentedly into oblivion.

UKALIQ AND THE
GREAT HUNT

DAVID D. LEVINE

When you view it one way, the story of human life is one continuous tale, weaving and dancing like the serpents growing out of Medusa's head, but all still connected, one long sinuous story, one generation after another.

Viewed another way, however, each generation sucks life out of the one before, drinking in memories, and then, at the first opportunity, setting aside the older generation and taking over. The older generation might be revered or it might be reviled, but one thing is certain: It will be replaced.

It all depends on whether you believe that the parents give gifts to their children or that the children steal the parents' treasure and flee with it.

Is it not the story of each child's life, that when he finds the magic beanstalk and climbs into the treasure house of the giant, he will steal the music and the magic and then cut down the beanstalk to bring the old giant tumbling down to destruction?

There is more truth than we know in those old stories, those old lies, though sometimes the truth itself is so frightening that we need to disguise it well and hide its face.

There are no wicked stepmothers. Just mothers. There are no evil giants. Just parents.

Or is that just another monstrous lie?

WHEN RAVEN FIRST LED the people from the third world to the fourth, the sky was black and empty all day long. A great chief kept the sun and the moons and the stars hidden in a cedar box with some icy rocks to keep the box from burning up.

Greedy Raven wanted these pretty baubles for himself. He changed into a lichen flake and floated into the drinking cup of the chief's daughter, who drank him up. Raven grew in her belly for one-third of a year, and then was born as a beautiful boy. The chief doted upon this grandson, and would give him anything he wanted.

One day Raven pointed to the box and cried and cried until the chief gave it to him. Once he had the box in his hands, Raven returned to his natural form and flew out the smoke hole with it. But the box fell open as he flew, scattering its contents in the sky.

Released from the box, the sun shone hotly down on the world. So fierce was its heat that all the water and even the air began to boil away. Raven tried to pull the sun down from the sky, but he could not fly high enough. He went to Black Cedar and asked the tree to lift him up, but even then he could not reach. So he cut a hole in the tree and packed it with caribou tallow. Then he built a fire at the base of the tree and climbed up into its branches. The tallow inside the tree caught fire, and the tree burst into the air with Raven clinging desperately to it.

Raven and the tree flew through the air for many days until they came to the sun, but it was wedged firmly in the sky and Raven couldn't move it. Nearby, though, he found some of the icy rocks that had been in the cedar box. He gathered up as many as he could and brought them back to the people. The rocks made it a little cooler and a little wetter, but everyone could see that many, many rocks would be needed to make the world cool and wet again.

That is why the sun and the moons and the stars shine down from the sky, and why the world is dry, and why the people build totems of black cedar and go to capture the ice boulders.

That is why we have the great hunt.

WHEN I WAS A YOUNG MAN, just a few years older than you, the elders saw the signs in the sky and declared it was time for the great hunt. They sent all the clan's hunters to cut a black cedar tree, while the gatherers set up camp at the traditional carving place.

Every step in the preparation of the great hunt totem must be performed exactly according to the ancient ways, or the totem will lose its way. Or even worse! In my father's day a clan near Irkaluit was destroyed by a great fire while carving their totem.

Only the wisest elders and the hunters with the surest hands do the actual carving. I was with another group of hunters, who went to the encampment of the glass people for trading.

No, they are not made of glass! Who told you that? Well, your sister is wrong, and you can tell her Grandfather Ukaliq told you so. We call them the glass people because they make so many things of glass. Even their houses are made of glass! In my great-grandfather's day they wore glass hats that covered their heads completely, but they are not so vain today.

Even the biggest glass person is no bigger than you, and as skinny as a hare's foreleg. They always wear bulky clothing—to keep them warm, they say, but I think they are ashamed of their tiny, sunken chests. Their skins are very pale, and they smell like burnt antler. But they are much stronger than they look.

Some say the glass people are very stupid. It's true that they are poor traders, but they are excellent healers and great travelers. And great liars! One tried to convince me he was born on a star!

Despite their lies, the glass people can be trusted to provide the things we need for the great hunt. We brought many fine carvings, which we had been making and saving for just this purpose ever since the last great hunt, and traded them for sheets of glass, rings of metal, special carving tools, and other objects used only for the great hunt totem. We needed special tools because the outer wood of the black cedar is so strong and hard. But the heartwood is soft, and burns hotter and faster than any other tree.

You probably think the great hunt totem is like the totems we carve for the summer longhouse. It is much bigger—as tall as five people, and so big around that two people can barely join hands around it at the base—but that is not the most important difference. Ordinary totems are solid wood, but the great hunt totem is riddled with hollows and channels. Some are so big a person can crawl inside; all are decorated with the bright glass and metal objects we get from the glass people. Everything must be prepared according to the elders' wisdom (even though much of it cannot be seen) or the totem will surely lose its way.

Another difference in a great hunt totem is that the figure on the top, not the bottom, is the most important. In our totem the topmost figure was Raven himself. He was carefully carved out inside, and the space within was decorated with the finest and most elaborate pieces in the most ancient patterns. The other figures—Bear, Badger, and Hare—were mostly solid inside; smaller hollow spaces were made and decorated between the figures, as tradition dictates.

While the totem was being carved, the great hunt candidates spent each day being instructed in the rituals of the hunt. We learned to read the patterns of the stars: Whale and Seal and the other legendary creatures became our guides and companions. We learned the rituals of purification and cleansing that must be performed before and during the hunt. We learned the traditional chants and the dances that went with them. Grandmother Tiriganiaq would strike me with her stick if I dropped a phrase or chanted too fast; many candidates failed because they could not keep proper time.

Most important of all, we learned to wear and care for our ritual garments. The great hunt costume is vital to the hunt; it protects the wearer from malicious spirits who would steal his soul. It is made of a special fabric we get from the glass people, more supple than doeskin but tough and waterproof, and must be kept completely clean and free of any holes or tears. Mine was made for me by my mother and my grandfather Udjuk. It represented Porcupine, with bold red and black stripes on the arms and legs and a grand headdress that covered my whole head and face.

In the end, ten of us knew all the chants and dances. Our bodies were strong and purified, and our minds were full of knowledge. Finally, on the day the carving of the great hunt totem was complete, each of us was taken away from the camp by three elders and made to perform the entire ritual alone, while they watched stony-faced.

I cleansed myself three times. I struggled into the heavy and awkward ritual garments, and carefully sealed all the openings to keep my soul from being stolen. I stood in a circle drawn in the dirt, the exact size of the hollow inside Raven, and executed each chant and dance, speaking the name of each sacred object as I pretended to touch it in the prescribed way.

The watching elders were silent, offering no assistance or criticism, but I could see their heads nod as they chanted along with me under their breath. When the test was done I stood panting while they conferred on my performance. Finally Grandmother Koovianatuklook spoke: "You have performed adequately." That was all. They left me there to cleanse the ritual garments and haul them back to camp by myself.

The next day the elders called a council of the whole clan. When all were gathered, Grandfather Umingmak raised both hands and spoke: "Six of the candidates have performed adequately, demonstrating a complete command of our most sacred traditions and rituals. Of these six, it is traditional for the elders to select the one with the greatest strength and agility to represent our clan in the great hunt. But on this occasion we have been unable to reach a consensus. There are two candidates of equal qualification: Natsiq and Ukaliq." The blood roared in my ears, nearly drowning out his following words: "These two will compete in the pole game to select our representative."

Once again I cleansed myself, carefully inspected my sacred costume, and sealed myself inside it. This time Natsiq—my father's brother's daughter, and my companion in many games and hunts—performed the same rituals beside me as she donned her own costume. Finally we faced each other, two creatures of legend, and raised our hands in salute.

The poles were brought out, as tall as a person and brightly painted, with two crossbars fixed at the top of each. The other candidates raised the poles, two strides apart, and held them while Natsiq and I scrambled to their tops. I hooked my thighs over the top crossbar and my feet under the bottom one, to lock myself to the pole. My balancing rod, a long straight wand of yew, was handed up to me. I was given a moment to find the center of the rod and position it horizontally across my chest.

I saw that Natsiq had done the same. Then the other candidates released the poles, and the pole game began. The last one remaining upright would be the victor.

For the first few moments we just teetered, rods wavering. The people outside the circle of candidates shouted and cheered at each movement. The muscles of my chest and back strained as I used my rod to counter each motion before it could turn into a fall, and my legs and stomach burned from clenching the crossbars.

Then I saw Natsiq's rod swinging around toward me. I moved my rod to block it, but nearly unbalanced myself in doing so. My left shoulder felt as though it were tearing open, but by sheer luck I managed to knock Natsiq's rod with my own, so she was also distracted while I fought back to center.

I took advantage of this opening to strike at Natsiq's head; my rod seemed to move as slowly as the greater moon in its path through the sky. Natsiq managed to slip her rod under mine, and pushed up. But I pushed down, sending both of us into a frenzy of waving and dipping to stay upright. The crowd yelled encouragement; my breath roared in my headdress.

I nearly toppled, but saved myself by pushing at the ground with my rod. Seeing me defenseless, Natsiq struck quickly, landing the end of her rod squarely in the center of my chest. As I started to fall back, I did the only thing I could: I pushed with my planted rod. A great cheer exploded from the crowd as I overbalanced and started to fall toward Natsiq instead.

Natsiq's rod still hovered before my chest. I released my own rod and grabbed the end of hers. Natsiq's eyes were wide behind her ceremonial mask as I pushed wildly to stop my forward movement, pushing Natsiq back. Her eyes never left mine as she tipped back, back, back, and landed in the arms of the other candidates. I was left atop my pole with no rod, waving my arms frantically, for a long moment before I too fell.

Natsiq and I struggled to our feet and saluted each other. The noise of the crowd doubled as I unsealed my headdress; I waved at them, then embraced Natsiq. She stiffened at first, then squeezed me back. After a long hug we held each other at arms' length. There were tears in Natsiq's eyes, but she held her chin high and smiled as she shouted above the din of the crowd: "You have performed adequately!"

After that my training only increased in intensity. The final ceremony of the great hunt would begin in just two days. I drilled constantly, until my muscles ached and the rhythms of the traditional chants controlled even my dreams. I ate only sacred meals, building up my spiritual energy for the hunt. I cleaned and inspected every part of my ceremonial garments over and over. Meanwhile the elders and hunters completed the preparation of the great hunt totem, moving it from the carving place to the rocky valley nearby and standing it erect.

The morning of the final ceremony found me fully awake before first light. I had slept, but fitfully; I was too excited. I was even a little scared. I knew that not every hunter returns from the great hunt. Totems lose their way; hunters' souls escape through unnoticed tears in their garments; ice boulders crush hunters by accident.

I reminded myself that even if I did not return, I would represent my clan in the great hunt and bring honor on us all. Some clans are too poor to trade with the glass people. Some do not complete their totems in time, or do not find any successful candidates among their young people. Our clan is great, and has participated in every great hunt since time began. Be proud of this.

I walked alone in the predawn light to the valley where my totem awaited me. The rising sun shone on the bold red, black, and white patterns. I greeted noble Bear, brave Badger, clever Hare, and mighty Raven—who glittered in the sun with the bits of glass and metal worked into his design—and wished them well for the great hunt. Then I returned to camp, where the whole clan was beginning preparations for the day's ceremonies.

My day began with a substantial breakfast, to sustain me for the hunt. I would eat only the most consecrated foods on the hunt itself. Then I cleansed myself three times and donned once more the ritual garments. The elders inspected them carefully before I dressed, and again once I was fully costumed, to be sure my soul would be properly protected from the hazards of the hunt. Finally I sealed the headdress onto my shoulders, and the elders and I walked slowly down to the rocky valley.

The other candidates were there, standing in a ring around the great hunt totem, all wearing their ceremonial garb. Around them in a larger ring was gathered the whole clan. As soon as we came in view, a great shout went up from the crowd, and they all chanted my name song as I walked with the elders to the center. Once we had seated ourselves, the drums began pounding and the candidates leapt into the ice boulder dance, to bring me luck on the hunt. I was very proud of them.

After the dance, the candidates stood panting before me and the elders. Grandfather Umingmak thanked them for their efforts and encouraged all the people to bend their thoughts toward success in the great hunt. Then a climbing pole was brought in for me to ascend the totem. My heart leapt in my chest as I realized that the great hunt itself was about to begin.

My mother and father held the pole steady, and I formally thanked them for birthing and raising me before I clambered to the top. There I found a pot of paint and a brush waiting. As I spoke the words of the awakening chant, I carefully painted in the pupils of Raven's eyes so he would guide the totem safely. I made them as big and as round as I could so that he could see clearly. When I was finished I lowered the pot and brush on a cord to the elders below, then stepped inside Raven's body. The climbing pole was pulled away as I fastened the door behind me.

The hollow space inside Raven was glorious with color. The entire space was painted with a single giant image of Raven, centered on the seat carved into the floor where I positioned myself. Raven's beak rose over my head, and his wings—encrusted with the most sacred objects and punctuated here and there with glass—enfolded me in their embrace. I was honored to know that only I would see this marvelous work, and I knew Raven would be pleased by it and keep me safe. I continued the awakening chant as I fastened the clasps of the many necklaces and belts that would protect my spirit. The chant concluded with the words: "Mighty Raven, hear my voice: guide me well and bring me success in the great hunt!"

Next after the awakening chant came the Bear chant. Through the glass in Raven's feathers I could see the people gathered, far in the distance, while I touched each bead and carving as prescribed by the chant. Bear began to stir below me as he responded to the demanding rhythms of the chant. He shrugged and rumbled louder and louder, and I chanted harder just to hear my own voice. Finally, touching the amulet of Bear fastened beneath my left hand, I firmly chanted: "Noble Bear, hear my voice: awaken and carry me to the great hunt!"

Bear responded with a mighty shout. The sound of his voice was a thousand thunders, so great it shook the world and turned the sky from blue to black. I felt the spirit of Bear standing upon my chest as he roared in my ears, but I did not omit one syllable of the chant.

Now began the Badger chant. This was the most critical chant of all; the slightest deviation in timing would bring down Badger's immediate wrath, and not even Bear and Raven together could keep me safe. I do not understand how Bear and Badger could hear me, so loud was Bear's voice. But just as I spoke the words: "Brave Badger, hear my voice: bend your back and carry me on in the great hunt" and touched the Badger amulet under my right hand, Bear stepped off my chest and Badger began to roar instead.

Badger is not so large or fierce as Bear, but he is powerful. The mere sound of Badger's growl rattled my bones and drummed on my belly, making my whole body tremble. Badger's spirit walked from one end of my body to the other, but as I chanted I felt him tread more and more lightly. Finally he leapt away from the totem with a great jolt, leaving me alone with silent Raven and Hare.

A great lightness came upon my soul then. Some may tell you that Raven and the other spirit beings do not exist, that they are only tales we tell ourselves to help the world make sense. I know this is not true, for I have heard their voices. If that mere sound was enough to make my head spin and my stomach tumble for days, imagine what would happen to you if you actually saw mighty Raven in the flesh! Surely your poor body could not withstand it.

I thanked Bear and Badger for their help, then began the great hunt chant. Like the Caribou chant, it politely asks the ice boulders to come and give themselves, and promises that we will remember them in our songs and stories. We must always show respect for those we hunt.

As my mind settled into the rhythms of the chant, the whole world, red and ochre, seemed to spread out below me. Twinkling lights in the distance were my fellow hunters; I knew that they were chanting with me in their own totems. The sun rose and set, but it seemed to me that each day passed in just a few breaths. And whether or not the sun was shining, the sky was as black as when the world was new.

Finally the ice boulders heard the hunters' chants and came before me. At first they were just tiny lights, smaller than the stars, but they grew until I could see them clearly, slowly tumbling against the black of the sky and the red of the ground.

I chose carefully, as the elders had taught me; I knew I would have only one chance. I wanted to pick a boulder that was large, but not too large, and not tumbling too quickly. I also needed to observe my fellow hunters to be sure we all chose different prey.

After careful consideration I set my eye on a fine large boulder that turned slowly at the near edge of the pack, and began the stalking dance. In this dance and the accompanying chant, the hunter must bring all his skills to bear. It is not simple memorization; each movement and word must be carefully chosen for the current situation.

The pole game is important to the great hunt because it is preparation for the stalking dance. In the pole game, you must learn to move your body *this* way so you do not fall *that* way. The stalking dance uses the same moves, but the dancer's movements cause the bells and rattles on the ceremonial garments to sound in certain ways. Raven and Hare hear these sounds, and move the entire totem in the desired direction. The belts and amulets on the sacred garments must be positioned and fastened exactly properly for this to work.

Gingerly I moved up on my chosen prey, quietly chanting reassurances. Ice boulders will never attack a person deliberately, but they are stubborn, and that makes them dangerous. Many hunters have been killed simply by getting between two boulders intent on each other. Raven and Hare muttered in my ears as they nudged my totem closer and closer to the boulder's gray, pockmarked surface. The closer I got, the bigger it appeared and the faster it seemed to tumble, but I fought down my fear; I was determined to bring down this boulder for the sake of our clan and the whole people.

Finally I was within striking distance. With a great cry I lunged with my whole body; clever Hare heard the rattling beads and shoved the totem forward to meet the boulder. Raven's open beak bit into the boulder with a mighty crunch. I wiggled my shoulders a bit to sound the bells there, and I felt Hare try to move the totem in response, but Raven's beak was firmly set. We had captured the boulder!

The stalking dance concluded with a series of moves that stopped the boulder's tumbling. Next came the Hare chant, which thanks Hare for his assistance in the stalking dance, then concludes with these words: "Clever Hare, hear my voice: send this boulder home for my people from the great hunt!" Hare stretched his legs, propelling Raven, the boulder, and myself forward with a shuddering jolt, then leapt away. I saw the Hare totem tumble away behind me, empty, as Hare's spirit departed.

The great hunt was nearly concluded. Thanks to Hare, the ice boulder was now headed toward the red world below, where it would give its life so that all the people can have air to breathe and water to drink. I thanked the boulder for this sacrifice and promised once more to remember it in my songs and stories, then began the Raven chant.

The Raven chant combines elements of the stalking chant and the Hare chant, and ends with these words: "Mighty Raven, hear my voice: spread your wings and carry me home from the great hunt!" But though I spoke the words properly and pressed the Raven amulet firmly, Raven did not release his hold on the boulder.

I was so shocked I did not even complete the final phrase. Raven had been so kind and helpful so far, I could not believe he would let me down now. But Raven is the Trickster as well as the Creator, and he had chosen this moment to play a trick on me.

Not knowing what else to do, I repeated the entire Raven chant, raising my voice as loud as I dared and pressing hard on the amulet with the final words, but again nothing happened.

For long moments I simply sat, open-jawed, there in Raven's embrace. What could I have done wrong? I had performed every chant, every dance, faithfully and well. I did not recall missing any steps or dropping any syllables. Yet for some reason Raven refused to cooperate.

Then I remembered Raven's greed, and how he stole the sun. Yes, Raven put the sun into the sky and brought light to the people, but it was not only for our benefit; it was because *he* wanted it! Obviously Raven was particularly fond of this ice boulder, and had decided to hold onto it. I had to convince him to let go, or he and I would join the ice boulder in its sacrifice.

The sun glinted over the horizon of the boulder clutched in Raven's beak. Suddenly I had an idea.

I returned to the stalking chant, improvising madly to change it into a plea to Raven. I sang of the sun, of its great light and noble power. I compared the glorious sun to the gray and dingy boulder. I rattled my beads in the stalking dance, and Raven heard those at least, because he turned the whole boulder so he could look on the sun in its splendor.

Eagerly I chanted, praising the sun, praising Raven's judgment and taste, imploring him to reconsider his choice. The sun shone hotly on one side of Raven's beak; the other side was black against the icy boulder. I heard a creaking noise and felt Raven's beak twitch indecisively. Perhaps my words were having some effect.

Once again I began the Raven chant, blending with it words of the stalking chant and my own improvised chant of praise for the sun. My mask filled with my words as I pressed the Raven amulet: *"Mighty Raven, hear my voice: open your beak and carry me home from the great hunt!"*

There was a grinding, creaking sound and Raven released the boulder at last. Then, with a great shuddering thrust, Raven spread his wings and beat forward. For many breaths Raven pressed on, as I watched the boulder fall away toward the red world below. Finally the sound of Raven's wings faded away, leaving me alone with the silent stars.

There was no sign of the glass people's village, which I had to locate in order to return to the people.

Anxiously I peered in every direction. I did a few steps of the stalking dance to turn Raven's gaze around, but apart from a few stray ice boulders and the tiny twinkling lights of some distant totems, there was nothing to be seen anywhere. I had taken too long to convince Raven to release the boulder.

I was lost.

At first I was angry. Greedy Raven had doomed me by refusing to release the boulder. But after a time I realized that it was not Raven who had failed me, but I who had failed him. Raven is what he is, like everything in the world, and it is up to us to respect him for that and treat him fairly. I had tempted Raven with a boulder that was too large and too fine, and he had merely followed his own nature in preferring to hold on to it.

There were no more chants for me. I sat quietly, with the voices of the spirits ringing in my ears and the world seeming to turn around me. I was sad, but I knew I had done my best and my clan would remember me in their songs. I closed my eyes and waited patiently for my unknown end.

Suddenly there was a splintering crash, and my eyes jerked open, expecting to see an ice boulder bearing down on me. Instead I saw a tiny figure clambering on the outside of my totem. It was one of the glass people, wearing a crude imitation of my own ceremonial garments! He waved and pointed at the door, beckoning me to come out. I carefully unfastened my belts and necklaces, then drifted to the door and opened it.

The glass person was waiting for me right outside the door. Quickly he pulled me away from Raven's embrace, bundling me into his own conveyance. It was something like a house, only smaller and rounder and painted all in white and blue, and it floated in the air, attached to Raven by a harpoon on a cord. Raven looked sad and alone without Bear, Badger or Hare to keep him company. His bright colors were streaked from nose to tail; his beak was scarred from the ice boulder, and even his bold staring eyes seemed to weep. I spared one brief moment to thank him for all he had done for me, then let the glass person pull me into his house.

The air inside the house was oppressively hot and moist, and smelled of metal and burnt antler. I tried to thank the man for helping me, but he waved impatiently at my words and jabbered in his own tongue. He helped me remove my ceremonial garments, then removed his own and ushered me into the tiny main room of the house. Blinding white light glared from glass panels everywhere, and the walls, ceiling, and floor were crowded with meaningless decorations in the glass people's awkward style.

Although the glass person could not speak the people's speech, he had a machine that did. It explained that the man's name was Maqandisen, and that he had been sent to help me by the glass people's village in the sky. The machine's tones were calm and pleasant, but Maqandisen's eyes and the tone of his voice were hard.

Maqandisen seated himself in the room's one chair and turned his back to me. Astonished at his rudeness, I could only watch as he busied himself with the tiny glowing squares fastened to the wall there. I have often noticed that the glass people are more interested in machines than in other people. After a time of this, there was a rushing sound and a pressure against my back; Maqandisen nodded once at his machines, then finally turned to face me. He said nothing, but his face clearly indicated that I was not welcome in his home. "Machine," I said, "tell Maqandisen that I am profoundly grateful for his assistance and his hospitality. I was lost, and would surely have died before long if he had not come by."

The machine repeated my words, then translated his response: "I came because I was ordered to come. The journey to the village of the watchers will take one-third of a day. Sit quietly and do not touch anything." Once again he turned his back. This was the glass people's hospitality! But I was a guest in his house, so I was determined to respect his ways.

For a long time I simply watched the man as he stared intently at his little colored squares and occasionally poked one with a finger. Every once in a while he glanced over his shoulder at me, but when he saw I was watching he always looked away quickly. Finally I had to ask: "Is there nothing I can do to express my gratitude?"

Angrily he turned and spat: "No! I never wanted to risk my life and my house to save you. The watchers have been watching you for too long. They have forgotten why we made you."

I scarcely knew how to respond to this arrogant lie. "You didn't make me. My mother and father made me."

He rolled his eyes. "My people made your people. All of them. We started with tiny pieces from our own bodies, then changed them to make you more suitable for this world. We gave you Whale's lungs so you could breathe the thin air, and Owl's eyes for the thin light."

"That is a lie. Raven made the people!"

"We made your Raven too. We put together your bodies from pieces of our people and animals, and we put together your legends from pieces of our people's legends." There was a smile on his face, but it was a grim smile. "We built your whole culture to keep you alive in the bad weather and make you respect the animals and plants."

I knew this tiny man didn't make Raven. I had felt the power of Raven's wings. All I had to do was show how his words crossed themselves, and he would be forced to admit his lies. "You didn't have to make the people respect the animals and plants. People are smart. They know that we all depend on each other."

At that he laughed. "Your people know that because we made them know it. My people were not so smart. They had to learn it the hard way."

"How can you say your people made mine, if they are not even smart enough to respect the other animals in the world?"

"Oh, my people are very clever at putting things together. But we are lazy, and short-sighted. We never stop to think about what will happen once we've built something and set it in motion." He stared out the glass into the black sky. "We built machines to do our work for us, but we didn't build machines to clean up after the machines. Not until too late. Then we had to start over, here." Suddenly he turned back to me with eyes full of hate. "We never do anything ourselves if we can make a clever tool to do our work for us. We made the lichens to turn the rock to dirt. We made the caribou to control the lichens. We made the wolves to control the caribou. And we made you to control the wolves. But who will control you when you get out of hand?"

"No one controls us. We are a proud and free people!"

"I know that. But the watchers think they control you through your legends. They give you thruster trees and other things to make you more useful. They don't understand that the most useful tool is also the most dangerous."

"Your lies are outrageous. No one can make a whole people!"

"I told you we are clever, but lazy. We do not build a whole people. We build just a few, then they make more of themselves." He laughed again, short and bitter. "We made you because you were a good trade. A small effort expended, a little patience, and in the end we get a whole world."

"Lies built on lies. Arrogance piled on arrogance!"

"The arrogance is not mine, it is the watchers'. The lies are theirs as well. I am just a simple pilot who speaks the truth." He stared straight into my eyes. "Not all of my people are like the watchers. Some of us believe it would be better if you had never been made. But now you are here; what should be done with you?"

"We have always been here, ever since this world was new. We should be left alone to live our lives in peace."

"I wish that we could."

There was a long silence then. Maqandisen turned away from me and stared at his colored lights, and I watched the stars turn slowly outside the glass.

We did not exchange another word until we arrived at the glass people's village in the sky—the village of the watchers, as Maqandisen had called it. It floated in the sky, round as a sun hat, and hundreds of totems and glass people's houses were gathered around it. Just before we entered the village, Maqandisen looked at me and said, "I did not want this task. I do not like the watchers or the things they have made. But I am glad to have met you."

"Thank you. I am indebted to you for saving my life. But you have terrible manners, even for a glass person."

At that he just smiled sadly.

The great hunt participants from all the other clans were there in the village of the glass people, and they greeted me as one returned from the dead. The glass people there asked me if Maqandisen had told me any strange tales, and I told them that he had not. I don't know why—Maqandisen had told me nothing but lies, why should I protect him with a lie of my own? But I felt it was the right thing to do.

Soon after I arrived, we were all bundled into one of the glass people's strange houses, which carried us to their largest city. There we held a great dance to celebrate our successful hunt and commemorate the lives of those who had not returned. In the evening we shared tales from our different clans, and there was much hilarity over the differences in customs between us. The next day we said our good-byes and began the long trip back to our homes.

When I returned to my own clan there was much rejoicing. The people held a mighty feast in my honor, and I told the tale of my great hunt—the tale I am telling you now—for the first time. Then I returned to my life as an ordinary hunter.

For some years I was troubled by Maqandisen's words. Could he have been telling the truth? It would explain much. But in the end I recalled Bear's mighty roar and the powerful thrust of Raven's wings, and I knew in my heart that the old tales are true.

Maqandisen, like all of his people, was a great liar. Never doubt that it was Raven who made the people, and the caribou and all the other living things, and put the sun and moons in the sky so that we could have light. Maqandisen's claim that his people made us was nothing more than an arrogant boast. But sometimes there is truth to be found inside a lie.

What if the glass people believe their own lies? What if they really do believe they made us as a tool to shape the world for them, and someday they decide the world has been sufficiently shaped? The glass people may emerge from their cities and seek to assert their domination over us and all the world. We must prepare weapons and strategies against that day.

I know that some consider me insane. Others look on me as a prophet. I am neither; I am just an old man who had a great adventure once, and learned a lesson from it that I think is very important. When you are grown and meet the glass people yourself, I hope you will remember my words, and then you will tell your children and they will tell their children.

Trade fairly with the glass people. Be alert for their lies. But watch them carefully and learn from them. They know many things we do not. But they do not know how much *we* know. Some day I think we will surprise them.

Now my tale is done, and the winter is just a little shorter.

WARRIOR HEART

DAVID JOHN BAKER

*Not just swords: All weapons have two edges. For as soon as
you use a weapon, your enemy can learn from it, and build a
better one to turn back on you.*

*For a brief moment in history, only one nation had atomic
bombs, and the use of it made that nation irresistible in war.*

*How many years was it—how many weeks—before that na-
tion's rivals had their own bombs? And then rockets to carry
them.*

*Stones to throw. Shields to block the stones. Spears to stab,
atlatls to fling a javelin, swords to cut, arrows to kill from a
distance. Every weapon countered by another.*

But what if there was a perfect weapon, an irresistible force?

A perfect monopoly on power, no rival now to face you.

*In such perfect safety, perfect dominance, what is left for the
weapon's owner but to play? What once was a weapon now is
a toy.*

*In Rome, blood spilled on the sand of the arena for the
amusement of the crowds. But the real weapon Rome used to*

conquer the world was not sword or spear or arrow, but the legion itself—the disciplined men fighting rank on rank in perfect obedience.

Only one thing could be counted on to beat that weapon, and it took no time at all for the Romans to realize it.

We change little from age to age, always relearning the same lessons, always replaying the same games.

THE SHADELESS WINDOW of Robert's room granted him a wide-ranging view of the lands surrounding the Peduman castle. Low hills, crusted with a thick and bushy grass that never seemed to ripen beyond an unhealthy brown, played host to a modest sunrise. The landscape of Jau boasted little to recommend it over the rest of the Twenty Worlds; all had been modeled after Mother Earth with little variation. Over the steepest of the near hills, he knew, the Peduman troops were making camp. Today would be the last day of inspection before he joined their campaign. Perhaps he would find some clue to the Emperor's logic in dispatching him to assist this pitiful, barbarous band.

He turned from the window, eyes seeking his weapons. The *keshrai* blades remained dormant and sheathed above the mantel where he had hung them last night. *Keshrai*—weapons of a Warrior, inspirations of balladeers throughout the Twenty. He lifted one from the rack and unsheathed it. The blade was short and wide, single-edged, and its sharpness was the only certainty in his life. With a strong blow, he knew he could cleave through the stone walls of the castle. *If Collin were here,* he thought, *he would recite some quote from the Covenant—* "*the* keshrai *is the Warrior's soul metaled over," or some such nonsense.*

He put the weapon away, then threw on a gray, hooded cloak and slung a scabbard over each shoulder. Round his neck he clasped a pewter pendant marked with the lizard glyph of the Emperor. This was the extent of his equipment; so clothed, this world and its concerns were a backdrop, a setting for the execution of his duty. He opened his door and descended the stairs.

At the foot of the staircase waited his host, Ulger, Baron Peduman. The Baron was not a fat man, but his skin hung from him loosely like a badly-fitted shirt and on his face it seemed to drip from his chin and jowls. "Warrior Robert," said the Baron, "for the fifth morning you grace my castle. The fifth and last morning of our inspection. Soon your work here may begin." The Baron was eager, Robert could tell, to see the brown fields of his domain reddened with Eophel blood.

"If all is found to be satisfactory, I will begin tomorrow," said Robert. *Though I think that unlikely. But perhaps today His Majesty's reasoning will become apparent to me.*

"Our escort is prepared," said the fleshy Baron. As they left the castle the row of guards snapped into line behind them, composite shock armor clicking and clacking like so much medieval metal.

At first sight of the camp, Robert's spirits sank, though he kept the confident gait he'd been bred and trained into. A hum of mingled screams hung over the valley like smoke, punctuated by the occasional rock-hard crack of gunfire. Here was a camp of spiritless soldiers, a blood-minded mob—this much he knew already. The only point of descending the slope was to survey the extent of the destitution. But he pressed on, aware of the Baron's eager eyes at his back.

Though the soldiers deferentially shrank away from his Imperial pendant, they made no effort to hide their despicable pursuits. A village raid had been conducted the previous night and the loot consisted largely of young women, now strapped to poles as the soldiers put them to unsavory use. Further into the camp, hastily-constructed tents housed the fervid auctions of an enterprising slave trade. Prisoners in the uniform of the Baron Eophel stumbled about blindfolded in a deep and dirty pit as the Peduman troops fired down on them with rifles.

Robert controlled his face with the adamant discipline of a Warrior, carefully concealing all traces of disgust as he met the Baron's expectant gaze. "I will inform my superiors of my recommendation. By tomorrow morning, the decision will be made."

That night, Robert composed a message to the planet's Guildmaster, which he immediately transmitted to the Guild Hall on the orbiting moon. It read:

> *Upon reviewing the assembled forces of Ulger, Baron Peduman, I find that I must object to my assignment here. The encamped troops are engaged in all manner of unethical and illegal practices: the torture and murder of prisoners of war, the physical abuse of women, the keeping and trading of slaves. It is my opinion that leading these forces to victory will in no way advance the honor or authority of His Imperial Majesty.*

The response came within the hour, from the Guildmaster himself:

> *The Imperial authorities are aware of the conditions you describe. Execute your duty as ordered.*

THE NEXT DAY Robert was again up with the sunrise, again fitted in his gray cloak, his *keshrai* blades and his Imperial lizard. This morning the Peduman camp was relatively quiet, if only because the troops were assembled in their ranks and ready to march. He walked resignedly at the side of Baron Peduman, face cowled in his hood, the anger boiling in him with no available release. Why was this armed rabble, this barbarian band, being granted the favor of the Emperor and the service of one of his Warriors?

The Baron, who had been animated with a mischievous glee since learning of Robert's assignment that

morning, now grew more cautious as the troops neared
their objective. These petty feuds between vassals usually centered on possession of profitable resources, so the
Baron had chosen a uranium mine as the first day's target. As their ranks crested another high hill, the smooth
metal mining complex confronted them. Above it flew
the panther flag of Geoffrey, Baron Eophel. Robert's new
enemy. Eophel's troops had arranged barricades around
the facility. An armored car was parked within the
perimeter with an officer perched on top, surveying the
field. A formidable force, far outstripping Peduman's
meager band.

The Baron put a hand on Robert's shoulder. "I wish
you would not announce your presence so openly," he
said. "Why not preserve the advantage of surprise?"

"Surprise is an advantage I do not need," said Robert.
"These troops may surrender at once when they see me."
You may wish to maximize bloodshed, Baron, but I do not.

Robert loosened the *keshrai* in their scabbards. His warrior heart was thrumming in his chest, finding the rhythm
of the local time. He tested it once, switching to battlespeed and holding it for just a moment, watching the
Baron's eyelids freeze shut in mid-blink. Stillness held all
around him like a paused film in a silent room. He let it
go and activity resumed—the clanking of armor, the
movement of troops, the gentle pressure of the wind. . . .

He strode down into the valley of Eophel troops, still
shrouded in his hood, lizard glyph held high so they
could see he was no Peduman. When he was within
shouting distance of the officer on the car, he halted and
lowered the glyph back to his neck. Slowly and ceremo-
nially, he pulled back his hood, freeing his shoulder-
length hair. With his arms he pulled his cloak back away
from his waist, revealing his *keshrai* to the assembled
troops.

"I am Robert," he called to them, "Warrior Robert of
His Majesty's Guild. I bring the mandate of our Emperor:

Baron Peduman is to be given victory and control of these disputed lands. I now offer you the chance to lay down your arms and surrender."

The mounted officer spoke in a voice free of fear. "We will surrender to no army of Peduman. Strike us down, Warrior, if you must." And to Robert's surprise, a cry of assent rose from the barricaded troops. It seemed a demonstration would be necessary.

Flexing the warrior heart in his right breast, Robert took hold of battlespeed. At once the sound of the soldiers' yells was stilled, all was stilled, motion and sound unknown to him. His mind and body were moving impossibly fast, so that none of these men would see him even as a blur. He jogged over to the armored car and climbed up its side to stand by the brave officer. He drew one *keshrai* from its sheath and cut a clean, shallow wound on each of the man's cheeks. Returning to the spot where he had been standing, he put away his blade and let go of time.

The officer put his hands to his cheeks, and blood ran thin through his fingers. "I warn you," said Robert, loudly enough for the troops to hear, "none are safe from my blades. If you defy the will of the Emperor, you will die at my hands. That is certain."

"So be it," cried the officer, and his troops chorused their approval once again. Robert saw some of them training their weapons on him. Now was the time to act. At once, he drove himself to battlespeed.

For a moment he considered killing the officer, but banished the thought. The man had been shown his own weakness, yet his fighting spirit remained. Robert would not kill him unless he was forced to. He ran up to the second rank of troops and drew his *keshrai* from their scabbards. There were six men in this barricade. The first he beheaded, severing the neck and watching the head hang in air, impervious for the moment to gravity. The next two he stabbed though the hearts and the fourth he sliced cleanly in half at the waist. The fifth and sixth he dismembered rather gruesomely, telling himself that the more sickening their deaths, the more bloodshed he might avoid in the long run. His work was done; the men were dead without knowing it, killed in a period of time too small to measure. He sheathed his blades.

He was beginning to feel the strain of the stillness, so he jogged behind a tree and let time return. Gasps and screams from the back ranks of troops were audible as they discovered their slaughtered brethren. But when Robert peered around the tree, he saw that they held fast, warily eyeing the landscape.

So be it, he thought, remembering the officer's words. He recited to himself the one line of the Covenant he had memorized: *The keshrai is a Warrior's secondary weapon. His primary weapon is fear.* He felt ready again, rested, and with a deep breath he shifted back to battlespeed.

This time he dealt a painful but non-lethal wound to one man in each barricade. Some suffered severed fingers or ears, others stinging cuts or punctured lungs. This at last was enough. When he let time slide back to normal speed, the screams of the wounded caused pandemonium in the ranks and the Eophel army began to flee. First in packs of a few, then by dozens, they ran from their fortifications as Peduman's men fired into their midst from the safety of the overlooking hill.

But the officer in the armored car stood his ground, firing his vehicle's laser cannon at the Peduman formations even as his men broke and ran all around him. He did not attempt to rally them, perhaps because he knew he would only be sending them to their deaths, but still he battled on. Robert wondered for a moment what to do next. He did not want to kill the valiant officer, but he was duty-bound to assist the Peduman troops.

At last he steeled himself and clenched his warrior heart. Time froze around him once more, and he sprinted across the field toward the armored car. He was beginning to tire and did not want to hold onto battlespeed for much longer. He drew a *keshrai* with his left hand and jumped onto the body of the vehicle. With a single motion he chopped off the barrel of the laser cannon. Meanwhile he lifted the officer from his seat with his right hand and threw him to the ground beside the vehicle. Jumping down beside him, he disarmed the man, and then cut the car's axles with his *keshrai*. Looking around, he found no more Eophel soldiers in sight. At last he let go of time.

The officer groaned, then adjusted quickly to his new position. He climbed to his feet and, seeing Robert at last, groped at his empty holster. His hands fell limp at his sides. "You'd better kill me, Warrior," he said. "I've seen what the Peduman do to their captives, and I'll not be taken prisoner."

"I have captured you myself, under Imperial authority." Robert showed him the lizard pendant. "You are my prisoner, not Peduman's."

The valiant man bowed his head. "I understand."

By now, the Baron's soldiers were swarming over the facility, looting corpses and taunting the wounded. Five had circled Robert and his captive, their weapons leveled at the officer, mouths curled in hungry hate. "This man is my prisoner," Robert announced to them. "Bring him to my quarters in the castle. If he is harmed or mistreated, all five of you will die." He tucked his *keshrai* blade away beneath his cloak and stalked off to find the Baron.

WHEN ROBERT RETURNED to the castle that evening he found a guard at his door and his prisoner sitting on the bed, unharmed as he had ordered. He had expected no less. A Warrior could always count on the power of fear to bend the will of others.

The man's name was Thar Feldell, he learned. As a youth, he had been inspired by the bravery of the Baron Eophel in his war against Peduman, and had joined the army at an early age. Now, as a captain, he was still cer-

tain of the cause, and his opinion was only reinforced by
what he had seen in the Peduman camps he had captured.

"Why has the Empire chosen to assist the Peduman?"
he demanded. "They are the aggressors, the butchers and
slaveholders."

"I don't know, Thar," said Robert. "I have tried to protest
my orders, but the Guild seems resolved." He found himself speaking easily with this captive; indeed, he had more
in common with this man than with any of the Peduman.

"Has this ever happened to you before?"

"I have never before received an assignment I thought
was unjust."

"And how many assignments have you carried out?"

"Dozens. The Emperor's lords and vassals are feuding
constantly, on each of the Twenty Worlds, except Tiercen,
of course. Without the Guild, His Majesty would need an
army millions strong to keep them in line."

"Have you been to Tiercen?"

"Of course. The Warriors' Guild is headquartered on
Tiercen. It is where we are raised and trained. And any
appointment of a Warrior to active service must be con-
firmed by the Emperor himself. He never leaves the capital world."

"You have met His Majesty?"

"Several times."

"And the Princess? Is she truly as beautiful as they say?"

"Oh, yes," said Robert, his eyes slipping shut for just a
moment. Nadine, the Crown Princess—fairy creature,
budding goddess. He knew her, knew the sloped and
delicate face, the clear and purposeful laugh. She was a
woman perfect enough to make any man feel lonesome,
no matter his fortune. To a cold and distant Warrior it
was all the more painful to be in her presence.

He realized that he had slipped into battlespeed without realizing it. Immediately he let time resume. He
would need his strength for the next day.

But he must have moved slightly in fast time, for Thar noticed and raised an eyebrow. "Is it difficult to do that?" he asked.

"It puts a certain strain on the warrior heart," said Robert, tapping his right chest where the organ pulsed. "Holding battlespeed is like holding your breath. You can keep it up longer with training, but it tires you, and eventually you must let go."

"I see."

"Soon I will need to sleep," Robert said, rising from his seat and stepping to the window. "I've arranged a room for you next door." He peered out the window for just a moment. Stars were visible, pinpricks of white beauty. But tonight there was something more: a blue burst, like a nova in monochrome, a cloud of brightness drowning out the surrounding sky. The tiniest dot of blackness lay at the center of the blue cloud. "That's strange," he said.

"What is it?" said Thar, joining him at the window.

"A starship in transit."

"It's not the one you arrived on?"

"No. A departing craft would appear as a cloud of red light. This ship is approaching, decelerating." He shook his head in wonder. "I can't think who it might be."

After a moment, Thar bid him goodnight. The prisoner waited at the door just a moment, steeling himself to speak. "I suppose it's back to business for you tomorrow."

"I am under strict orders."

The captive nodded and was led away.

An electromag air barge was a nearly silent form of transport, and Robert was thankful for the quiet. A cliff face lay ahead, a gray and earthy sheer slope crested with brushes of green. A few hundred meters beyond lay a sprawling forest. The contrast of the treed highlands against the jagged rocks of the slope reminded him of the mountainous lands of Tiercen, capital of the Twenty Worlds. Among cliffs like this he had sparred with the other young Warriors of his litter. That had been the dawn of his life.

Now it was the dawn of the day, and this cliff would be a battleground before the day was through. The Eophel had arranged artillery missiles atop the cliff. This was their only battery capable of striking the Peduman Castle, making it a logical target for Robert's second attack.

The air barge flew past the cliff face, staying safely out of range of any anti-aircraft defenses, and set down in a clearing some distance from the artillery base. Soldiers filed out from the barge and formed up behind Robert. Only a few platoons today, but it would be more than enough once he was finished with the defenders. The Baron had remained in the castle this morning, and this strike team was commanded by a lesser officer. Robert was glad. He had grown tired of dealing with the shameless man.

At the fringes of the forest, where light began to leak between the trees in front of them, Robert told the troops to halt and dig in. He would go on alone. After he had finished with the defenders, they would be summoned to occupy the area and deal with prisoners.

These arrangements made, he stepped from the woods onto the sun-blessed grass. Today he wore a scanning bug in his ear that warned him when a sniper was training on him so that he could shift to battlespeed and dodge the bullet. Surprisingly, it did not go off even once as he drew closer to the emplacement. He loosened one *keshrai* blade in its sheath. Might they have some trap in mind?

At last he was only ten meters from the installation. He could see the helmeted heads of the enemy, visors lowered like insect eyes. He raised the lizard glyph above his head. "I am Robert, Warrior and servant of our Emperor. This land is now the rightful property of the Baron Peduman. Set down your weapons and surrender."

And from the midst of the Eophel army there rose a figure, cloaked and cowled in gray like Robert himself. Something hanging at his neck gleamed in the daylight. He pulled back his hood to reveal his face. Hair cut to the shoulders in a Warrior's style, hawkish nose and clean, angular cheeks, a face that looked forged in a fire. A face Robert recognized. The man parted his cloak, hand moving to his waist, gripping the hilt of a blade, a *keshrai* he could see. Then in an instant he was out of sight.

And at once Robert was in battlespeed, both his *keshrai* drawn and held out to parry. He was just fast enough, for the blow came a second later, a cut to his throat that he deflected with his left-handed blade. He stepped back and let time flow back, for he saw that his opponent had done the same.

"Collin," he breathed.

The other nodded, his *keshrai* held ready. At these close quarters, their warrior hearts were tuned together—if Robert shifted time, Collin could sense him and do the same in an instant.

"What are you doing here?" said Robert, blades still carefully on guard.

"By order of our Emperor, these lands belong to the Baron Eophel," said his friend. "I am duty-bound to defend them."

"Collin, I am under Imperial orders to secure these lands for the Peduman."

"I know this, my friend."

"Has there been a mistake in the Guild?"

"No. Your orders are genuine, and so are mine."

This was impossible, Robert knew. The Guild had never pitted one Warrior against another, except in training. He and Collin were charged to protect the Emperor's interests, to see that these local feuds ended in his favor. The Emperor could not support both sides in such a conflict. The very idea was ludicrous.

"Come, Robert, fight for the Peduman," said Collin. "I am ready to begin." He drew a second *keshrai* with his left hand. They circled each other warily, their warrior hearts pulsing as one.

"Collin, this is unheard of. Has our Emperor gone mad?"

"He is quite sane."

"How do you explain this? He can't favor both Peduman and Eophel!"

"Peduman and Eophel are inconsequential. He favors neither."

"Then why are we here?"

"Strange days are upon us, Robert. The Emperor has ordered the construction of a Crystal Ship." Collin teased the air with his right-hand blade.

"What has a Crystal Ship to do with this?"

"Read your Covenant, Robert. *Prophecies*, verse twelve." And with that, Robert felt a mighty burst of time as Collin lunged at him. Again he shifted just fast enough. He blocked the cut and shoved Collin away. Time slowed again.

"Fight me, Robert!" cried his friend. Another flash of battlespeed, another blow barely parried. Collin's lip curled. He seemed truly eager, suffused with the urge to kill.

Robert's mouth opened, but he had no words for the confusion that coiled in him. His fingers tensed around the grips of his blades. Setting his jaw, he let his warrior heart flutter and take hold of time, bending it to his will, funneling it into battlespeed. And when time was his, in the moment before Collin could shift up himself, he turned and ran for the forest.

He held time as long as he could, an inhuman length, minutes on end. His legs pumped beneath him in a sprint born of terror. His warrior heart felt like a fist clenched around a hot cinder, burning from the inside, begging his nerves for release. He risked a glance behind him and

saw that Collin had not followed. At last he let his warrior heart uncurl and he fell to the forest floor. He
breathed hungrily.

To his back he could hear the cries of the Peduman
troops. Collin was slaughtering them to exact punishment for Robert's own cowardice. But it had not been
cowardice, he told himself. It had been confusion, the
surrealism of facing his closest friend in a battle to the
death. No one could fault him for that, not even the im-
peccable Collin.

Presently, his breath returned. The screams to his back
had died out, and he rose from the ground and walked to
the grounded air barge. He did not regret what he had
done. He needed time to make sense of this. With that
thought he lifted off.

THE BARON PEDUMAN'S FLESHY CHEEKS were now taut with
rage. "A hundred of my men are dead, Warrior."

"Would you rather have me dead?" said Robert. "I'm
worth more to you than a thousand men." He swept his
arm at the formation outside the castle window.

"I'd rather have this Collin fellow dead and that artillery emplacement under my control. Why didn't you
kill him?"

"I'm not sure that I can. He may be better than me."

"Then it's best we find out now, isn't it? You won't be
getting any better in the next few days, and you'll have
to take him on eventually."

Robert fixed the Baron with a glare that halted the
man's tongue. "I think it's rather likely, Baron, that there
has been some mistake within the Warrior's Guild. I can
see no other reason why two Warriors would be called to
assist opposing sides in a feudal war. If you'll allow me
to use your microwave transmitter, I will iron this out
with the Guild Hall right now."

"It sounds as though your opponent was quite sure of
his orders. Sure enough to begin killing off my troops."

"Yes, he was sure of them. Perhaps my own orders were assigned in error." Robert's tone made it clear that he felt this was the most likely scenario.

Peduman's eyes narrowed. "Go about your business, then."

"YOUR ORDERS are accurate?" Thar Feldell was agape with surprise.

"Yes." The Guildmaster's response had been cruelly concise. Both Robert and Collin held genuine Imperial orders. The Emperor was backing both sides in this war.

"Did he give any explanation?"

Robert shook his head with angry vigor. "He made it clear that I had no right to expect one. The conversation was short. I think he expected my protest and had rehearsed his answers."

Thar's tone turned persuasive. "They can't ask you to kill a friend, or to join the wrong side in a war. You should leave this planet."

"For a Warrior, it is death to disobey the Emperor. He made that clear enough, as well."

"But Collin is your . . . your brother, isn't he?"

"Close enough. Warriors have neither father nor mother. Our parents are the Guild's biogen tanks. My closest friends were my trainsibs—those in my generation of trainees. Collin and I are the only graduates from a class of five. I suppose you might call him my only living relative."

"What happened to the other three?"

"Training is harsh." Robert drew one of his *keshrai* from the sheaths dangling above the mantel. "It's been a long time since I've sparred with another Warrior," he said, falling into a fighting stance. The last time he'd fought another of his kind had been with Collin, the night of their appointment to active duty. They had fought in slow time, for the amusement of the Princess. Collin had bested him that night. He remembered the reddish envy inside him as she laid the laurels on his trainsib's head. She had smiled at Collin then, that soul-taunting smile.

He took a few cuts at the air, recalling tactics he had not used since his days of training. The best method he had found against a two-bladed foe had been to use his left-handed weapon for parrying, saving the right hand for attack.

"You're serious about this aren't you? You're going to kill him." The awe and disgust in his prisoner's voice angered Robert, and with a rush of strength he stabbed the *keshrai* through a stone table. It cracked and split in half. Thar flinched in his seat.

But when Robert turned to him, he had calmed his face and slacked his muscles. Breaking the table had softened his anger's deadly edge. "I haven't yet decided," he said honestly. "Collin certainly seemed ready to kill me. And there was something he said—"

"What?"

"He mentioned a passage from our Covenant. The *Book of Prophecies*. And a Crystal Ship."

"I'm not familiar with the sacred documents of the Warrior's Guild."

"That is as it should be. We are forbidden to distribute the Covenant outside the Guild membership. I've never had much use for the Guild metaphysics myself, but I do remember most of the *Prophecies*. After the Twenty Worlds were cut off from the Earth and the Empire began with the Halloche Dynasty, the first Warriors prophesied a return to Earth. The Covenant states that the last Emperor of the last dynasty will construct a starship of quartz and crystalline carbon in orbit around Tiercen. His daughter will be named Emissary to Earth, and this Crystal Ship will carry her there."

Thar sat back, fingering his chin. "And Collin seemed to think these Prophecies might be on their way to fulfillment?"

"He claimed that the Ship was under construction."

"Then the Princess Nadine would be the Emissary."

"Yes."

They waited in silence for some time. Outside the night was deepening. At last Thar said, "I find it hard to believe that His Majesty would risk his daughter's life, sending her alone to Earth." Even public legends still spoke of the cruel last days of the homeworld, the blood gangs that roamed the used-up cities and the spent countrysides. A planet of harsh, scarred nature and exhausted fuel. It was no wonder that the folk of the Twenty were forbidden to return until the time of the Emissary.

"She will not be alone. A single warrior must be named her Escort."

"And how will he be chosen?"

"The Emperor will select him."

"Well," said Thar, rising to his feet, "perhaps he's narrowed the possibilities down to two." He bid Robert goodnight and left.

As soon as he had gone, the Warrior reached beneath his bed and drew a wooden chest from where he had stowed it the day his starship dropped him onto this world. His fingerprint and an imperceptible bit of skin cells were enough to open the lock, and he rummaged for a minute through the box. At last a leather-bound book presented itself. He cracked it open and laid it in his lap.

Prophecies, Prophecies. What verse had Collin mentioned? Twelve. Here it was. He read the paragraphs, and then reread them. Nothing had impressed upon his mind. But Collin was a scholar and a lover of myth. He pored over his own Covenant religiously. This would be a subtlety, a detail of the text, no more than a few words. Robert read through the passage once again.

And there it was, hard to pick out but clearly worded once he found it. Numbly, he lifted the cover of the book and shut it. His *keshrai* was on the floor beside him; he picked it up in his right hand. In his left he took the

Covenant. And in a moment's purifying release, he threw the book in the air and met it with the blade at the apex of its flight, shearing it in half. Pages flushed out across the room.

In his rational mind he knew he had sinned, destroying a holy text of his Guild. Another part of him knew he didn't care, that the myths and mysticism of the Guild were nothing to him, that the Guild itself meant nothing more to him than the next day's fight. But he knew what did mean something. His childhood with Collin played back in his skull, followed closely by that moment of terror and reverence when he sat down to dinner across from the Princess Nadine. The night Collin bested him, stopping his blunted *keshrai* just a centimeter from Robert's chest.

He sat on his bed, tapping the flat of his blade against his hand. Another night on this planet Jau—his last, maybe. Another night pondering his mission here, his duty to the Empire and what he wanted from tomorrow. He watched the window, waiting for the first merciful light of the next day's sun.

HE SET OUT ON FOOT, accompanied only by his *keshrai*, his cloak and his lizard pendant. By a roundabout path that would take him half the day to follow, he knew he could safely climb to the cliff face where he and Collin had met the day before. He would not stop for food or rest. He knew the limits of his strength and how to pace himself, and the nutrient patch on his chest would keep his hunger satisfied.

He had not informed the Baron of his departure. With luck he would never see the man again. He understood now the nature of his mission. As Collin had said, it had nothing to do with the Peduman or the Eophel. This war was a pretense.

The journey passed quickly. The cloud-shrouded sun was faint today and Robert pulled his cloak tightly around him. The trails he followed took him in a winding path up a steep but negotiable slope that would end in the forest, the scene of yesterday's escape. All the while he exercised his warrior heart, clenching and unclenching it, building endurance. Like the rest of his body, it needed to be stretched and warmed up before it could take the strain of activity.

He threaded through the forest now, five hours of travel behind him, only minutes in his memory. The next hour would be remembered as one remembers a day or a week. He was in the open now, watching again for snipers. But as he expected, the Eophel soldiers had their orders. Their ranks parted as he neared the artillery station. From the part came the hooded form of Collin.

"I hoped you would return, Robert," he said, the hood thrown back with a toss of his head. Behind him the sun peeked from a split in the clouds.

Robert simply shrugged. "I have discovered the truth."

Collin nodded, pleased. "It will be better this way. Better that you know what is at stake."

As if acting from a script, both men unbuckled their cloaks and let them fall, in perfect sync. Both drew their *keshrai* blades, the right and then the left. Both warrior hearts beat together, and time stood still.

They ran at each other.

Collin's first cut was low, with his left-handed blade. A surprising move, and difficult to block. He had probably rehearsed it. Robert executed the proper defense, turning the blade aside, and made his own attack: a head cut. A flick of the wrist was all Collin needed to bat it away and set up his counter.

They stabbed and sliced, feinted and fleched. There was no intensity like combat. Each motion was a separate life-or-death struggle, each twitch a lethal risk. Robert almost had him once. Dancing with a rhythmic bounce, swinging his blade with each step, he drew Collin into a false pattern. When he broke his rhythm with a slash for the throat, the other Warrior barely reacted in time, and was forced to parry with the stabbing point at the end of his hilt. A narrow escape.

But Collin became more cautious, and Robert's tricks no longer drew him in. Once he pretended to block an elaborate feint, only to strike back with a cut across Robert's chest that drew blood. Robert felt his warrior heart skip. Any wound now might shock him out of battlespeed. Even a moment's freeze would be enough for Collin to step in and kill him. The next cut might be his last.

He backed away, weapons up to defend himself. Blood trickled down his chest into his trousers, and he cursed. The wound was not deep, but it was enough to distract him. He could not hold battlespeed for much longer. It had already been three or four minutes, the longest he'd ever spent in fast time.

Collin struck at him several times and Robert retreated, backing toward the cliff. He felt himself slow once on a parry, and though he blocked Collin's blow, he did not draw back as he should have to lessen the force on his weapon. Collin hit his right-hand blade with the sharp edge of his *keshrai*, and it shattered.

Cursing again, Robert dropped the broken blade and shifted his remaining weapon to his right hand. He knew he was doomed. With just one blade, he could not attack Collin without exposing himself, and his warrior heart was pounding with exhaustion. He had only seconds of battlespeed left.

And as he backed away, he could feel Collin's own heart, still firm and in control, attuned to his own . . .

And he thought of his training. Sparring in fast time was an exercise of reflexes for the young Warriors, but it was also dangerous. If one lost his grip on time for only a moment, the other might kill him by accident.

So they were taught to reflexively shift back to normal time if their opponent lost it . . .

And all at once, Robert let go of time completely. It snapped back in an instant. Things around him were moving again. And he saw that Collin had snapped back, too.

Robert read confusion on his enemy's face, but he himself was ready to act. With mighty and painful effort, he forced himself back to fast time and lunged at Collin. The other Warrior began to speed up, but he was just a moment too slow. Robert's *keshrai* plunged through his right breast.

His enemy froze, eyes and mouth wide, and joined the rest of the world in stillness. Robert examined the face for a moment, then let his exhaustion take hold of him. Time snapped back.

The soldiers crowded around him, mumbling among themselves, clearly disappointed. They had expected a show, an epic battle. Instead, they had watched two gray blurs race across the field, too fast to follow, then shape into a man and a falling body. Robert stooped over the unconscious form of his friend. Collin would surely live, but he would never shape time again. His warrior heart had been split open by Robert's *keshrai*.

The stunned circle of men parted for him, and he picked up his cloak from the grass. He thumbed a control on his Imperial glyph, calling for a shuttlecraft from his orbiting starship. Enough of this planet. The next world he saw would be Tiercen. And then Earth, with the Princess beside him.

For, as the Covenant read, *"The Escort will be a worthy Warrior, strong enough to cut the fighting heart from a foe."*

THE COLDEST PLACE

LARRY NIVEN

In "My Universe and Welcome to It!" which serves as the in-troduction to Tales of Known Space: The Universe of Larry Niven, *published by Del Rey in 1975, Larry writes: "Twelve years ago I started writing. Eleven years ago I started selling what I wrote."*

Some of the Phobos Award winners will be able to make the same claim—that they started selling their work shortly after starting to write it.

To put in perspective the work of the emerging authors col-lected here, we thought it would be fun and instructive to reprint the story that launched Larry Niven's career—his first published story, "The Coldest Place."

Larry writes that he "dithered" over including this story in the Known Space collection because, in his words, it simply "wasn't that good." And he added a special note before the story saying: "This, my first story, became obsolete before it was printed. Mercury does not have an atmosphere, and ro-tates once for every two of its years."

Science moves quickly. The tension between science and fiction keeps us all running to catch up. We love Larry's abashed description of his story. A master who can see the flaws in his own work is the greatest master of all.

IN THE COLDEST PLACE in the solar system I hesitated outside the ship for a moment. It was too dark out there. I fought an urge to stay close by the ship, by the comfortable ungainly bulk of warm metal which held the warm bright Earth inside it.

"See anything?" asked Eric.

"No, of course not. It's too hot here anyway, what with heat radiation from the ship. You remember the way they scattered away from the probe."

"Yeah. Look, you want me to hold your hand or something? Go."

I sighed and started off, with the heavy collector bouncing gently on my shoulder. I bounced too. The spikes on my boots kept me from sliding.

I walked up to the side of the wide, shallow crater the ship had created by vaporizing the layered air all the way down to the water ice level. Crags rose about me, masses of frozen gas with smooth, rounded edges. They gleamed soft white where the light from my headlamp touched them. Elsewhere all was as black as eternity. Brilliant stars shone above the soft crags; but the light made no impression on the black land. The ship got smaller and darker and disappeared.

There was supposed to be life here. Nobody had even tried to guess what it might be like. Two years ago the Messenger VI probe had moved into close orbit about the planet and then landed about here, partly to find out if the cap of frozen gasses might be inflammable. In the field of view of the camera during the landing, things like shadows had wriggled across the snow and out of the light thrown by the probe. The films had shown it beautifully. Naturally some wide ones had suggested that they were only shadows.

I'd seen the films. I knew better. There was life.

Something alive, that hated light. Something out there in the dark. Something huge . . . "Eric, you out there?"

"Where would I go?" he mocked me.

"Well," said I, "if I watched every word I spoke I'd never get anything said." All the same, I had been tactless. Eric had had a bad accident once, very bad. He wouldn't be going anywhere unless the ship went along.

"Touché," said Eric. "Are you getting much heat leakage from your suit?"

"Very little." In fact, the frozen air didn't even melt under the pressure of my boots.

"They might be avoiding even that little. Or they might be afraid of your light." He knew I hadn't seen anything; he was looking through a peeper in the top of my helmet.

"Okay, I'll climb that mountain and turn it off for awhile."

I swung my head so he could see the mound I meant, then started up it. It was good exercise, and no strain in the low gravity. I could jump almost as high as on the Moon, without fear of a rock's edge tearing my suit. It was all packed snow, with vacuum between the flakes.

My imagination started working again when I reached the top. There was black all around; the world was black with cold. I turned off the light and the world disappeared.

I pushed a trigger on the side of my helmet and my helmet put the stem of a pipe in my mouth. The air renewer sucked air and some down past my chin. They make wonderful suits nowadays. I sat and smoked, waiting, shivering with the knowledge of the cold. Finally I realized I was sweating. The suit was almost too well insulated.

Our ion-drive section came over the horizon, a brilliant star moving very fast, and disappeared as it hit the planet's shadow. Time was passing. The charge in my windpipe burned out and I dumped it.

"Try the light," said Eric.

I got up and turned the headlamp on high. The light spread for a mile around; a white fairy landscape sprang to life, a winter wonderland doubled in spades. I did a slow pirouette, looking, looking . . . and saw it.

Even this close it looked like a shadow. It also looked like a very flat, monstrously large amoeba, or like a pool of oil running across the ice. Uphill it ran, flowing slowly and painfully up the side of a nitrogen mountain, trying desperately to escape the searing light of my lamp. "The collector!" Eric demanded. I lifted the collector above my head and aimed it like a telescope at the fleeing enigma, so that Eric could find it in the collector's peeper. The collector spate fire at both ends and jumped up and away. Eric was controlling it now.

After a moment I asked, "Should I come back?"

"Certainly not. Stay there. I can't bring the collector back to the ship! You'll have to wait and carry it back with you."

The pool-shadow slid over the edge of the hill. The flame of the collector's rocket went after it, flying high, growing smaller. It dipped below the ridge. A moment later I heard Eric mutter, "Got it." The bright flame reappeared, rising fast, then curved toward me.

When the thing was hovering near me on two lateral rockets I picked it up by the tail and carried it home.

"No, no trouble," said Eric. "I just used the scoop to nip a piece out of his flank, if so I may speak. I got about ten cubic centimeters of strange flesh."

"Good," said I. Carrying the collector carefully in one hand, I went up the landing leg to the airlock. Eric let me in.

I peeled off my frosting suit in the blessed artificial light of ship's day.

"Okay," said Eric. "Take it up to the lab. And don't touch it."

Eric can be a hell of an annoying character. "I've got a brain," I snarled, "even if you can't see it." So can I.

There was a ringing silence while we each tried to dream up an apology. Eric got there first. "Sorry," he said.

"Me too." I hauled the collector off to the lab on a cart. He guided me when I got there. "Put the whole package in the opening. Jaws first. No, don't close it yet. Turn the thing until these lines match the lines on the collector. Okay. Push it in a little. Now close the door. Okay, Howie, I'll take it from there . . ." There were chugging sounds from behind the little door. "Have to wait till the lab's cool enough. Go get some coffee," said Eric.

"I'd better check your maintenance."

"Okay, good. Go oil my prosthetic aids."

"Prosthetic aids"—that was a hot one. I'd thought it up myself. I pushed the coffee button so it would be ready when I was through, then opened the big door in the forward wall of the cabin. Eric looked much like an electrical network, except for the gray mass at the top which was his brain. In all directions from his spinal cord and brain, connected at the walls of the intricately shaped glass-and-soft-plastic vessel which housed him, Eric's nerves reached out to master the ship. The instruments which mastered Eric—but he was sensitive about having it put that way—were banked along both sides of the closet. The blood pumped rhythmically, seventy beats a minute.

"How do I look?" Eric asked.

"Beautiful. Are you looking for flattery?"

"Jackass! Am I still alive?"

"The instruments think so. But I'd better lower your fluid temperature a fraction." I did. Ever since we'd landed I'd had a tendency to keep temperatures too high. "Everything else looks okay. Except your food tank is getting low."

"Well, it'll last the trip."

"Yeah. 'Scuse me. Eric, coffee's ready." I went and got it. The only thing I really worry about is his "liver." It's too complicated. It could break down too easily. If it stopped making blood sugar Eric would be dead.

If Eric dies I die, because Eric is the ship. If I die Eric dies, insane, because he can't sleep unless I set his prosthetic aids.

I was finishing my coffee when Eric yelled. "Hey!"

"What's wrong?" I was ready to run in any direction.

"It's only helium!"

He was astonished and indignant. I relaxed.

"I get it now, Howie. Helium II. That's all our monsters are. Nuts."

Helium II, the superfluid that flows uphill. "Nuts doubled. Hold everything, Eric. Don't throw away your samples. Check them for contaminants."

"For what?"

"Contaminants. My body is hydrogen oxide with contaminants. If the contaminants in the helium are complex enough it might be alive."

"There are plenty of other substances," said Eric, "but I can't analyze them well enough. We'll have to rush this stuff back to Earth while our freezers can keep it cool."

I got up. "Take off right now?"

"Yes, I guess so. We could use another sample, but we're just as likely to wait here while this one deteriorates."

"Okay, I'm strapping down now. Eric?"

"Yeah? Takeoff in fifteen minutes, we have to wait for the ion-drive section. You can get up."

"No, I'll wait. Eric, I hope it isn't alive. I'd rather it was just helium II acting like it's supposed to act."

"Why? Don't you want to be famous like me?"

"Oh, sure, but I hate to think of life out there. It's just too alien. Too cold. Even on Pluto you could not make life out of Helium II."

"It could be migrant, moving to stay on the night side of the pre-dawn crescent. Pluto's day is long enough for that. You're right, though; it doesn't get colder than this even between the stars. Luckily I don't have much imagination."

Twenty minutes later we took off. Beneath us all was darkness and only Eric, hooked into the radar, could see the ice dome contracting until all of it was visible: the vast layered ice cap that covers the coldest spot in the solar system, where midnight crosses the equator on the back of Mercury.

ABOUT THE AUTHORS

David John Baker was born in Traverse City, Michigan. Aged twenty-two, he completed his Bachelor's program in physics and philosophy at the University of Michigan, Ann Arbor. His Bachelor's thesis discussed the philosophy of space and time and he had previously done research in high-energy physics at the Fermi National Laboratory's collider detector in Batavia, Illinois. Baker plans to enter a graduate program in philosophy. His love of science fiction was fostered by his father, John Baker, and both his parents have greatly encouraged his writing. In addition to his fiction Baker writes poetry which can be found on his homepage http://www.personal.umich.edu/~djbaker.

Rebecca Carmi took time off from full-time work as a Cantor four years ago to stay home with her children and pursue her life's dream of writing science fiction. Since then two of her short stories, "First Love Twice" and

"Gujarat Prime," appeared in *Zoetrope All-Story* online and in *Artemis*, respectively. She has also written two children's books for Scholastic, Inc. Carmi has a Bachelor's degree in semiotics and comparative literature from Brown University, a Master's degree and investiture from Hebrew Union College, and a Master's in voice performance from the Cleveland Institute of Music. She has sung opera and chamber music professionally. Carmi is a two-time winner of the Phobos Fiction Contest. Her story "22 Buttons" was included in the first Phobos anthology, *Empire of Dreams and Miracles*, and received favorable reviews from *Locus* and on *Slashdot*. Carmi lives in Cleveland, Ohio, with her husband, Irad, their sons, Amnon and Aryeh, and their baby daughter, Yardena. She is a member of Cajun Sushi Hamsters, Cleveland's professional science fiction writers' workshop.

Eugie Foster, residing in Metro Atlanta, shares her writing space with her husband, Matthew, and her pet skunk, Hobkin—which makes for some interesting writing experiences. After receiving her Master's degree in psychology from Illinois State University where she co-authored a child development textbook, she retired from academia and became a corporate computer drone. She finds that writing science fiction gives her an outlet for her scientific interests. Her first published fiction appeared in the YA literary magazine *Cicada*. Foster has sold stories ranging from folktales to erotic horror and says that writing for a diverse audience "keeps things edgy." Visit her website at home.attbi.com/~eugienmatt for updates on her forthcoming works.

Carl Frederick is a theoretical physicist, theoretically. Even though he left the comforts/confines of academia years ago and hasn't published in his field of quantum relativity for some time, he still thinks of himself as a physicist. In his mind, physics is not so much a field of employ as a way of life and perhaps even a religion. Frederick is "Chief Scientist" of a small A.I. software company in the academic community of Ithaca, New York. Previously, he held a junior faculty position at Cornell University, and before that, had a Post Doc position in astrophysics at NASA. He designed and built balloon-borne telescopes for far-infra-red astronomical observations. After leaving Cornell, he co-founded a small computer hardware/software company, Wolfdata. They created the first digital modem. Several years ago, Frederick decided that he'd like to write science fiction. Frederick was a double winner in last year's Phobos Fiction Contest, and his stories "Great Theme Prisons of the World" and "Messiah" were published in *Empire of Dreams and Miracles*. He was also a first-place winner in the 2002 Writers of the Future contest. He has written a respectable corpus of short stories, and put an interactive novel on the Web. While reading the story at www.darkzoo.net, a reader can click to change the point of view and to expose subplots. In his spare time Frederick fences and plays Scottish bagpipes. He has two children—boys. Frederick is a graduate of Jeanne Cavelos's Odyssey Writers Workshop, and asserts that he learned to write there.

Harold Gross has been a writer most of his life and a professional writer since 1994. He is represented in *Star Trek: Strange New Worlds III* with "An Errant Breeze," written with partner Eve Gordon under the name Gordon Gross. Their contributions also appear in the recently published *A Cup of Comfort Cookbook*. Other stories with the Gordon Gross moniker have appeared in *Fantasy & Science Fiction* and *Analog Science Fiction and Fact*. Gross works as a technical writer and a professional actor, both of which compete for his time at the keyboard. When not attempting to earn his keep, Gross can be found reading, playing computer games or creating in the kitchen. His story

"RUWattU8," was named by the Phobos jury as one of the top three "Best of the Best."

Kyle David Jelle was abducted by aliens in 1973. They never brought him back. The duplicate left in his place—only slightly damaged in transit—lives in Tacoma, Washington, and drives a truck for the local daily newspaper, *The News Tribune*. Jelle began writing—mostly science fiction and horror—in the sixth grade, but didn't begin to take writing seriously until the third time he dropped out of college. This isn't Kyle's first success in a writing contest. His short story "Black on Black" won first place in the second quarter 1996 Writers of the Future contest. He is currently working on a novel. You can visit his website at www.kylejelle.com. "Hidden Scars" was named by the Phobos jury as one of the top three "Best of the Best."

Rosemary Jones collects children's books, an addiction that she blames on her grandfather, who sent her *The Wizard of Oz* when she was five, and the rest of the Oz books on birthdays and Christmas. From there, it was a short hop to Narnia, Middle Earth, and other points east of the sun and west of the moon. As an adult, she's co-authored four books on collecting children's books with her mother, Diane McClure Jones, as well as a guide to alternative medicine colleges. She has a great wealth of experience writing for newspapers, magazines, catalogs and websites; and she has worked as a bookstore manager. She circumnavigated the globe in the opposite direction of Jules Verne's Mr. Fogg, thus permanently losing one day. Jones discovered science fiction in grade school through the works of Andre Norton and Alexander Key, and George Lucas' *Star Wars*. Rosemary's story "The Takers," was ranked highest overall by the jury of the 2002 Phobos Fiction Contest, topping the list of three "Best of the Best." The optimistic anti-war message at the heart of Rosemary's tale resonated with the Phobos jury and editors.

David D. Levine has been reading science fiction as long as he's been reading. He wrote his first SF novel in fourth grade, and annoyed his teachers by turning in SF stories for every creative writing assignment. After graduating from college he became a technical writer, and writing SF was a little bit too much like work. Fifteen years later he shifted to software engineering, partly to get his writing energy back. It worked. In 2000 he spent his sabbatical at Clarion West, and in 2001 made his first pro short story sale. Since then his stories have appeared in *Interzone*, *F&SF*, and David Hartwell's *Year's Best Fantasy #2*, among others. He lives in Portland, Oregon, with his wife Kate Yule; together they produce the highly regarded fanzine *Bento*. Their web address is http://www.BentoPress.com.

Paul Pence's writing usually skims along the edge of the genre, where mainstream characterization and drama begin to meet the awe and flash of the fantastic. For most of his career, he's written in borrowed universes, primarily *Star Trek*, creating new stories for his fellow fans, but recently he has begun writing stories in original universes. His fiction and poetry have appeared in *Jackhammer*, *Planet Relish*, the *Providence Journal*, the *Goblin Market*, and other publications. By day, he is managing editor of *Rhode Island Roads Magazine* (http://www.riroads.com).

Matthew S. Rotundo is a 1998 graduate of the Odyssey Writing Workshop. His work has appeared in *Absolute Magnitude* and *Thin Ice XVI*. He has written two novels—*The Watermasters* and *The Lonely* Stars—and continues to write more short stories. He and his wife, Tracy, live in Omaha, Nebraska.

Christine Watson lives in Southwestern New Mexico, where she worked in radio before shifting to full-time writing. A member of SFWA, she's been published in *The*

Dune Encyclopedia, Survey of Modern Fantasy Literature, Asimov's and *Rapport*. In her spare time she reads, spins, knits, gardens and spoils her dogs.

Jake West, a rare native Californian, grew up in Bakersfield and has lived most of his adult life in the Los Angeles area. The struggling writer's usual mixed-bag of jobs eventually led to his teaching developmentally disabled, emotionally disturbed and learning-handicapped populations. His publication credits include stories in *The Magazine of Fantasy & Science Fiction* ("Halls of Burning," August 97); *Amazing* ("Digital Hearts and Minds," Winter 99) and *Plot Magazine* ("A Dearth of Ravens," Spring 97). He has also collaborated with his partner Taenha Goodrich on television sales to *Airwolf* and the syndicated anthology series *Monsters*. They have written several screenplays together, including a series pilot, *The Archer*, and a first novel, *Steel Stallions*. He lives in Torrance, California, with his wife Janet, who, "thirteen years of marriage later, continues to put up with all my weird quirks (only some of which have anything to do with writing SF)."

ABOUT THE JUDGES

ORSON SCOTT CARD

Nobody had ever won the Hugo and Nebula Awards for best novel two years in a row, until Orson Scott Card received them both for *Ender's Game* and its sequel *Speaker for the Dead*. Card continued the evolving saga of Ender Wiggin in *Xenocide* and *Children of the Mind*, and returned to the events of *Ender's Game* through the perspective of one of Ender's fellow battle school cadets, Bean, in a novel published by TOR in 1999 entitled *Ender's Shadow*. The Ender series has reached over 20 million readers worldwide, and the original novel is currently being developed as a movie by Lynn Hendee and Robert Chartoff, co-producer of *The Right Stuff*, *Raging Bull* and the *Rocky* series, with Card writing the screenplay. These books comprise only the beginning of this prolific author's bibliography.

Card has broken new ground with each of his major works. "The Homecoming Saga" (the novels *The Memory of Earth, The Call of Earth, The Ships of Earth, Earthfall* and *Earthborn*) was a retelling of ancient scripture as science fiction. *Pastwatch: The Redemption of Christopher Columbus* is the sine qua non of alternative history novels, in which time travelers return from the future to keep Columbus from discovering America. Card's innovative "American Fantasy" series (*The Tales of Alvin Maker*) reexamines American history in a magical version of the Western frontier.

Card served as Editor of Note on the first Phobos Anthology *Empire of Dreams and Miracles*, writing in his introduction, "Science fiction, of all genres of storytelling, is the one that hungers most for new writers. These stories stood out from an array of many, and are offered to you now because they meant something to the judges, and we think they'll feel important, entertaining, truthful to you." He was happy to once again serve as a member of the jury in the 2nd Annual Phobos Fiction Contest, and reprises his role as Editor of the new contest anthology, *Hitting the Skids in Pixeltown*.

Card has written two books on writing, *Character and Viewpoint* and *How to Write Science Fiction and Fantasy*, and has taught writing courses at several universities and workshops at Antioch, Clarion, Clarion West, and the Cape Cod Writers Workshop. Card says he enjoys teaching dedicated writers because he believes they will contribute to the overall quality of literature available to avid readers like him.

Card received degrees from Brigham Young University (1975) and the University of Utah (1981). He currently lives in Greensboro, North Carolina, with his wife Kristine, and their five children: Geoffrey, Emily, Charles, Zina Margaret, and Erin Louisa.

CATHERINE ASARO

Catherine Asaro was born in Oakland, California, and grew up in El Cerrito, just north of Berkeley. She received her PhD in Chemical Physics and MA in Physics, both from Harvard, and a BS with Highest Honors in Chemistry from UCLA. Among the places she has done research are the University of Toronto in Canada, the Max Planck Institut für Astrophysik in Germany, and the Harvard-Smithsonian Center for Astrophysics. Her research involves using quantum theory to describe the behavior of atoms and molecules. Catherine was a physics professor until 1990, when she established *Molecudyne Research*, which she currently runs.

A former ballerina, Catherine has performed with ballets and in musicals on both coasts and in Ohio. In the 1980s she was a principal dancer and artistic director of the Mainly Jazz Dancers and the Harvard University Ballet. After she graduated, her undergraduate students took over Mainly Jazz and made it into an organization at the college. Catherine still teaches ballet in Maryland.

Catherine's fiction is a successful blend of hard science fiction, romance, and exciting space adventure. She has published nine novels, seven of which belong to her Saga of the Skolian Empire. *Spherical Harmonic*, the most recent novel in this series, came out in hardcover in December 2001 from Tor. Her previous novel, *The Quantum Rose* won the Nebula Award for best novel of 2001 and is now available in paperback. Catherine has also published short fiction in *Analog* magazine and in several anthologies, as well as reviews and nonfiction essays, and scientific papers in refereed academic journals. Her paper, "Complex Speeds and Special Relativity" in the April 1996 issue of *The American Journal of Physics* forms the basis for some of the science in her novels.

Catherine recently completed the next installment in the Skolian series, entitled *Moon's Shadow*. It will arrive in bookstores in February 2004. Also appearing next February will be her first anthology as an editor: *Irresistible Forces* will feature new novellas by six top authors in the genres of science fiction, romance, and fantasy: Mary Jo Putney, Lois McMaster Bujold, Bo Beverley, Jennifer Roberson, Deb Stover, and Catherine herself. Catherine was also recently elected vice president of Science Fiction and Fantasy Writers of America, Inc. (SFWA). Her husband is John Kendall Cannizzo, an astrophysicist at NASA. They have one daughter, a young ballet dancer who loves math.

VINCENT DI FATE

For more than three decades Vincent Di Fate has held an international reputation as one of the world's leading artistic visionaries of the future. *People Magazine* has said "One of the top illustrators of science fiction, Di Fate is not all hard-edge and airbrush slickness. His works are always paintings—a bit of his brushwork shows—and they are all the better because of it." And *Omni Magazine* made the observation that "Moody and powerful, the paintings of Vincent Di Fate depict mechanical marvels and far frontiers of a future technocracy built on complicated machinery and human resourcefulness. Di Fate is something of a grand old man in the highly specialized field of technological space art. Stirring images of far-flung environments have been his trademark." In his prolific career, he has produced art of science fiction, astronomical and aerospace subjects for such clients as IBM, The Reader's Digest, The National Geographic Society, and the National Aeronautics and Space Administration.

Di Fate has received many awards for his paintings, including the Frank R. Paul Award for Outstanding Achievement in Science Fiction Illustration (1978), the Hugo Award (Science Fiction Achievement Award) for Best Professional Artist (1979), the Skylark Award for Imaginative Fiction (1987), the Lensman Award for Lifetime Contribution to the Science Fiction Field (1990), and the Chesley Award from the Association of Science Fiction/Fantasy Artists for Lifetime Artistic Achievement (1998). He was also Guest of Honor at the 50th World Science Fiction Convention in Orlando, Florida, in 1992 and has been an honored guest at numerous regional SF and fantasy conventions throughout the United States since the late 1960s.

Di Fate has published two major books, *Di Fate's Catalog of Science Fiction Hardware* (Workman Publishing Co, 1980) and *Infinite Worlds: The Fantastic Visions of Science Fiction Art* (Penguin Studio Books, 1997). The award-winning *Infinite Worlds* is the first comprehensive history of science fiction art in America. In addition, Di Fate has lectured extensively about the methods, meaning and history of his craft and has been a consultant for MCA/Universal, 20th Century Fox and MGM/United Artists. He served two terms as president of the Society of Illustrators (1995–1997), an organization of which he is a Life Member, chaired the Permanent Collection Committee for the Museum of America Illustration (SI) from 1985 to 1995, and has served on the Illustration Committee for the Sanford Low Collection of the New Britain Museum of American Art since 1993. He is also a founding member and a past president of the Association of Science Fiction/Fantasy Artists.

MARSHA IVINS

Marsha S. Ivins is a NASA Astronaut, an avid science fiction reader, and the only Phobos Jury Member who has actually traveled in outer space. A veteran of five space flights, (STS-32 in 1990, STS-46 in 1992, STS-62 in 1994,

STS-81 in 1997, and STS-98 in 2001) Ms. Ivins has logged over 1,318 hours in space.

Born on April 15, 1951, in Baltimore, Maryland, Ivins graduated from Nether Providence High School, Wallingford, Pennsylvania, in 1969, and received a Bachelor of Science degree in aerospace engineering from the University of Colorado in 1973.

Ivins has been employed at the Lyndon B. Johnson Space Center since July 1974, and until 1980, was assigned as an engineer working on orbiter displays and controls and man machine engineering. Her major assignment in 1978 was to participate in development of the Orbiter Head-Up Display. In 1980 she was assigned as a flight engineer on the Shuttle Training Aircraft and a co-pilot in the NASA administrative aircraft (Gulfstream-1).

Selected in the NASA Astronaut Class of 1984 as a mission specialist, Ivins' technical assignments to date include: review of Orbiter safety and reliability issues; avionics upgrades to the Orbiter cockpit; software verification in the Shuttle Avionics Integration Laboratory; Spacecraft Communicator in Mission Control; crew representative for Orbiter photographic system and procedures; crew representative for Orbiter flight crew equipment issues; Lead of Astronaut Support Personnel team at Kennedy Space Center in Florida, supporting Space Shuttle launches and landings; crew representative for Space Station stowage, habitability, logistics, and transfer issues.

Ivins was on the space shuttle *Atlantis,* January 12–22, 1997, during a 10-day mission, the fifth to dock with Russia's Space Station *Mir,* and the second to exchange U.S. astronauts. The mission also carried the Spacehab double module providing additional middeck locker space for secondary experiments. In five days of docked operations more than three tons of food, water, experiment equipments and samples were moved back and forth between the two spacecraft. She was part of the *Atlantis* crew again February 7–20, 2001, and continued the task of building and enhancing the International Space Station by delivering the U.S. laboratory module *Destiny*. The Shuttle spent seven days docked to the station while *Destiny* was attached and three spacewalks were conducted to complete its assembly. The crew also relocated a docking port, and delivered supplies and equipment to the resident Expedition-1 crew.

DAVE MCDONNELL

David McDonnell is Editor of *Starlog*, a 26-year-old monthly magazine devoted to science fiction & fantasy film, television, and literature, and to their creators. He has also served as Editor of *Fangoria* (a sister magazine chronicling horror), *Comics Scene* and *SCI-FI TV*. Dave edited the official *Star Trek: The Next Generation, Deep Space Nine* and *Voyager* magazines. A movie magazine specialist, McDonnell has produced editions showcasing some 30 films including *Aliens, Terminator 2, Starship Troopers, Willow* and several *Star Trek* and James Bond adventures. He graduated in 1978 from West Virginia's Bethany College and has an MA in Advertising from Syracuse University. His career began in 1972 with work in fanzines. He began working for *Starlog* in October 1982, becoming Editor in April 1985.

LARRY NIVEN

Larry Niven was born in 1938 in Los Angeles, California. In 1956 he entered the California Institute of Technology, only to drop out a year and a half later after discovering a bookstore jammed with used science-fiction magazines. He graduated with a BA in mathematics (minor in psychology) from Washburn University, Kansas, in 1962 and completed one year of graduate work before he dropped out to write.

His first published story, "The Coldest Place," appeared in the December 1964 issue of *Worlds of If*.

He won the Hugo Award for Best Short Story in 1966 for "Neutron Star" and again in 1974 for "The Hole Man." In 1975 the Worldcon voters awarded *The Borderland of Sol* the Best Novelette Hugo. His novel *Ringworld* won the 1970 Hugo Award for Best Novel, the 1970 Nebula Award for Best Novel and the 1972 Ditmar, an Australian award for Best International Science Fiction; it has been followed by two sequels to date, *The Ringworld Engineers* and *The Ringworld Throne*. Many of his best stories are set in this long-spanning "Known Space" universe.

But while the Ringworld is an artificial, made construct, Niven's Smoke Ring could exist in nature: a doughnut-shaped region of breathable atmosphere in null-gravity, centered on and orbiting an ultra-dense object, which is itself in orbit around a star (and in an infinite universe, it should exist somewhere). Two novels have explored this fertile realm thus far, *The Integral Trees* and *The Smoke Ring*, both with outstanding cover art from Michael Whelan and set in the same milieu as an earlier novel, *A World Out of Time*.

Niven has written several landmark novels with longtime friend and collaborator Jerry Pournelle, including *The Mote in God's Eye*, an outstanding first-contact novel, and its sequel, *The Gripping Hand*; *Lucifer's Hammer*, an excellent comet-collides-with-Earth novel; and *Footfall*, a great alien invasion novel. Other collaborations with Pournelle include *Oath of Fealty* and *Inferno*. With Steven Barnes he wrote the acclaimed *Dream Park*. With both he wrote *The Legacy of Heorot* and its sequel, *Beowulf's Children*.

JOHN G. ROCHE

John G. Roche has been a connoisseur of literature and film since his youth, developing a particular enthusiasm for science fiction. An admirer of Philip K. Dick, he once negotiated an option on *Clans of the Alphane Moon*, and wrote a screenplay himself. In 2000, he became a founding partner of Phobos Entertainment Holdings, a company that is devoted to developing and producing quality science fiction entertainment.

After selling his companies Telecommunications Reports (to Commerce Clearing House) and Wellspring Media, Roche became a film producer and financier. His first movie, *Firedancer*, became the first film from Afghanistan to qualify as an Oscar contender for Best Foreign Language Film. *Firedancer* has since been selected to premiere at the Tribeca Film Festival, a new and vital New York City cultural event founded by Robert DeNiro and Jane Rosenthal. *Return to Afghanistan*, Roche's second film will be completed in the fall of 2003.

Roche's early career was distinguished by his partnership in John Hay Whitney's Whitcom Investment Company. He served as Executive Vice President of Whitney Communications Corporation and, in that capacity, helped build the Whitney newspaper, magazine and cable interests—including *The International Herald Tribune, Parade Magazine, Interior Design Magazine,* and *Art in America.*

Born in Rochester, New York, Roche earned a BA with honors from Georgetown University, and an MBA from the Harvard Business School in 1963. Active in multiple NYC business and civic affairs, Roche is a longtime trustee of the Film Society of Lincoln Center, and treasurer of The Kitchen, an avant-garde performance and technology center.